THE CHINA
CONSPIRACY

Also By Doug Hall

THE BRITTLE THREAD
THE GIRL IN 906
NOT MADE FOR DEFEAT
THE LONG WAY DOWN
THE KIRSTY AFFAIR
THE WORSHIPPERS
SECONDS TO DISASTER

THE CHINA CONSPIRACY

by Doug Hall

NELSON CANADA LIMITED

© Doug Hall 1981

Published in 1981 by
Nelson Canada Limited
1120 Birchmount Road
Scarborough, Ontario M1K 5G4

ISBN 0-17-601737-2

Cover Design: Rob McPhail
Cover Photo: Canadian Press

Printed and bound in the United States
of America

1 2 3 4 5 6 7 8 9 10   D   987654321

The author gratefully acknowledges
the assistance of the Ontario Arts Council
in the publication of this book.

Canadian Cataloguing in Publication Data

Hall, Douglas, 1929-
  The China conspiracy

ISBN 0-17-601737-2

I. Title.

PS8565.A44C55   C813'.54   C81-095014-6
PR9199.3.H325C55

For My Daughters-In-Law
Michelle and Barbara

1

The Right Honorable Christopher Jennings hated Cole Harrison with a passion that was growing with each breath. He had never fully realized that he had the capacity for such violent and blind hatred. Less than three hours ago the man the media labelled his 'right arm' and 'the power behind the throne' had been his closest friend and confidant. Now he was a dangerous and detested adversary.

The emotions that surged through Jennings' body and mind clashed and contradicted each other, swept over him with a fury he could barely control. For over twelve years he and Harrison had been more than friends. They had been comrades in political wars, co-adventurers in sexual conquest, brothers in spirit. And they had become an unbeatable team on Parliament Hill. If it had not been for Harrison's political savvy, infighting and skilful manoeuvering Jennings would still be the Honorable Member for Bonnachere/Renfrew sitting on a backbench instead of in the Prime Minister's office in the East Wing of the Parliament Buildings.

Jennings leaned back in his study chair and slowly sipped his third sherry of the evening. His study window looked out upon the well-manicured lawn of 24 Sussex Drive, the Prime Minister's official residence in Ottawa. Normally, when the problems of State pressed, his private moments with a sherry were usually enough to allow him time to collect his thoughts and weigh the pros and cons of any argument. This time it was not working. If ever he needed concise, objective, logical thinking it was now. Three events rotated in his conscious thinking like the sherry in his glass.

The first was a late afternoon call from Lao Chengtu, Press Attaché at The People's Republic of China's Ottawa Embassy, asking for a brief appointment the following morning. It was too premature to second guess the call from Lao. It could be nothing more than a courtesy call from Ottawa's most popular member of the diplomatic corps, but courtesy calls usually came from an Ambassador or First Secretary and never in the pre-noon or during days the House sat.

The second was a private call just as he was leaving his office, from James Cairns, the Liberal Leader of the Opposition and a bitter parliamentary foe. Cairns suggested that it would be in his interest to watch Channel 11 between nine and ten. Cairns would give no amplification beyond the fact that he would be the guest on 'Meet the Lawmakers', a nationally syndicated public affairs show with the acerbic host, Winston Morrant.

The call bothered Jennings greatly. Unlike most politicians who set aside their personal animosity or partisanship and presented a facade in public, Jennings and Cairns never spoke outside the House. The call was the first contact between the two, without a Speaker to referee, since their nationally tele-vised debate one week before the election. It was during the debate that Jennings accused Cairns of electioneering conduct unbecoming a Prime Minister. When Jennings captured the office with a large majority, Cairns could only attempt to re-build his shattered party and retain his leadership. Privately, he vowed to get Jennings if it was his last conscious act before death. He began his crusade during the very first Question Period in the new parliament and he never let up.

The call could only mean that Cairns had something, some bombshell to drop that would wound Jennings badly. He was not the sort of man to call out of kindness. He was going to stick in the knife and he wanted Jennings to feel every slow twist of the blade.

The third and most unnerving event of the day came between the main course and dessert when his wife, Diane, announced in her annoying, matter-of-fact tone that win or lose she was leaving him after the next election. She was in love with Cole Harrison.

Jennings' musing was interrupted by the opening of his study door. "Will there be anything else, sir?" asked Copeland, the steward.

"No thank you, Mr. Copeland."

"Perhaps a pot of tea?"

Jennings shook his head and looked at the ornate clock on the mantel. It was two minutes to nine. "Please make sure I am not disturbed until after ten. I want no interruption for the next hour."

"Very well, sir. Good night."

Just as the door was closing Jennings turned in his chair. "Mr. Copeland. Should Mrs. Jennings return before ten would you please tell her that I'll look in on her before I retire."

"Of course, sir," replied Copeland as he gently closed the door.

2

At 7:15 p.m. the clatter of Kevin Ingram's manual Underwood typewriter echoed throughout the nearly deserted editorial room of Dominion Press' Ottawa Bureau. Management had long since given up the battle for neatness. The deserted desks were cluttered with yellow telex copy, empty and half-empty plastic coffee cups, pop cans and well-thumbed copies of the evening edition of the *Ottawa Gazette*. Without exception the top of every oak and metal desk was scarred by carelessly dropped cigarette butts. The atmosphere reeked of stale tobacco smoke mixed with the peculiar aroma of a news room.

It had not been a good day for Ingram, and his drawn face, ashen complexion and round-shouldered stance made him look old beyond his 38 years. The day had begun with a blistering confrontation with his live-in lady of six-and-a-half months. Their battles were becoming less civilized and even though he enjoyed what he called a rational battle of wits, vitriol unnerved him more than he would care to admit. The main point of contention was ownership; ownership of each other. Ever since his divorce six years ago, he had kept a personal vow that he would never give of himself totally to any woman again. But 26-year-old Cindy Morris wanted more of him than he cared to give.

Ingram's casual breakfast announcement that because of a deadline they'd have to take a raincheck on a firm dinner and theatre engagement with friends triggered a violent outburst. His defence that he was being pressured because of a late deadline only exacerbated the confrontation. It culminated in a slammed door and a "fuck you" instead of the customary memorable goodbye kiss.

It was not uncommon for Ingram to produce his best work during periods of deep personal problems. His pinnacle as an investigative journalist came when he won the National Press Award for a series on the mercury poisoning of two Northern Ontario rivers by a pulp and paper mill, and the effects of the mercury on the native people. He researched and wrote the series during the drawn out and bitter divorce proceedings. He was accused of yellow journalism by the industry but his facts were irrefutable. A Royal Commission was launched on the basis of his revelations which enraged many Canadians.

But tonight the harder he pounded his ancient typewriter the more his frustration grew. The story was not coming together. There was a major hole in it and try as he would he could not write around it.

As much as possible he was a creature of habit and enjoyed his late afternoon beer with his colleagues in the Press Room Bar on Sparks Street. Tonight, for the first time in recent memory he passed up the early evening ritual and stayed at his desk. It wasn't only the story. He was in no particular hurry to face Cindy and cover familiar ground one more time. He told her that just before she told him what to do. Her cryptic retort was that she would be more than happy to compete with another woman but could not defend against a typewriter and an ego bigger than the Peace Tower.

Ingram was not conscious of the telephone ringing on a desk at the far side of the editorial room. Nor was he conscious of the night editor grumbling and shuffling across the floor.

"Ingram!" he shouted above the clatter of the teletypes. "It's for you. Are you here?" His hand was firmly clamped over the mouth-piece.

"Who is it?"

"Some broad! How the hell do I know?" His irritability was

10

evident. Ingram nodded as he walked to the desk and took the receiver from the outstretched hand.

"Hello."

"It's me."

"Hi," replied Ingram. His voice softened.

"Coming home?"

"Want me to?"

"If you have to ask a dumb question like that you don't know me very well." Ingram responded with a gentle laugh, then silence. "Don't sulk. Are you coming?"

Ingram chuckled slightly. "I'm coming. Have you eaten?"

"No. I lost my appetite early this morning."

"So did I, but it's coming back. Do you want me to bring in something?"

"How about a pizza? I'll open the wine and let it breathe. How's your story?"

"It's cooking," Ingram laughed.

"Sure you can pull yourself away from it?"

"I can now."

Cindy was tempted to make a caustic comment about the relative importance of the story but held back. She felt she had won a minor victory and there was no sense spoiling what appeared to be the beginning of a promising evening.

"Kevin," said Cindy in a quiet voice. "I love you."

"I'm on my way." Ingram dropped the receiver into its cradle and began humming as he walked back to his desk. With a sweep of his hand he pulled the copy paper out of the typewriter and jiggled the pages of his uncompleted story into a neat stack. Walking quickly across the editorial floor, he came up behind the night editor who was huddled over his desk with a heavy marking pencil poised.

"Harry!" said Ingram in a loud and guttural voice.

"Christ!" responded the startled man as he stiffened upright and dropped his pencil. It clattered to the floor. "How many times have I told you and the rest of your goddam crowd to knock it off? It isn't funny. Some day you'll regret it. I'm capable of violent and uncontrollable outbursts. Don't try me."

"Sorry, Harry. I just got good news." Ingram bent down and retrieved the pencil which had rolled under an adjoining desk.

11

"I hope the good news has something to do with your feature. I saw a memo from our fearless Assignment Editor about it."

"I didn't get a memo."

"It wasn't to you. It was to the Managing Editor."

Ingram's face changed expression abruptly. "What did it say?"

"Something about you maybe needing help to finish the story."

"Bullshit. It's my story and nobody jumps on it. I'm nearly done and it's going to be a dandy. I've got one hell of a problem. I can't reach the Chinese Press Attaché, and the story's dead unless I can get him to talk."

"Go without him."

Ingram shook his head. "I've no story without him. I've got to get their side of it. It's driving me crazy. The bastard's dropped out of sight."

"What's the Chinese Embassy say?"

"What do any of them say when you call. Nothing! He's not there, they don't know where he is nor when he's expected back in his office."

"Try his apartment?"

Ingram nodded. "That's where I was this afternoon. Closed up tight as a drum. I looked in his mail box in the lobby and from what I could see through the window there's about three to four day's mail. The superintendent was no help. I couldn't find anyone who knows a damn thing."

"Try the Mounties. You have good contacts."

"Nothing there. They even asked me to let them know if I got a line on Lao. They don't know where he is."

"You're kidding. They have a tail on all Commie diplomats, especially when they stray further than fifty miles from Ottawa."

"That's the damndest part of it. They're either putting me on or he's given them the slip. I have a pretty good contact in security, right on the Soviet/Chinese desk and up to now reliable."

"It could be a smoke screen."

"Of course, but again it could be on the level. It's the first time I've been asked to volunteer any information. The Mounties are usually light years ahead of any of us. But not this time. I think Lao is playing games. But I'm not sure why."

"How about External Affairs? If I remember correctly you had a good contact there, or has she gone on to new affairs?" The tone was suggestive.

"I haven't talked to her in over a year and God knows I don't want to resurrect that pain-in-the-ass."

"It's worth a try. Haven't lost your touch have you?"

Ingram shrugged. "You'll never know."

"You guys will bugger around. Hey, I just had an idea. If your little piece at External Affairs doesn't come across, in more ways than one, what about trying to get a line on Lao's girlfriends. It's my guess he's shacked up. All orientals are horny as hell."

"Filthy mind, and racist to boot."

"Give it a try. You can't afford to pass up anything. You're in deep shit if you don't file that story before too long. I'd go after all of them if I were in your shoes, or bed for that matter. Take advice from an expert."

"External it is, Harry. You've made your point."

"At the risk of repeating myself, get that story filed. I'd hate to see it reassigned."

"Don't worry, they'll get their goddamn story."

"If you can't track him down through one of his ladies check the wives of the more libidinous cabinet ministers. Most are bored to death and have the odd fling to add spice to their lives and stick it to their husbands. We've all heard rumours." There was not a journalist in Ottawa who couldn't name cabinet ministers with homosexual, bisexual or questionable heterosexual predilections, but it was an unwritten rule that such deep background was not used unless it was pertinent to a story, such as Pierre Sevigny's association with Gerda Munsinger, the German prostitute accused of being a security risk.

"Want a bit of fatherly advice?"

"From you?" replied Ingram in mocked surprise.

"I'm serious. Could your story stand up as it is now?"

"Yes, but I wouldn't be happy with it."

"You're not paid to be happy. File it and forget Lao. You can always do a followup once you get to him. Don't back yourself into a corner. They want the story so give it to them." Ingram lapsed into pensive silence. "Did you hear me?" asked Harry.

"I heard you. Here it is." Ingram handed the copy to Harry with reluctance.

"A wise decision. I'll have a look at it and if it needs anything I'll give you a call at home and hopefully we can do it over the phone."

"Thanks, Harry. You are a human being after all," said Ingram as he walked slowly toward the door.

Just as he gripped the doorknob and opened it Harry called out. "You're a betting man. Ten bucks says Lao is shacked up with a cabinet minister's wife."

"You'll have to give name, place and time before I'll pay off," said Ingram as he shut the door and hurried to the elevator. He was not humming.

It didn't take him long to reach the apartment, even with the detour for the pizza. All thoughts of reactors, plutonium and warheads disappeared, forced from his mind by visions of Cindy – her thighs, her mouth, her breasts. As he saw himself devouring her body and saw her devouring his, his pace quickened. Reality matched fantasy as he opened the door and saw her silhouetted against the bright June sky visible through the window. Her open shirt hung to just below her navel. She was wearing nothing else. He undressed in front of the door as they looked at each other, unspeaking. They slowly walked towards each other then fell to the floor, rolling on top of one another on the soft carpeting.

Their lovemaking was as energetic as their fighting and left both just as spent.

"That pizza nearly ready?" called out Ingram. "I'm half starving."

Cindy leaned out of the kitchen. Her face was slightly flushed and bore no trace of makeup. Her skin still tingled from the shower they shared. "You didn't think about food half an hour ago," she replied as she checked the re-heating pizza in the oven.

Ingram picked up the TV guide and flipped the pages as Cindy handed Ingram a plate and wine glass. "How would you like to watch 'Meet the Lawmakers'?"

"How'd you like to go back to bed for one more go?"

"Give me an hour to get my strength back and you've got yourself a deal. How about it?"

"I suppose so, but it's not my idea of a way to spend a sparkling hour. Who's on?"

"Jim Cairns."

"He won't say anything."

"You never know," replied Ingram as he positioned the TV trays in front of the two-cushion chesterfield and reached for the remote control unit.

"Sure you want to watch it?" asked Cindy as she carried in the cardboard carton with the steaming pizza.

Ingram flicked the channels and nodded. "Just give me an hour."

"I mightn't be in the mood in an hour."

"I couldn't do anything about it right now even if I wanted to. Pass the pizza."

3

Diane Jennings eased her four-year-old, inconspicuous green Mustang into the rear parking area of the *Chez Gatineau* Restaurant in Hull, Quebec.

The *Chez Gatineau* was formerly what the real estate agent called "one of the gracious homes of Hull," but Yves Bouvier was more interested in its potential than in its history and financed a total renovation. His vision became a reality and his restaurant became the "in" place for gracious dining and total privacy. Politicians quickly made use of *Chez Gatineau* for rendezvous, both political and personal. Many political deals were consummated between the hors d'oeuvres and a selection from Bouvier's celebrated cheese tray. Just as many sexual conquests began in one of the rear booths. Bouvier knew his patrons by name and was not above a bare-faced lie to protect their privacy, especially from prying reporters.

Diane switched off the motor and glanced about at the other cars in the lot. She was looking for one in particular. It was a silver grey Mercedes 450SL two-seater. Much to her irritation, she found it parked under a lone light standard, a favourite parking location for such an expensive automobile. Obviously the owner wanted it in an illuminated area as a means of protection against vandalism or theft.

Diane hurried up the front steps and walked through the heavy oak door with the brass adornments. While she was adjusting her eyes to the semi-darkened interior she felt a gentle touch on her arm. "Bonjour, madame. Right this way." With the accentuated body movements of a skilled maitre d', Bouvier led her to the rear of the private dining room which was reserved for the 'important' people.

A table for two was surrounded by three-quarter-ceiling high panelling with plush burgundy drapes filling in the remaining openness. Cole Harrison rose as Bouvier seated Diane. "A martini, very dry, for the lady and another gin and tonic for me, Yves. We'll order our meal later. We're not here," said Harrison as his voice dropped.

"Certainly, monsieur," replied Bouvier in a slightly petulant tone. He resented being reminded that Diane Jennings liked her martinis very dry and especially being asked to protect the privacy of his guests.

Diane waited for Bouvier to get beyond ear shot. "Why the hell don't you put a neon sign on the roof of your car and have searchlights to draw crowds?"

"What's that supposed to mean?" asked Harrison as he lit a cigarette and offered one to Diane. She shook her head.

"I thought we agreed that we'd either use our old cars or arrive by cab and walk the last three blocks. If I can forget about a chauffeur and government cars you can forget about showing off with your fifty-thousand-dollar toy."

Harrison held up his hand in surrender. "Sorry. What's up? I didn't expect to see you until tomorrow night."

"I told Chris."

16

"Told him what?"

Before Diane could reply Bouvier appeared with two drinks on a silver tray. "A very dry martini and a gin and tonic," his tone was patronizing. Both Diane and Harrison nodded and smiled slightly as the drinks were positioned.

"You told Chris what?" asked Harrison after Bouvier disappeared.

"I told him I was in love with you and that I would file for divorce after the election regardless of whether he won or not."

Harrison took a large swallow of his drink and choked slightly. He stabbed at the quarter piece of lime in the glass with his swizzle stick. Looking directly at Diane, he began to laugh. It was a soft laugh beginning in the back of his throat. "You're kidding. We did agree to hold off until after the election." Diane nodded her head slowly. "Shit!" breathed Harrison as he thumped his nearly empty glass on the table. The ice made a tinkling sound as it bounced off the sides of the glass.

"It just came out. It was so natural. I couldn't hold off any longer. Chris didn't take it badly. He just looked at me. He almost wasn't listening to what I was saying but he heard me."

"Shit."

"Will you stop saying that? Surely there must be something more intelligent to say."

"What do you want me to say? Congratulations! Well done!"

"How about you love me?"

"How about it! You have probably just signed the death warrant to my career and our future."

"Chris won't say or do anything. We'll just have to come to an unstated understanding. He can't win without you and he knows it. He can't win without me for that matter. If his family image is tarnished the party will turn on him even if the voters don't care anymore. You've always said that."

Harrison nodded his head. "God how I wish you'd called me first." .

"And just what would you have said?"

"I'd have told you to keep your damn mouth shut and not rock the boat."

Diane's eyes narrowed. She could feel the frustration and

hurt of the moment swelling up in her body. "Don't you tell me to keep my damn mouth shut now or ever. I'll say what I want, when I want! Do you understand?"

Harrison waved his hand. "Don't get on your high horse. We need to think this thing out before it destroys both of us."

"I'm glad it's out in the open. It's about time. He'll play the game."

"How can you be so sure?"

"I know my husband. He never comments immediately. He'll ponder the problem and take his own sweet time. You know that as well as I do. How many times has he received shots in the House and let them go by only to respond when he's good and ready?"

"That's what bothers me. He's a master of timing."

Diane reached across the table and laid her hand on Harrison's. "This time we have the advantage."

"I hope you're right. He can be a son-of-a-bitch. If you don't believe me just ask Jim Cairns. He's been burned more than once."

"You forget one thing, my darling. Cairns is his enemy."

"What the hell do you think we are now, especially me?"

Bouvier appeared with two menus in his hand. "May I recommend the Pheasant Normandy. It's . . . "

Harrison held up his hand. "We're in your capable hands, Yves. Surprise us. I so enjoy a surprise. I get so few." Discreetly, Diane extended her foot under the table and gently caressed his leg.

4

Christopher Jennings took advantage of the third commercial break to place a quick call to Brian Beacom. He had given Beacom, the chairman of the party's Strategy Committee, a rundown of his call from Cairns, but now both men expressed surprise at how deadly the interview was. They agreed to suffer through the rest of the program, however. They knew Cairns too well. Hurrying back to his chair, he had just settled when Winston Morrant's face completely filled the television screen.

"Welcome back. My guest is the Honorable James Cairns, Leader of the Opposition. Mr. Cairns, if I may recap and make an observation. We are almost through this interview and you haven't really said anything that the average Canadian doesn't already realize or know."

Cairns shifted his weight awkwardly in his chair. "If I may . . ."

"Excuse me, Mr. Cairns," interjected Morrant, "I shall give you ample time to respond but it seems to me that you have just covered old and familiar ground. No Canadian needs to be reminded that unemployment is creeping up to $8^{1}/_{2}$ per cent and just about everyone knows that our dollar is worth 81.67 cents American."

"But why isn't the present government honest enough to face up to the seriousness of the problems instead of hiding behind the smokescreen of regionally adjusted unemployment figures and World Bank pronouncements on the state of the international monetary system?" Cairns interjected. "A little honesty and candor would be refreshing."

"I've covered Parliament Hill for more years than I care to remember, Mr. Cairns, and I think I can safely say that your Minister of Manpower and Minister of Finance did precisely that very thing during their term."

Cairns shifted uneasily in his chair. "We took positive action. Our record stands," he snapped. "We're proud of it."

Jennings felt like turning the set off and getting back to his reports as Cairns droned on. There was nothing that Jennings hadn't heard in the House. In his gut he knew Cairns had some surprise, although as time ran out he began to have doubts.

Morrant received a 30-second cue from his floor manager. "We shall take a break and will be back in a moment for the conclusion of this program."

Cairns closed his eyes and turned his face upwards as the makeup lady patted his moist forehead with a puff.

"What do I have left for the extro?" asked Morrant.

"They're adding the time up now," replied the floor manager as he pressed his headset to his ear. "One minute and fifty-eight seconds."

"Good," replied Morrant. "Well, Mr. Cairns, let's end on something current and new. Any suggestion?"

Cairns leaned forward.

"Try not to lean too far forward sir," suggested the floor director as he moved off the riser and stood beside camera three. "Coming up. Twenty seconds."

"Ask me about the Bonnaventure sales to China," said Cairns hurriedly.

"Fifteen seconds."

"We covered the Bonnaventure sale."

"Ten, nine, eight," counted the floor director as he held up both hands in line with the camera lens and began flicking his fingers as he counted down.

"You want something new?"

Morrant turned to face the camera.

"Four, three, two, one." The floor director's index finger sliced through the air as the red tally light on top of the camera flicked on.

"Mr. Cairns. Most Canadians viewed the sale of our Bonnaventure reactors to The People's Republic of China as something very positive. How do you see it now that another sale may be in the offing?"

"A scandal. The relaxation of the safeguards on the use of the fuel was foolish. We said so at the time but the Prime Minister said they were still strong enough to prevent the Chinese from substantially adding to their nuclear stockpile. But that is what they're doing. They . . . "

"What? You are saying the Chinese are . . . "

"Using our reactors for military purposes."

"Wait a minute . . . "

"And that's not all. The financial aspects of the sale were highly questionable. There is evidence of an even greater scandal that reaches into the heart of this administration. Canada has been betrayed."

Morrant leaned forward. In spite of his experience it was his turn to block one of the cameras. The cameraman reacted before being ordered to do so by the director. Morrant's senses were razor keen. "Details!"

"I'll be making a statement, with full corroboration, in the House. There are a few questions I wish to ask the Prime Minister."

"Will you be naming names?" Cairns smiled. Morrant caught the one-minute cue from his floor director. "Are you charging the government with malfeasance?"

"I will make my statement in the House." Cairns relaxed in his chair.

Morrant turned to face the camera. "My guest has been the Right Honorable James Cairns, Leader of the Opposition. I trust you have found what he had to say provocative. Won't you join me again next week as we talk to another interesting guest on 'Meet the Lawmakers'. Until then, as always. Good night."

It was customary for Morrant to lean over and shake his guest's hand while the credits rolled. This time he did not. The moment he was certain his mike was dead he swung to face Cairns and fixed him with a penetrating stare. "That was dirty."

Cairns smiled. "My statement or my timing?"

"Oh your timing was impeccable. You knew damn well that there would be no time to speak to the question. Why didn't you introduce it earlier in the show. You owed the viewers that much."

"I owe them nothing. They'll get their bushel of dirt when I stand up in the House."

"Planning a motion of non-confidence?"

"You don't expect me to answer that at this point, do you?"

"I thought you were a champion of fair play and honesty?"

Cairns smiled. "I'm going to be Prime Minister again. How I do it is my business."

"Politicians," snorted Morrant as he undid his microphone and quickly walked off the set without looking back at Cairns. "Goddamn politicians."

5

It had been nearly an hour since Diane Jennings and Cole Harrison left the *Chez Gatineau,* separately and in opposite directions. Harrison drove directly to downtown Ottawa and his apartment while Diane absentmindedly crossed the Macdonald-Cartier Bridge separating Hull from Ottawa and, instead of turning left on to Sussex Drive, turned right.

Time and distance ceased to have meaning as she drove aimlessly along Rideau Street, passed the Parliament Buildings and turned left on Bank Street which intersected with the Queensway and Highway 17. Her mind was a jumble of memories and she was concentrating more on her relationship with Harrison than she was on where she was going. As the beam of her headlights illuminated the highway sign for the small village of Antrim, some 30 miles north-west of Ottawa, she was suddenly jolted back to reality.

Looking at her gas guage, which registered three-quarters full, she rolled down the window, took a deep breath and depressed the accelerator. Another half-hour would take her to Renfrew. Memories of Chris and their daughters flashed through her mind as she recalled some of the best days of her marriage, when she was simply Mrs. Christopher Jennings, wife of the elected member for Bonnachere/Renfrew and not the wife of Canada's Prime Minister. She also remembered the ten hours she spent in the Sunshine Motel on the outskirts of Renfrew with Cole Harrison.

Diane switched on the interior light and quickly glanced in the rear view mirror. She was pleased with what she saw. Her hair was neatly tucked up under a colorful bandana which was coordinated with her blouse and slacks. With no make up and her face freshly scrubbed her appearance was totally changed once she put on her tinted glasses with the fashion design frames. While she would attract admiring glances, only those who knew her intimately would identify her as the wife of the Prime Minister.

The clandestine meetings with Cole had ranged from a high point in the VIP suite in Toronto's Royal York Hotel to a basic room in the Sunshine Motel. The Royal York interlude pleased both of them and appealed to their sense of the bizarre. It also provided many moments of fantasy for her when they could not be together.

Jennings, at Harrison's urging, accepted the invitation to be guest speaker at the International Congress of Evangelical Baptists. While he did not personally identify with the Baptists he needed their vote. The invitation had included Diane and she readily accompanied him to Toronto on the Canadian Armed Forces 707 executive jet along with the entourage which included Harrison. A life-long sufferer of migraine headaches, she had little trouble in convincing Jennings that one was building with intensity. She blamed it on the change of barometric pressure while flying. Jennings was solicitous, as he had nursed her through many blinding migraines during their marriage. He suggested that she stay in the VIP suite instead of attending the dinner. He would make the apologies to the Baptists. The scenario of deception had been carefully orchestrated by Harrison.

The moment Jennings and the head table guests entered the Canadian Room, led by a pipe major from the 48th Highlanders, Harrison rushed to a telephone and asked the RCMP security officer to come to the registration desk in the main lobby and pick up an envelope for the Prime Minister. It was to be delivered to the VIP suite. By the time the officer returned to his post and handed the envelope to Diane, Harrison was safely in the suite, undetected. Another call would take the officer away from his post long enough to allow Harrison to return to the Canadian Room before the dinner was scheduled to adjourn at 10:45 p.m.

Diane started to laugh as Harrison stood in the bedroom doorway and held out both arms. "Do you want this envelope?" she asked.

"You keep it as a memento. You never know when you might need half a dozen blank pages," replied Harrison as he threw it on a chair and took her in his arms. He had no problem reaching behind her and slowly lowering the zipper of her fashionable cocktail-length dress. Diane put both arms around his neck and pulled herself closer. She felt his rising hardness.

Neither said a word as Harrison slowly removed the dress from her shoulders and exposed her highly tilted breasts held firmly in place by a low-cut brassiere. His eagerness to possess her body was difficult to control but he had learned through bitter experience not to rush. On more than one occasion Diane had accused him of being selfish and only thinking of his personal gratification at her expense. On those occasions the moment was irrevocably spoiled for both of them.

Diane removed her dress and after carefully laying it across the chair she stripped off her pantyhose and stood before him in her panties and bra. Harrison undid his shirt studs, removed his black patent leather shoes and dropped his trousers to the floor. They were unceremoniously kicked aside.

For a long, tender moment they stood in a silent embrace. Slowly, Harrison began to move his hands up and down her back and with a cultivated gentleness, undid her brassiere and freed her rounded breasts with their firm and erect nipples.

Diane started to lower his jockey shorts and they fell to his feet. Her panties followed quickly. With the drapes securely pulled shut, their bodies were silhouetted in the darkened room. Diane took Harrison by the hand and they groped their way to the bed conveniently turned down by the maid.

At the precise moment that Jennings began to congratulate the assembled 1,500 Baptists, in their rented tuxedos and plastic corsages, on the unanimous passing of a resolution demanding a return to traditional family life, Diane and Harrison began to make love.

With tenderness and consideration, each explored the other's body and fought to prolong the exquisite foreplay as long as possible. Suddenly, Diane laid Cole on his back and spread her legs to straddle him. She helped Harrison enter her and their bodies met in blinding passion.

Their supreme moment of ecstasy was juxtaposed with the newly elected President of the I.C.E.B. rising to his feet to thank the Prime Minister for his support of historic Baptist precepts. He droned on for twenty-three minutes to the total boredom of the head table guests. He applauded Jennings for his leadership and example in politics, family life and marriage,

24

and the hardshelled Baptists signalled their approval with murmured "Amens" and fervent "Praise Gods".

Diane Jennings was not a promiscuous woman in the classic sense. She was sensual and had been sensual since the first stirrings of puberty. It was only with great forebearance that she reached her eighteenth birthday still a virgin. The only child of a staunch Wesleyan Methodist grocer who revelled in his Christianity and his Loganville, Nova Scotia roots, Diane lived in constant fear of incurring his monumental wrath by becoming pregnant before marriage. Her fully developed breasts, combined with a lithe body and finely moulded features, made her fair game for the local studs or the more adventurous who drove the twenty-three miles from Truro looking for a good time. It was only her father's reputation as a defender of his only daughter's virtue that kept them at arm's length.

Unbeknown to her father, who prided himself on her innocence in a lascivious world, she lost her virginity three months following her eighteenth birthday. It happened in a secluded spot on the shore of Northumberland Strait near the small Nova Scotia hamlet of Knoydar.

Diane remembered it with clarity and in her more melancholy and reflective moments relived the experience. It was one of her more frequent fantasies. She was attending the Sunday School picnic, the annual highlight of the church calendar. Because it was church and she was in the company of "fine young Christians" her father had no objection when Jamie Blackthorn asked her to walk along the beach and look for shells. After all, Jamie Blackthorn was the son of the minister and highly regarded by the congregation, especially the mothers.

It was a bittersweet experience. Neither was schooled in the art of love. Their moment of supreme passion was preceded by an awkward fumbling and juvenile embarrassment. It was Diane who took the initiative and became the aggressor. Without her persistence it would have been nothing more than a heavy petting session ending in predictable frustration for both.

Following a momentary blinding flash of pain for Diane, both rose to heights of ecstasy as their bodies thudded against one another under the shade of a weeping willow. Neither appreciated the irony of the sounds of the church choir drifting across the water as they sang the old hymn "I Surrender All".

In a moment of confession Diane told her closest friend, Mandy Crozier, that losing your virginity must be like dying. You'd only do it once, then heaven. Diane enjoyed sex and fed her new found appetite whenever and wherever possible within the limits of parental control. She never made love to Jamie Blackthorn again but was always grateful for the initiation.

A life-long Progressive Conservative, her father insisted that she and her mother attend a major political meeting in the auditorium of the Sir John A. Macdonald Collegiate Institute in Truro. Both Diane and her mother hated politics and only went under duress. The meeting was predictably boring, with long introductions followed by longer speeches from local and national representatives. Diane began to fidget and continued to do so despite her father's withering stares. She only stopped when the last speaker walked to the lectern. He was Christopher Jennings, the newly elected President of the Progressive Conservative Youth Federation. He was tall, lean, tanned and in total command. It was his eyes that attracted Diane. She had never seen a man with such magnetic eyes before. Her whole body stirred. She knew the feeling. She also knew that she had to meet Christopher Jennings.

By the time Jennings was scheduled to move on to the next stop in his Maritime itinerary their lovemaking was satisfying and their romance budding. Over the next nine months they kept it alive through long passionate letters and telephone calls. They were married the following June with the Reverend Denzil Blackthorn officiating. Jamie Blackthorn played the organ.

The early months of their marriage were punctuated by extended bursts of passion. It was as though they could not slake their sexual appetites. As the months grew into years the frequency of their lovemaking reduced even though the passion maintained its high level. More times than not Diane initiated the foreplay but Jennings didn't object. Tired or not he could always respond once they began. While he wouldn't admit it even to Diane, he enjoyed the passive role. Bed was the only area in which he submitted, willingly or otherwise.

They were an attractive couple and precisely what the party needed to symbolize its revitalization. They embodied all the

26

attributes to spearhead a major advertising and public relations campaign.

Their married life blossomed as did Jennings' political fortunes. It wasn't until the decision was made to stand for election that Cole Harrison entered their lives. Jennings found his enthusiasm, drive and political acumen refreshing. It was the beginning of a strong professional and personal relationship. Harrison liked to win and no cost was too great. He was determined to make Jennings a winner. This he was to accomplish.

His first major assignment was campaign manager for the neophyte Christopher Jennings. The party could not have given him a greater challenge. The incumbent, a popular Renfrew doctor, had held the seat continuously for eighteen years and was considered unbeatable. The only drawback was his age. At 69 years he was too closely identified with the "old guard" and did not fit into the new vibrant image the party desperately needed if it were to capture the imagination of the electorate. In a spirit of face-saving the party executive suggested that it would not stand in the way of any candidate over 65 retiring. A number, including Dr. Desmond McConnell, were offered a seat in the Senate should the party win. With the exception of Dr. McConnell, all accepted. He adamantly refused to retire and told the party president to go to hell. The only way he'd retire would be to be defeated at the polls.

Jennings won the nomination. It was not by a landslide but the margin was comfortable. McConnell, magnanimous in defeat, walked to the platform, raised Jennings' hand in victory and moved that the executive make it unanimous. It was so recorded.

The victory enhanced Harrison's image within the party and further cemented his relationship with Jennings. Dubbed the "Canuck Twins" both were hailed as being politically invincible.

Early in her seventh month Diane became severely toxic and her physician, fearing for what was now confirmed to be her unborn twins, ordered her to bed for the balance of her term. He also ordered the cessation of all sexual activity. Jennings readily acceded to the order without complaint, a fact that bothered Diane. She welcomed his consideration as an act of love, but their marriage was never to be the same again.

The birth was protracted and difficult. It took much longer

than the customary six to eight weeks following birth for Diane to even consider resumption of a normal marital life. The resumption of sex was awkward, fumbling and embarrassing. It was a throwback to the time she gave of herself to Jamie Blackthorn. For once Diane did not assume the aggressor's role. Neither was satisfied.

Jennings' immersion into politics was total. His only relaxation was devouring every book he could lay his hands upon that featured a Canadian political theme. His favourite reading was biographies, and he was a near expert on the lives and times of the sixteen Prime Ministers who held office from Sir John A. Macdonald to Pierre Trudeau. He was particularly fascinated with some of the lesser known men such as Mackenzie Bowell and Sir Charles Tupper who held office in the 1890's.

He once told Diane that one of the most succinct epitaphs ever written about a Canadian Prime Minister was penned by one of Bowell's biographers who quoted Sir Joseph Pope, Clerk of the Cabinet: "When the Governor-General called Mackenzie Bowell to form the government he took him one step over the edge down into the abyss of his own conceit."

He would quote from biographers and historians to make a point to an infuriating degree at times. Diane once told a close friend that he was beginning to make political dissertations an integral part of their foreplay.

His performance in the Commons and his untiring work on committees did not go unnoticed by the party. It was not too many months into his first term that he was being singled out as possible heir apparent to the aging leader. A high profile, many eighteen-hour days and Cole Harrison's behind-the-scenes guidance and influence helped propel him into residence at 24 Sussex Drive. Initially the success he so ardently sought was mutually shared by Diane. Their greatest pleasure was seeing his popularity and influence blossom. But the schism that appeared following the birth of their daughters widened as time passed. No longer did Diane comment on his speech drafts or adjust her calendar to suit his public appearances. Like many Prime Ministers' wives she began to resent political life. She barely maintained her composure when around party members or politicians. In moments of extreme frustration she would berate Jennings with the fact that most were shallow opportunists and that he was becoming like them. When necessary she would accompany him to functions and play the game, with the fixed smile, the handshake and the small talk artfully employed. It was warmth and sincerity that was lacking.

The only time a crack appeared in Diane's façade came during the second day of an exhausting two-day riding tour with Jennings. It was a by-election. The sitting member had died and the party candidate was far from strong. In desperation the riding association appealed to the national office for help. It was decided that nothing short of an appearance by Jennings would save the day. Jennings agreed but insisted that Diane accompany him, in spite of Harrison's objections. The itinerary was gruelling.

Diane's reserves began to dwindle when she was asked to accompany Jennings on a mid-afternoon handshaking walk down Main Street. She hated this aspect of politicking because she felt it was a sham. The more it was orchestrated to give the appearance of being informal the more ludicrous and contrived it became.

It was not the fault of the coffee hostess that Diane fell from political grace. Rather it was Diane's inability to cope with what she considered to be a charade. She was to regret the moment.

Trying to be solicitous the hostess asked Diane if there was anything she could get her to make her more comfortable while Jennings addressed the bevy of adoring matrons. "A stomach pump would be appreciated," replied Diane in a voice loud enough so that there was no mistaking what she said or the tone in which she said it.

The reporters were delighted to be thrown such a human interest angle. The wire services and broadcast news picked up the story and it was national news by mid-evening. The editorial writers and cartoonists had a field day, to say nothing of the opposition.

Publicly Jennings laughed it off and complimented Diane on her sharp wit. Privately it became the focal point for the bitterest quarrel of their marriage. Jennings insisted that Diane write a letter of apology to the hostess he felt she had insulted. Diane refused. Neither spoke for over three weeks unless absolutely necessary. Diane moved into a separate bedroom; she never moved back. Three months later Diane looked in the mirror and decided that precious few years were left for her to attract admiring glances. It was time to accept whatever happiness came her way. If it included no-strings-attached sex or sex with a deeper relationship she was ready for either one and not necessarily on her terms.

Cole Harrison was to supply the sex, practically on demand. It would be deeply fulfilling sex, but total happiness would be elusive.

The memories were still flooding her mind as she sped along the Queensway, parallel to the Central Experimental Farm. She was suddenly startled by the glare of a flashing red light on the right fender of a police car as it pulled along side. Taking her foot off the accelerator she eased her car to the right of the throughway and depressed the brake pedal. By the time she rolled down the window a uniformed police officer was standing beside the car.

"What's the matter officer?" she asked in a startled voice.

"May I please see your driver's license and proof of insurance?" His tone was firm but pleasant.

Diane released her seat belt and fumbled in her purse. It took her a moment to fish the wallet from out of the cluttered purse. She handed it to the officer.

"Would you please remove the license and proof of insurance?"

Diane nodded and leaned back in the shadows to lessen the chance of recognition.

"Have you been drinking?"

"I had two small glasses of wine with my meal but that was," Diane looked at her watch, "over four hours ago." It was 1:48 a.m.

"I've been following you for the last three miles. Didn't you notice the 80 kilometer signs for that stretch of construction between Churchill and Fisher Avenue?"

Diane shook her head. "I'm sorry, I guess I wasn't paying proper attention to my driving. I have a lot on my mind."

"I clocked you at 113 kilometers. I'll have to give you a summons. If you want to plead guilty you can sign the back of the summons and send in a payment to the address shown or you can appear in court on the day indicated."

Diane nodded and waited patiently as the officer finished filling out the summons.

"Are you still residing at 37 Ridgefield Crescent, Nepean?"

Diane shook her head. "Not exactly."

"Could you be more specific?"

"It's still my home but I haven't lived there for a while."

"Where do you live?"

"You're not going to believe me."

"Try me."

"24 Sussex Drive."

"That's the Prime ...". The officer leaned down to get a better look. Diane nodded and smiled slightly. "I wouldn't have recognized you, but then I've only seen you on television or your picture in the papers. Why didn't you tell me?"

"Would it have made any difference?"

"Of course."

"It shouldn't."

The officer looked embarrassed. "I can't do anything about this ticket, Mrs. Jennings. Once we start to make one out we have to complete it. That's regulations. Only a superior can cancel a summons. I'm sure the Inspector would be pleased to see what he can do."

"Don't bother. I broke the law. I should be treated no differently than anyone else. I'll take my medicine and be more careful next time."

The officer flushed and finished the summons. He handed it to Diane. "Could I ask you a favour?"

"Certainly."

"Could I have your autograph. I'd like to give it to my wife. She heard you address the National Coalition of Canadian Women. She thinks you're great. She's liberated, like you."

"What's her name?"

"Wendy."

Diane wrote "To Wendy. I just got pinched by your husband. Sincerely, Diane Jennings." She handed the slip of paper back to the officer. They both laughed. Carefully, she put the car into gear and swung around the parked police cruiser. She was

31

just passing the intersection of Sussex and Stanley when her legs began to shake. She suddenly felt ill. With care she guided the car to the curb and switched off the motor.

6

Six weeks following his election as Prime Minister, Christopher Jennings fulfilled a party promise and created a special twelve-member strategy committee, an elite group of caucus members and senior party organizers. Their mandate was straightforward. The members would act as a sounding board for the cabinet and Prime Minister on such wide ranging concerns as interpreting public opinion polls, advising on election strategy, second guessing the opposition and recommending courses of action to repair political fences or improve party fortunes. One imaginative opposition member dubbed the committee "Jennings' Jerks".

The strategy committee also provided a useful tool for currying favour and feeding egos. Appointment was eagerly sought. To be a member was a mark of being in the inner circle. It was also a salve that healed the deep wounds of losing the leadership battle. Defeated candidates were high on Jennings' short list and their appointment to the committee brought a sense of coherence to a party that was fragmented by a bitter convention.

Chairman Brian Beacom was a dour Scot who used his considerable influence and wealth without apology. An entrepreneur in the classic sense he parlayed a one-tug operation into the largest salvage fleet on the west coast. Respected internationally for his innovative salvage techniques, Beacom's fleet roamed the Pacific. The company flag was regularly seen in Far Eastern ports. When Jennings announced formation of the committee it was a foregone conclusion that Beacom would be the first one approached to be chairman. A loyal, hardworking party member, Beacom could be relied upon to keep any dissidents in line and uphold party interests at all times. He accepted the position with alacrity and immediately turned control of Pacific-Orient Tugs over to his three sons and moved to Ottawa to be accessible to the Prime Minister. His enthusiasm for the job made him popular with the cabinet ministers.

Tonight, his enthusiasm was lacking. The conversation with Jennings after the Morrant show unsettled him. He thought the P.M. sounded distant, uninterested in what were very serious charges, even if Cairns had not deigned to substantiate them. He called the committee members quickly, arranging for an emergency session early in the morning.

Then he had to make the hardest call of the night. He drummed his fingers impatiently on the top of his desk and with obvious frustration pressed the receiver closer to his right ear.

"We are ready with your call to Vancouver, sir."

"Thank you," mumbled Beacom. "Duncan."

"Hello, Dad". The voice sounded haggard.

"I just heard the news about the typhoon. What's the latest?"

"It's not good. The Sea-Queen left Hong Kong two days ago and was just entering the Formosa Strait when it hit. The tow line broke and we lost six barges."

"Christ," breathed Beacom. "Did they sink?"

"We don't know. The Captain thinks they might be beached on the China coast but he can't go into their waters to look for them."

"Any damage to the Sea-Queen?"

"Moderate. We're lucky she didn't go down."

"Have you advised Taipei?"

"Yes. They're madder than hell. We have forty-eight hours to locate the barges or they'll start legal action."

"Let them. They can fight it out with the underwriters."

"There's a problem. We weren't fully insured."

Beacom rubbed his forehead. "We weren't what?" he bellowed.

"We weren't fully insured. If we can't recover the barges intact we're liable for eighty per cent of book value."

Beacom sucked in his breath and struggled to control his anger. "Since when does Pacific-Orient leave port without full coverage?"

"Since we lost our shirts on the Philippines salvage contract. You ordered us to cut back on costs wherever possible."

"I never meant on insurance, for God's sake."

"We could have saved fifty thousand if everything had gone right. We had no warning of a typhoon."

"How much?" asked Beacom.

"Taipei International are talking 2.5 million."

"All for the sake of a measly fifty thousand! Is the *Sea-Queen* still in the area?"

"Yes. She's seaworthy and I've ordered the captain to keep searching until ordered back to port. We've asked other boats in the area to keep a lookout so we may get lucky."

"Any chance of entering Chinese waters?"

"Not without permission. That takes days the way they operate."

"Not if I get someone leaning on them it won't. Stay put. I'll get back to you." Beacom hung up the phone without saying goodbye.

He had spoken to Jennings about resigning his position as Strategy Committee Chairman following the Philippines disaster but Jennings had talked him out of it. While he had an unquestioned loyalty to his party he was not about to see a company which had been his life-blood sink into bankruptcy through mismanagement. It was obvious his sons needed his active participation if Pacific-Orient was to survive. But right now he needed Jennings to intercede on his behalf with the People's Republic of China. Running his finger down a page in his telephone index, he squinted and began dialling Jennings' private number.

7

The clock on the wall ticked towards two as Lao Chengtu waited patiently for the door to open to Ambassador Wu Tai Shan's private office. Unconsciously he smoothed back his straight, jet-black hair with the open palms of both hands. The gesture had been carefully cultivated during his early years in the diplomatic corps but now was conditioned and became more pronounced as stress intensified. Most men found it theatrical but for some of the women it was a mark of individuality with sexual overtones. "The Ambassador will see you now," said an aide as he bowed slightly and held the door open. Wu's office was spartanly furnished even by Third World embassy standards. The basic oaken desk with its non-padded swivel chair appeared starkly out-of-place in what had once been the mahogany-panelled library of a gracious Ottawa mansion. Three wooden straighbacked chairs faced the desk. A smaller chair for a recording secretary stood empty by the side of the desk.

Lao bowed deeply. "Mr. Ambassador," he said with respect.

Wu nodded in response and pushed a button on the telephone. The door opened almost immediately and First Secretary Yuan Tzu, followed by a secretary, entered. Lao and Yuan bowed toward each other then turned to face Wu. The secretary quickly positioned her chair by the side of the desk and made ready to take notes. The sound of the turning pages was accentuated in the early morning silence.

Lao was casually dressed in dark brown corduroy pants with a matching turtle-neck pullover and a straw-colored, hand-knitted, cardigan. He contrasted sharply with the Ambassador and First Secretary, both of whom were dressed in conservative, grey, high-collared suits.

"You arrived within the expected hour," said Wu with a pleasant smile. Nodding toward the secretary, he continued. "Are you prepared to report?"

Lao flexed his shoulder muscles and once more smoothed down his hair, one side at a time. Glancing at the secretary who had pencil poised, Wu turned and fixed his eyes on Lao. "Before you begin, Comrade. Question. Are you aware of Mr. James Cairns' appearance on television this evening?"

Lao nodded. "I heard the report on the eleven o'clock news as I was driving back to Ottawa. It sounded like the babblings of a desperate man."

Wu spread the fingers of both hands apart and, settling back in his chair, began matching the fingers of the right hand with those of the left slowly, one at a time. "Yes, Comrade. The babblings of a desperate man and a dangerous politician. Did you have a pleasant visit with our friend at Atomic Power?"

"Yes, Ambassador, most pleasant."

"Your pre-arranged meeting place?"

"Yes, Ambassador. We spent a day-and-a-half fishing in White Partridge Lake in Algonquin Park. It didn't take long to catch our limit. The fish were biting."

"Secured?"

Lao smiled. "We met in the middle of the lake and camped on opposite shores."

"Where did you lose your RCMP friends?"

"They are still waiting for me to come out of the O'Brien Theatre in Pembroke. I hope they enjoy the film; it was dreadful."

Wu nodded. "Splendid. You seem quite adept at shaking your surveillance. Just be sure they're not playing your game and making it too easy for you."

Lao frowned. He didn't need a lecture from Wu Tai Shan on security procedures. Of all the senior embassy personnel he was the most skilled at countering RCMP intelligence. But Wu was the Ambassador so he listened in polite silence and nodded in agreement as Wu droned on.

"We could all do with a refresher course on security procedures," Wu said looking at Yuan Tzu. "I suggest that for the next month, two evenings a week be set aside for up-grading on security. It will be mandatory for all staff and no one will be exempt unless they have signed permission from me."

Yuan nodded and glanced at the secretary. Her head was down and she was writing in a smooth fluid motion. "We are entering into a very fragile period as far as our relations with Canada and the West are concerned. I expect a great flurry of interest in what we are doing and I do not want anyone in this embassy to be the means of embarrassing our government or jeopardizing what we have all worked so hard to accomplish. At this moment we are in a position of advantage with the Canadians. We shall stop at nothing to maintain that advantage. Is that clearly understood?" Lao and Yuan nodded their heads in unison. "Can we completely rely upon our friend at Atomic Power?"

"Absolutely. He has no choice."

"Everyone has a choice, Comrade."

"Not this man. He's in far too deep to ever back out."

"Is money his only weakness?"

"As far as I can tell. Sex would be no enticement and I don't believe appealing to his vanity would influence him either. He wants money, quickly and in large amounts."

"Is he in financial distress?"

"He certainly doesn't live beyond his means but he isn't suffering."

"Take a lesson from him Comrade. The love of money has ruined more men than the love of a woman, or of a man for that matter," pontificated Wu.

Lao nodded. Had he not been in the presence of his Ambassador and bound by diplomatic politeness he would have countered with a lighthearted aside that he liked both and neither had ruined him. Money provided creature comforts that he enjoyed and coveted and women personal pleasures that for a man such as Ambassador Wu must be foreign.

"I trust our friend was in a receptive frame of mind to your proposal?"

Lao nodded. "Most receptive. The offer of increasing his monthly retainer to $1,500 was most appreciated."

"Did you mention the incentive?"

"I did and that interested him greatly. I think we will find that the quality of his information will appreciate substantially."

"I trust so. Peking is not exactly ecstatic at what we have received so far."

Lao's expression changed. Any criticism of his contact was a direct criticism of his control efficiency. "I am surprised, Excellency. I would have thought the last delivery was of superior quality."

Wu tugged at the lapels of his suit coat and smoothed out

37

the wrinkles. "You thought wrong. While the information was interesting, it was not new. Our scientists were singularly unimpressed. We shall have to do better, much better." Wu inspected his finger nails. It was an irritating ploy which he used when emphasizing a point or lapsing into introspection.

"I shall have a full report on your desk late tomorrow, including an analysis of my meeting with the Prime Minister."

"Be prepared for the cancellation of your appointment, Comrade Lao," said Wu in a well modulated tone. "He may have other priorities as a result of the television pronouncements of Mr. Cairns."

"He will see me, Excellency," replied Lao firmly. "It's in his best interests to see me and I assume he realizes the fact."

"Don't assume too much, Comrade. Assumption is the luxury of the unwary and ill-informed." Wu swung his chair a full one hundred and eighty degrees. The meeting was terminated.

It was twenty after three when Lao snapped off the light in his office and left the embassy by a side door. The cool blast of air refreshed him as he hurried to his car. He noticed a small blue compact parked half a block down from the embassy's front door. The silhouette of a man and woman in an embrace made him smile. "Canadians have no class," he thought. "They'll do it anywhere and at any time."

The Ottawa streets were almost deserted. Instead of taking the direct route to his apartment he drove through the residential section, backtracking from one side street to another. Twice he noticed the headlights of a car but they were two blocks behind and quickly disappeared. Turning onto Laurier Avenue, he continued slowly to the intersection of Henderson. Two cars, a taxi and sedan, passed him on the left. Three cars were behind with half a block distance separating each vehicle. The third was a small blue compact with a man and woman in the front seat.

As he came abreast of Henderson and Laurier he gently applied the breaks and glanced at the bank of three telephone booths. All three were empty. On the glass of the middle booth which was well lit by the overhanging streetlight, was a white sticker with red block letters – GOD LOVES YOU. Lao stepped sharply on the accelerator. Pulling into the left-hand-lane, he turned onto Nelson and drove quickly to Laurier Avenue and his apartment. He did not see the small blue compact stop in front of the booth and the woman passenger get out and walk quickly towards it.

Lao Chengtu glanced at his watch as he turned his car into the parking lot across the street from the Lord Elgin Hotel. It was 7:48 a.m.

Casually he took the ticket from the attendant and parked at the far end of the lot. He sat motionless and scanned the cars coming into the lot in his rear-view mirror. Satisfied that he was not being shadowed by an unmarked RCMP car, he got out, locked his door and walked to the lobby of the hotel. He bought an early morning edition of the Toronto *Globe and Mail* and sat down in a chair which provided an unrestricted view of the lobby. Again satisfied that nobody was paying any attention to him, he slowly folded his paper and walked to the bank of telephone booths.

Closing the door of the end booth securely, he inserted two dimes in the slot and dialed. He let the phone ring three times then hung up. He counted slowly to thirty, re-deposited the dimes and dialed again. The phone was answered on the first ring.

"Hello," said a male voice.

"You wanted to speak," replied Lao." "I see that God loves me."

"Did you watch television last night?"

"No, but I know all about it."

"It's serious."

"That remains to be seen."

"It's serious, I tell you!" said the voice in an agitated manner.

"Again," replied Lao softly, "that remains to be seen."

"What shall we do?"

"Nothing! Absolutely nothing. It's probably just a tempest in a tea pot and will blow over by tomorrow morning."

"I don't believe it will. Cairns is on to something. Somebody's talked. I think we should wrap up everything."

"We'll wrap up nothing! Cairns is a desperate man and clutching at straws."

"He's no fool. He wouldn't have said anything if he was just blowing smoke. We have to wrap it up. I don't know how long I can stay in place. There's ... ".

"We'll do nothing differently. The stakes are too high. I have to go. Don't try to contact me again. If I need you I'll get in touch. We'll carry on as though nothing has happened. Goodbye."

Lao didn't wait for a response. He hung up the phone and, without being conspicuous, left the hotel and joined the morning rush hour crowd of office workers on the street. He walked at a casual pace to the Spark's Street Pedestrian Mall where he found a vacant table in a small coffee shop and settled down to read his morning paper over a coffee and a toasted Danish.

8

The Parliamentary grapevine was working at peak efficiency. The Prime Minister had not taken twenty steps from his limousine before word had filtered down that he had arrived, appeared to be in a black mood and would be in his East Block office in moments.

With the customary nods and "good mornings" to those he passed in the corridor, Jennings walked with brisk steps. By the time he reached his office Marcie Peckman, his personal secretary, had a cup of steaming black coffee on a coaster beside his telephone. She also had his schedule for the day with notations beside what she considered to be important items and ones demanding a briefing.

Jennings allowed Marcie to help him off with his suit coat. As she hung it on a large hand-carved hall tree, he sat down and reached for his coffee with one hand and his schedule with the other. He swallowed a sip and said, "Well, it hit the fan last night."

"You could say that," replied Marcie as she sat in a chair beside the desk which had served Canada's Prime Ministers since Mackenzie King. "Is Cairns having a breakdown or can he prove what he's hinting at?"

Jennings shook his head. "I just don't understand him. I assume the press are on the prowl?" Marcie nodded. "Tell them I won't issue a statement until I've spoken to the caucus. Anything we can cancel today?"

"I suppose you could get out of meeting the delegation from the Manitoba Farm Co-operative. Too bad to have them come all this way and not see you. They've been on the list for four months."

"See what you can do. Try and pawn them off on the Deputy Minister of Agriculture. It'll give him a break from worrying about the price of horse shit." Jennings looked at his watch and swore silently. "Where's Harrison? It's eight-thirty."

"I have no idea. I suppose he's preparing a position paper on last night. Cairns really opened a can of worms."

"It's an empty can. He'll rue the day he shot off his mouth." Jennings spat out the words. "Get hold of Lao Chengtu and tell him I won't meet him this morning after all. Let's see how the dust settles before there's any more dialogue with the Chinese. I'd like to see how desperate they are for a meeting. After that," he said, handing her a folder, "this is your top priority for the morning. I want it done by 9:15."

Room 371 in the West Block was not the customary meeting place for the Strategy Committee. It usually met away from the Parliament buildings in a party headquarters room, but because of the short notice of the 8:45 meeting the Chairman suggested Room 371.

Brian Beacom entered the room in a somber mood. Looking neither to the right nor left, he walked quickly to the table and took his seat. The undercurrent of conversation ceased abruptly as Beacom tapped the desk top with his gold Cross pen and said, with heavy tones, "Gentlemen, if you please, we have important matters to discuss without much time to discuss them. I apologize for my own lateness. I was unavoidably detained."

Beacom positioned his reading glasses and looked up. "Thank you, gentlemen. I don't have to tell you that ill winds are blowing and our good ship could be entering upon heavy seas."

One member in the second row nudged the man sitting to his right and whispered, "What he means is that all hell has broken loose." Both men smiled.

"To continue, gentlemen, we have to come to a consensus on how we think the Prime Minister should respond to Mr. Cairns' innuendo. He will have one shot at the target when the question is raised in the House. If he scores a bullseye the matter will be laid to rest. A miss and we shall need the services of Red Adair to smother the greatest political blowout in Canadian history."

Jack Hutcheson, the member for Crow's Pass, Alberta, and a defeated leadership candidate, raised his hand. Beacom nodded. Hutcheson lumbered to his feet. He was a big man and the quintessential western rancher. He was still smarting from being defeated for the leadership and determined to erase the blemish on his record at the next convention. "I won't waste time by rehashing what Cairns said on television. We all heard him and I think we are unanimous in what we think of such bullroar. But before we go off half-cocked, has anybody considered that Cairns may be on to something?"

Beacom stiffened in his chair. He could sense that his authority was about to be challenged. "Is the Honorable Gentleman prepared to make a formal motion of debate on the question?"

Hutcheson pulled at the end of his oversized aquiline nose. "Some of the best and most fruitful conversations that you and I have ever had have occurred outside this room or any other room we meet in. I call you Brian and you call me Jack. We both speak our minds. If we are to arrive at anything significant it has to be through hard informal discussion. What I suppose I am really saying is, let's forget the formality and for once get down to the issue before us without being hampered. If I could say what I really think without fear of it turning up in some minute book in years to come I might really tell you how I see this problem."

42

Beacom looked around the room for a dissenting voice. He could find none. A man of procedure such as Brian Beacom did not welcome such a radical departure. "We'll have to prepare a summary with recommendations for the Prime Minister. It's expected."

Hutcheson nodded. "Of course. That can be done once we've all had the opportunity to speak our mind and come to an agreement on what to recommend to the P.M."

Beacom tapped the top of the table with his pen. "Do I assume gentlemen that you do not wish minutes to be taken?" The affirmative response was unanimous. "So be it," responded Beacom as he nodded in the direction of the recording secretary and waited until she had collected her pencils and stood up. "Keep yourself available. I shall send for you. It goes without saying that what you have just heard is for these four walls only." The secretary indicated her understanding and left the room.

Hutcheson waited until the door was securely closed then turned to face Beacom. "Brian, the question has to be asked. What does the Prime Minister have to say about last night?"

Beacom shifted his weight awkwardly. "I spoke to him briefly after the program last night and told him that this committee would meet this morning. We did not discuss the charges in depth, so I have no idea what he has to say about it. I assume that he is as upset as we are."

"You assume!" thundered Hutcheson. "You mean to tell me that you haven't talked to him this morning?"

"What did you want me to say? I'll be able to speak more intelligently once I have had the benefit of this body's counsel."

Hutcheson shook his head vigorously. "How in God's name can we come to any consensus without knowing what's on the P.M.'s mind?"

D'Arcy Forrest, a slight, balding man with a decided paunch, stood up. He was finishing his fifth parliament and it was no secret it would be his last. He was one of the few parliamentarians who was generally respected by all sides. His counsel was eagerly sought and graciously given.

"If I may, gentlemen," he said in a soothing tone. Hutcheson sat down with a thud. "I have to agree with Jack. The P.M.

43

should have been consulted before we met in emergency session. However, since he wasn't we are only wasting time by begging the question. What we need to do is come to an agreement on what should be done. I also agree with Jack that it is imperative that we find out if any finger of accusation can be pointed at the government, any minister or, God forbid, the P.M. Should a plea of virginal innocence be made it must be made on firm ground. If Mr. Cairns has anything of substance we must know what it is before the question is raised in the House or in the press. In other words, gentlemen, we have to know precisely where we stand before opening our mouths or allowing the P.M. to open his."

"Seeing as how we're being totally candid," interjected Beacom, "I'm not going to allow myself to be criticized for what I have done or not done. I felt it best to meet with you all first then see the P.M."

"Accepted, Brian," said Forrest. "Faced with the same situation I would probably have done the same." Beacom was momentarily pacified. "But right now we are discussing party survival. Should there be a modicum of truth to what Cairns in charging, this party and government is in serious, very serious, trouble. We are all aware of this fact so let's not try and fool one another or evade the issue. We all know that the mores of the Far East are not the mores of North America. Kickbacks are a way of life in that part of the world and not even given a second glance. I believe, Brian, that you would be able to speak to that point."

"Just what do you mean by that, D'Arcy?" Beacom's eyes flashed surprise and anger.

"Haven't you been involved with demands for kickbacks?"

"I resent that, D'Arcy. Indeed I do. Pacific-Orient has always kept its bow headed into the wind and both screws in the water."

"I'm not implying anything, Brian. All I'm asking is if you've ever experienced any demands for favors or kickbacks. That's all. I'm not saying your company became party to such a thing; all I'm asking is if you've come across it."

"The Far East is a difficult marketplace."

"You haven't answered, Brian," Forrest continued to press.

"I said the Far East is a difficult marketplace. You have to be flexible and ready to compete if you want to do business."

"Is it unheard of to have to slip certain people favors which include money for a firm contract? No one will repeat what is being said in this room. We're just looking for background on which to build a solid defense recommendation for the P.M." Beacom nodded slowly. "How prevalent is the practice?"

"Are you inferring that either I or my company has been party to kickbacks?" Beacom's eyes now blazed with righteous indignation.

"I'm not implying anything. Since we are conducting this meeting *in camera* I feel I have complete freedom to say anything or ask anything."

"You haven't license to sully my name or the good name of Pacific-Orient Tugs."

Forrest made no attempt to hide his frustration. "Goddamn, Brian, no one, least of all me, is sullying anything. I'm merely asking."

Beacom paused then softly said, "Kickbacks, or whatever you want to call them, are accepted in the Far East. Unless you make it worthwhile to certain people in high places, you can kiss any contract goodbye. Does that answer your question?"

"Partially. Let's assume that there was a major contract in the offing. Would perhaps some sort of finder's fee be par for the course?" Beacom nodded. "Would that fee be based upon a percentage of the overall contract?"

"Probably."

"Is it conceivable that such a fee would find itself in more than one pocket?"

"It's not unheard of."

"Would such a practice be frowned upon by those in the Far East?"

Beacom placed both hands on the table and slowly folded them. "I believe I can speak with a degree of expertise on the subject. You have to understand how business is conducted in the Far East. The Chinese, especially, are scrupulously honest. Leave anything in a Peking hotel room and it will be delivered to you in Hong Kong. No reward would be expected, and to offer one would be considered an insult. Business is another matter. My company has had major dealings in Hong Kong, Taiwan, Korea and a number of Southeast Asian countries. I can't think of one contract that didn't have a built-in percentage for what we laughingly called expediting insurance. It's no different than building invisible shrinkage insurance into the cost of every item that we purchase in a Canadian department store."

"It's dishonest," said a voice from the second row.

"Not really. If you want your contract processed quickly or if you want someone to intercede with the bureaucrats you have to pay for it. No one works for nothing."

"Kickbacks we all recognize, but what about a finder's fee?" asked Forrest.

"I'm quite certain that such a thing exists. People are paid finder's fees in Canada. Lord knows we paid enough to the negotiators in the early reactor sales. Such a fee is not illegal."

"It is if you are a government representative, Brian."

"Precisely, D'Arcy, and that's what we have to wrestle with. If a Canadian government official has indeed taken a finder's fee from the Chinese for the use of his good offices then the law has been broken and Mr. Cairns is on safe ground. But there are a number of reasons why I seriously question the allegation. The greatest disservice we can do our Prime Minister and party is not to explore all avenues. But I must caution against jumping to unfounded conclusions or suppositions. I personally find it highly unlikely that, if there has been questionable financial dealings, it is at government level. It's more likely to be at the civilian level. That is not to say that a Canadian civilian could not get to a government official and work a deal. That is a very real possibility, but to have a direct line from someone in Peking to someone on Parliament Hill is unlikely. It would be too dangerous for the Chinese to contemplate. Any question of tarnishing relations would be avoided like the plague."

Forrest nodded approval of the point Beacom made.

Denzil McMillan, the only non-establishment member of the committee, raised his hand. A union business manager, he was accepted and liked primarily for his moderate approach to capitalism, free enterprise and government. It was considered refreshing.

"Since you did not speak to the P.M. before we gathered would you kindly refresh memories on exactly where the P.M.

46

stood on the question of the Bonnaventure sales?" said McMillan without rising to his feet.

"Good suggestion," replied Beacom. "Most of us here were closely allied with the P.M. on the question of the sales. For those who were not on the committee then, I must say it was a soul-searching period. On one hand there were those who publicly promoted the sales as being good for Canada. Jobs would be generated, to say nothing of the great spur to Canadian technology and to national pride. It was a very competitive sale. Peking was also considering reactors from Great Britain, the States, Germany and France. To be chosen was quite a coup for Atomic Power. On the other side there was a strong lobby against the sales, supported in a self-serving way by both the States and some of the European countries. It was feared that Canada was falling into a clever trap. Peking would take our technology then turn around and fight us with it. It was not unlike what happened during the late '30s. Japan sent scrap metal dealers all over Canada buying our junk then killed our soldiers with our own steel.

"The P.M. weighed all the arguments carefully. He was personally opposed to relaxing the safeguards, but eventually did so at the urging of many individuals, some of them on this committee. He listened to both sides, then, confident that the sales would be in Canada's best interest, threw his support behind them. It wasn't easy as even cabinet was split on the question. But he prevailed and eventually everyone saw it his way."

"Would it be safe to say that the P.M. has seond doubts at this point in time?" asked McMillan.

Beacom bristled. "We all have questions, not doubts. The Bonnaventures have brought Canada into the forefront of nuclear technology. No nation can match them for design, efficiency and potential."

"I'm not questioning their capabilities, Brian. They may be too good, too easily used for weapons. I'm concerned about the problem at hand. I ask again, do you think the P.M. is concerned?"

Beacom nodded. "Of course he's concerned and so is everyone in this room. It's our duty to give guidance in this matter and that is precisely what I intend to accomplish. I do not think we have to debate the question any further. What is your pleasure, gentlemen. What do I take to the P.M.? We cannot permit our leader to ride into battle with his lance sheathed."

D'Arcy Forrest raised his hand. "I say we reject Cairns' allegations totally out-of-hand. However, we must be cautious and not allow him to seize the advantage on mere speculation. To do so would only exacerbate the situation. Once the damage is done there is no turning back. Damage has been done but we must prevent any further damage and if possible return this garbage to the backyard of the opposition where it belongs. We have to hammer his credibility, attack him for smearing the administration, call him the new McCarthy. A simple put up or shut up. But before we do that, let's know our ass from our elbow. I suggest that we recommend to the Prime Minister that he personally contact the RCMP Commissioner and request an immediate top security investigation into all aspects of the Bonnaventure sales to China. I also suggest that he bypass the Solicitor General. It's within his prerogative to do so should he feel it is in the national interest. Because of the sensitivity of what I am suggesting I recommend that nothing goes beyond these walls. I also suggest that the P.M. be advised to avoid at all costs any debate or confrontation in the House until he has the benefit of a full report from the Commissioner."

No one missed the nuance. It could only be someone such as Forrest, with his political future behind him, who would dare to voice publicly what was common knowledge within the party. The Solicitor General, Lucien Gravelle, could not be trusted. It was not that he wasn't well liked. He was one of the most popular and accessible of ministers. His gregarious nature, however, was his greatest weakness. In an effort to ingratiate himself with the media he had on more than one occasion embarrassed the government and placed the Prime Minister in a position of extreme vulnerability through ill-timed and off-the-record remarks.

On the other hand, it was no secret that Commissioner John Chambers did not relish the prospects of another Liberal government. As Prime Minister, Cairns had used the question of illegalities within the force for political gain. Chambers publicly criticized him for the stance and held him personally responsible for the low morale and wave of public non-confidence. Privately, he would welcome any opportunity to contribute to the discrediting of Cairns.

Beacom pulled at his lower lip. "Being totally candid I feel that D'Arcy's suggestion has merit and I for one will support it. Agreed?" Every head nodded in agreement. Beacom tapped the top of the table with his pen. "Since we have agreed to dispense with formality might I suggest that I speak personally with the Prime Minister and convey our recommendations. Since there will be no minutes there will be no necessity of having the customary summary forwarded to the P.M. In other words, gentlemen, this meeting never officially occurred and no record will ever be made of what was discussed."

"As you would so succinctly put it, Brian," said McMillan with a broad grin, "we have just covered our asses."

Beacom nodded and returned the smile.

9

Marcie Peckman swallowed the last mouthful of her ten o'clock coffee and glanced at her "in" box. It was half full of work which had to be completed by noon. With a labored sigh she switched on her typewriter and was just positioning a letterhead of the Prime Minister's personal stationery when the door to her office opened. Lao Chengtu entered, bowed slightly and offered his card. Marcie stood up. "Mr. Lao. I've been trying to reach you at the Embassy since 8:30. I'm afraid I have bad news. The Prime Minister has cancelled all morning appointments. I tried to reach you, sir."

Lao's eyes narrowed slightly. "Cancelled! It was a firm appointment."

"I realize that, sir, but it was with regret that he advised me he'll not be able to see you this morning. Some pressing business has come up since he made the appointment."

"Most regretful. Did the Prime Minister reschedule the appointment?"

"He hasn't advised me." Marcie opened her pad. "I shall speak to the Prime Minister at the earliest opportunity and do my best to work you into his schedule." The light on Marcie's telephone flashed. "Excuse me," she said as she picked up the receiver. "Yes, Prime Minister. No, I haven't heard from him. I'll see if I can find him. He may have got sidetracked. Yes, I realize that." She hung up the phone and turned to look at Lao. "I'll get your request to the Prime Minister at the earliest moment. Can I reach you at the Embassy?"

"Yes. If I am not available please leave a message and I'll get back to you immediately. Thank you for your trouble."

Lao bowed and left the office.

The moment the door closed Marcie picked up the phone and pushed a button. "Mr. Lao just left my office, Prime Minister. He seemed upset and ..."

A steady stream of people entered and left the Parliament Buildings by the front entrance. Lao paid them little or no attention and was not conscious of a man who stopped in his tracks, wheeled about and followed him at a discreet distance.

Lao was less than half a block from his parked car when the man suddenly increased his pace to a near run.

"Excuse me," he said as he came abreast of Lao and touched his arm.

Lao jerked his arm violently away. He did not like to be touched by strangers. "Yes?"

"I'm Kevin Ingram of Dominion Press." Ingram awkwardly held out his press pass.

Lao stopped. He recognized Ingram. It was his business to know the media. "Mr. Ingram," he said smiling slightly. "Cloak and dagger on an Ottawa street?"

"Could I buy you a coffee? I would like to talk to you. I've been trying to see you for the past few days."

"I've been very busy."

"Could we talk for a few moments. I think you'll find it to your advantage."

"I'm rather pressed. Couldn't we get together tomorrow or the day after?" asked Lao looking at his watch. Ingram shook his head. "Very well," said Lao with a deep sigh. "How about Macdonald's? There's one in the next block."

Macdonald's pleased Ingram's sense of the bizarre. The fact that Lao acquiesced so easily told him he was on to something but it would not be easy. He was confronting a master tactician.

Lao set a brisk pace as he walked toward the golden arches which identified the fast food giant. It took them a moment to get served and seated at a rear booth.

"Now then?" asked Lao as he fixed his eyes intently upon Ingram's.

Ingram opened his notebook and checked to see that his pen was in order. "I've tried to reach you for the past couple of days."

"So you've said."

"Where were you?" Lao did not respond. "When did you request a meeting with the Prime Minister?"

Lao arched his eyebrows and took a long sip of coffee before replying. "You are well informed, Mr. Ingram."

"It's my business. When did you request the appointment?"

"What makes you think that's any of your affair?"

"I'm just curious. I have a fair reputation for tracking down people I want to talk to but you're the exception. You really know how to go undercover."

"You make it sound like cops and robbers."

"How about spy versus surveillance?" Lao bristled noticeably and began to stand up. "Sit down, Mr. Lao. Please sit down. You can't afford to leave before you hear what I have to say," said Ingram in a controlled voice.

"I don't have to account to you."

"True, but you do have to account to the Mounties, especially when you've given them the slip. They're not too pleased. In fact they're mad as hell."

"I don't know what you're talking about. I have nothing to hide from anyone, including your Mounties."

"Oh you're good, Lao, you're damn good. You sure as hell weren't in Ottawa unless you were shacked up with an M.P.'s wife. By the way, I hear most M.P.'s wives enjoy a little bit of variety, especially the oriental brand."

"What's on your mind?"

"The Bonnaventure reactors." Ingram's tone was patronizing.

"The Bonnaventures," repeated Lao.

"Did you want to discuss them with the Prime Minister?" Again, Lao made no response. "Why would you, a Press Attaché, be calling on the Prime Minister to discuss anything. Meetings with heads of governments are usually conducted by the Ambassador or First Secretary, at the very lowest."

"Nothing mysterious or sinister. My Ambassador suggested that I should be the one to speak to the Prime Minister on the matters in question. My background is, I'm sure you will admit, more western than that of any of my colleagues, including Ambassador Wu."

"Your English is much better as well." Lao nodded. "It must have been a delicate subject. Again, was it the Bonnaventures?"

"You seem preoccupied with the Bonnaventures. Canada and China have much more important matters to discuss than reactors that are past history."

"The sale may be past history but they are very much a matter of public concern. Particularly this morning. I assume you were able to watch Jim Cairns on television last night. It was quite a preformance. What is your reaction?"

"I cannot comment on what we consider to be an internal problem."

"Using a program for peace to make instruments of war isn't internal. Payoffs between high-placed officials is more than just an internal problem when two nations are involved. Wouldn't you agree, Mr. Lao?"

Lao smoothed back his hair. His eyes flashed. "You are fortunate, Mr. Ingram, that you did not say that in the presence of witnesses. Had you done so I am sure my Ambassador would have lodged the strongest protest possible with your publisher. You are a very foolish man with a tongue that needs shackling."

"I am simply repeating what the Leader of the Opposition

said on national television. Are you going to take issue with him?"

"That is no concern of yours. There is a saying in my country that 'to defend the truth only blackens the defender.' Can you follow that simple logic, Mr. Ingram."

"You're the one who is not following it. Why jump down my throat while turning a blind eye to Cairns. I would have thought he would be a prime target about now."

"Targets are only chosen when the time is opportune. First come the weapons, then the strategy, then the target. We Chinese always have a secondary target as well just in case something goes awry with the primary. Mr. Cairns is neither primary nor secondary. In fact, he doesn't count. There'll be enough people targeting in on him in Canada. We won't need to concern ourselves." Lao stood up. "A word of advice, Mr. Ingram. Please be careful and look after yourself."

"Sounds like a threat."

"Not at all. Who am I to threaten you? You are an excellent journalist. I enjoy excellence and look forward to your byline. I was referring to the coffee. Too much can injure your health. You should follow our example and drink tea whenever possible. I was just trying to make a friendly suggestion."

Ingram swished the remaining coffee around in the cardboard cup as he watched Lao leave Macdonald's and walk quickly toward his car. Shrugging, he gulped down the coffee. It was cold and bitter.

10

"Where in hell is Harrison?" snapped Christopher Jennings. With obvious irritability which he did not attempt to mask, he thumbed through a formal document that was required reading for question period.

The brittle edge to Jennings' voice startled Marcie Peckman. It was not only his tone but the way he snapped "Harrison". She had never heard him refer to Harrison by anything but his first name unless it was in public. Their casual, warm relationship was admired and envied by those close enough to witness it. For politicians it was remarkable.

"He left a message about an hour ago. He's delayed," said Marcie as she uncrossed her legs and opened her dictation book to a fresh page.

Jennings was tempted to ask if his wife had called but decided against it. He had not spoken to her since dinner last evening. "What's the problem?"

"I don't know, Prime Minister. I didn't speak to him. I was just given the message."

"From now on don't take messages from him. Speak to him personally. I want no more of this third-person nonsense." Jennings' mouth was set in a hard narrow line. "Goddamn him," he growled as his closed fist thumped the desk top.

"He shouldn't be too long," soothed Marcie.

Jennings glared. He clenched and unclenched his fist. Marcie had seen him vent his anger before but never with such venom. He stood up and arched his shoulders. "I want Harrison in here the moment he arrives. Any questions?" Marcie shook her head. "I'm not running some half-assed Baptist Sunday School, you know. I'm trying to run a goddamn government." Jennings' face flushed. The veins on both sides of his neck stood out in purple relief.

"Yes, Prime Minister," mumbled Marcie. His expression shocked her but it was his eyes that were most frightening. She had never seen them blaze with such emotion.

The torrent of anger slowly subsided. Jennings' face gradually lessened in colour and his breathing became more regulated. The blood oozed back into his whitened knuckles as he slowly unclenched his fists. While the release of pent up emotion might be welcomed by a psychiatrist it was terrifying for Jennings. Being a man who always prided himself in possessing total control he found it difficult to look Marcie in the eye. The Prime Minister of Canada was embarrassed.

With the inexplicable sense of timing that only a sensitive

woman possesses, Marcie stood up, closed her dictation book and said in a matter-of-fact voice, "I have a lot of work to get through before noon, Prime Minister. I'll be at my desk if you need me."

Jennings looked up. He was grateful that Marcie had taken the initiative. She had made the moment bearable. "Of course." It was with great difficulty that he controlled the tone of his voice. "Marcie," he said with a slight hesitation.

"Prime Minister," replied Marcie as she reached the closed office door.

"Send him in the moment he arrives." Following an uncomfortably long pause he added, "Please."

Marcie had just turned the doorknob half a revolution when it spun in the palm of her hand. Cole Harrison burst into the room. It was usual for someone entering the Prime Minister's office to be announced. Harrison was the only one on Parliament Hill who did not have to follow procedure. "Sorry," he mumbled. Marcie paused for a moment in the doorway. She watched Jennings and Harrison. Their eyes met momentarily, then both quickly looked away. She found their reaction foreign and uncomfortable. As she closed the door she heard Harrison say, "It's been a hell of a morning."

"You're late!" snapped Jennings.

"Apologies."

"Stick the apologies. What kept you?"

"I had some important business to finish."

"It's important that I see you when I want to see you, especially before I go into caucus."

Jennings stared at Harrison with unblinking eyes. He seemed unsure of himself. In all their association Harrison was always in control and never appeared to be anything but coolly calculating no matter the pressure. He was anything but cool and calculating.

"You can handle those clowns," offered Harrison. It had always been an in-joke between the two men that caucus was nothing more than a three-ring circus with Jennings the ringmaster.

"The clowns are restless, especially those who saw Cairns' TV act last night. They're going to have their say and I have to have the answers. What in hell kept you, today of all days?"

"It was personal."

Jennings was sorely tempted to ask if it concerned Diane but stopped short. "Keep your bloody personal life off Parliament Hill," he ordered.

"You can't buy me twenty-four hours a day, Chris."

The long silence was punctuated by the chiming of the Peace Tower clock.

"What's your evaluation of last night?" asked Jennings as he abruptly changed the subject.

Harrison was relieved that the subject matter was not Diane. "Cairns is either the most calculating bastard in Canada or he was totally suckered by Morrant."

"Suckered or not, this could be the most serious problem the government's had to face."

"Only a fool would take Cairns seriously if they gave any thought to what he said. It was all circumstantial, no substance."

"Substance or not it opened a can of worms that we can ill afford to have open. The press sure jumped on the bandwagon. It's on every front page and the lead item of every newscast." Jennings glared at Harrison. "So, what's your advice?"

"Play it down. Cairns didn't give chapter or verse. I'm inclined to believe that he's merely flying a kite to see if we rise to the bait. Don't give him the satisfaction. Tell the clowns to refuse comment other than to say it's typical Cairns. To be dismissed out-of-hand will really bite his ass."

"He could retaliate by naming names."

Harrison shook his head. "No. He would have done it on Morrant's show if he had anything. I told Kevin Ingram that this morning."

"What did he want?"

"A statement. He's filed another story on the Bonnaventures and wanted something from your office."

"Shit!" said Jennings in a guttural tone.

"Ingram's a good journalist. I can't foresee any problems with what he'll write."

"I can. It'll just keep the pot boiling and give Cairns more ammunition. Any chance of seeing it before it's released?"

"I wouldn't even ask. The last thing we want to do is appear worried."

Jennings stood up and turned his back on Harrison. He

thrust both hands in his pockets and stared out of his office window in silence. Suddenly, he wheeled on his heel and looked at Harrison. "Why in hell does every hack writer feel it's his duty to try to dig up dirt when there is no dirt to dig up?"

"If you want my opinion . . ."

"When I do I'll ask for it!" Harrison made a move to stand up. "Sit down. I'm not finished." Jennings began pacing from his desk to the wall and back. "I have to know what's in the shadows. Nobody, including you or the caucus, seems to have a ghost of an idea what's happening."

"Look, Chris, if you'll give me a minute. I spent nearly an hour with Ingram and he told me nothing I couldn't have read in the morning paper. He's on a fishing expedition. He's seen a bit of smoke and is trying to find the fire."

The colour drained from Jennings' face. "I've had it! That son-of-a-bitch has gone too far. I'm through being made to look like a bloody fool. I'll be goddamned if I'll allow Cairns or anybody to damage the image of the party or government." Jennings made no attempt to control his voice. "You can get the word out. I'll fight. I'm loyal to the people who put me in office and I'm loyal to those who deserve my loyalty." Jennings stared at Harrison, his eyes blazing with fury.

Harrison blinked and rubbed the back of his neck. There was no mistaking who Jennings was challenging. Cairns did not warrant such a dropping of the gauntlet. Far more impressive and worthy foes had been met and defeated. Harrison desperately wanted to tell Jennings that what had happened between him and Diane was not all his doing. At that moment he would have gladly volunteered to walk away from their personal conflict leaving him and Diane to work out their future. But he knew Jennings too well. Such a gesture would have been after-the-fact and rejected. Jennings was not a man to endure injury without demanding satisfaction.

Jennings slowly scanned Harrison's face. A strange feeling gradually crept over him. For a brief moment he felt sorry for his erstwhile friend. He appreciated his anguish. For the first time he was seeing Harrison subjugating his cardinal rule of meeting a problem head on and talking it out to a satisfactory and positive conclusion.

As he studied Harrison he recalled with vivid clarity Diane's dinner pronouncement. "I love Cole and you'll have to accept it because he loves me. We want to be together but we won't do anything to hurt your election chances. We'll do everything we can to help you. We know how important your image is to the party. All we ask is for you to be adult and accept the situation as being irreversible. There's no reason why we can't go our separate ways and still be friends. We have the girls in common. I won't end up hating you and I won't do a Margaret Trudeau. I promise."

Harrison leaned forward in his chair. He had a concerned look on his face. "Chris! Are you all right?"

Jennings reacted with a start. "What? Of course I'm alright."

"You look a bit pale."

"I didn't exactly have a vintage night. I trust you slept well?"

The wedge between the two men was being driven deeper and deeper with each exchange. It was acutely evident to both that the conversation had to be abruptly changed if the moment was to be salvaged. "Any word on when you can expect the Auditor-General to table his report in the House?" asked Harrison desperately.

Jennings' change of expression signalled his surprise at the question. He had expected Harrison to make the most of the opening and say something about their mutual problem. "Any day now." The reply was clipped. "Why?"

"There was no mention of any irregularity involving the Bonnaventure sales in last year's A.G. report. Correct?" Jennings eased back in his chair and nodded affirmatively.

"If there is nothing in this year's report it sure as hell will take the wind out of Cairns' sails. How could he continue to press if the A.G. gave the sales a clean bill?"

"Not bad, but it would only be a band-aid. I need something to shut up the bastard once and for all."

"Beat him at his own game. Stand up in the House and ask the A.G. to look into the sales. If there is nothing in this year's report and nothing in last year's, what can Cairns do? He can only flog a dead horse so long."

Jennings could not suppress a smile of satisfaction. His personal anguish was momentarily forgotten. "I could suck the mother in and blow him out. He won't get elected dogcatcher in

Sheep Dip, Alberta when I get through with him. The thought of not having to look at his face in the next House would be worth all the effort."

Harrison felt relieved. As long as he could keep Jennings' ire directed at Cairns the situation between them could be bearable.

Jennings pursed his lips. "God, how I'd love to nail him."

"This is your chance. The very fact that it's you who requests the A.G. to snoop around will signal the end to Cairns' little charade. He'd be laughed out of the House and the press would have a field day. Cairns never impressed me as having the smarts but he's not that dumb. Anyway, it would take the A.G. at least eight months, maybe more, to wring a report out of his staff."

"It would probably be longer than eight months," mused Jennings. "The Seaway dredging report takes precedence and I haven't seen any action on that one yet."

Harrison nodded in agreement. "By the time it is tabled you could be back in as Prime Minister and Cairns could very well be back to his shyster law practice."

"I can't help but think about the possibility of something small being turned up."

"Like what?" Harrison made no attempt to mask the irritation in his tone.

"Like finding an expense charged to the account by one of the lower echelon."

"Lower echelon are always charging expenses. Not to worry."

"Suppose the expense was for dinner or drinks with someone like Lao Chengtu?"

"So what?"

"So what? Are you losing your sanity? That's all we'd need. Turn up that kind of information and it would be game over."

"The chances of that happening even if some dolt was stupid enough to have gone out with someone like Lao and charged it are remote. We all know that the investigation would be at a high level."

Jennings shook his head in disbelief. "I just can't figure Cairns out. Why would he make such a statement if he had nothing to back it up? Why?"

"God only knows. I'll bet he's sweating about now if he can't deliver the goods. What we have to do is turn this around to our advantage and make yards. Another advantage will be jumping the gun on the editorial writers. They'll demand a full investigation at the very least or a Royal Commission at the most. By announcing that you've already started the ball rolling you'll shut them up. They'll have nothing to bitch about and you'll come off smelling like roses."

Jennings knew Harrison was right. He was always right. The strength of argument reconfirmed that, Diane notwithstanding, he had to have Harrison running his election campaign. After all, some of the most successful duos could not bear the sight of each other.

"Speaking of Lao," said Jennings matter-of-factly. "I cancelled an appointment to see him this morning."

"I didn't know he had an appointment."

"I don't believe I have to clear my appointments with you," replied Jennings testily. "He requested a meeting yesterday."

Harrison was finding it difficult to ride the waves of Jennings' emotions. "What did he want?"

"He wanted to sound me out on a suggestion from Peking before a formal request was made."

"Did he indicate what it concerned?"

"Evidently Peking is interested in accelerating the exchange program we announced last year. It's working very well. The pilot project with the University of Guelph that the Peking Agricultural College has been conducting is exceeding expectations."

"Interesting," mused Harrison. "It certainly wouldn't do us any harm. Did he mention an exchange between the nuclear community?"

"Not specifically, but I am certain that will be included. They are desperate to get the Bonnaventures on-line. I can't understand why they are having problems."

"There are always problems during the de-bugging period, no matter how complete the operational guidelines. How did he take the cancellation?"

"That's the least of my worries. Don't you find it strange that Lao would ask for a meeting the day before Cairns dropped his bombshell? He called me long distance."

"From where?"

"No idea."

"His call was probably pure coincidence. How would he know what Cairns was going to say? But keep him at arm's length. He's a lecherous bastard and I don't fully trust him. Then, again, anybody who can hit the sack with Milly Telford can't be all bad."

Jennings allowed himself his first smile of the morning as he thought about the 146-pound Lao making love to the 183-pound wife of the Honorable Member from New Bicton East. It had its comic overtones, though the Honorable Member failed to see the humor. The separation was bitter and the upcoming divorce gave all signs of being acrimonious. It took the promise of a cabinet position in the next government to pacify Telford and keep him from naming Lao in his action.

"It might be an idea to test the water and let a couple of the thought-leaders at Chalk River in on what's going to be proposed," suggested Harrison. "You can rest assured that Peking will include nuclear research and development in the list of disciplines."

Jennings stroked his chin. It was a sound proposal. Like the majority of Harrison's suggestions this one had merit. "Without being too obvious, find out when Rogers is scheduled to meet with Paul Innis. They're always getting together. Rogers is a stickler for keeping the Minister fully informed, and it gives him an excuse to get to Ottawa for a bit of fun and games. Can't blame him. Chalk River isn't the most exciting town in the province. Then call Rogers and invite him to a private and confidential luncheon with me at Sussex Drive. Tell him I wish to discuss a matter of great urgency. He likes to be stroked and a private luncheon should do the trick."

Harrison stood up. The shift to business had momentarily eased the building tension. "I might be able to get a line on what Cairns is planning for Question Period if I get moving."

"Your private pipeline?" Harrison nodded. "Make sure it's reliable."

"Isn't it always?"

"No," replied Jennings emphatically. The wall being built between the two former friends had not been forgotten.

"It will be."

"For your sake it had damn well better be."

Harrison walked towards the door. He regretted making the offer. Turning, he looked back at Jennings. "You haven't forgotten that the picture layout with you, Diane and the girls is scheduled for five tomorrow afternoon. You might want to remind Diane."

Jennings' features hardened. He was about to suggest that Cole would be in a better position to remind her, but he refrained. "Cancel it!" he snapped.

"It's too late."

"It's never too late."

"What do you suggest I tell them? You agreed to the front cover and an eight page layout. They've been promoting the feature in the last three issues."

"Shit. What's the storyline?"

"Canada's first family and how the family comes first with you and Diane," mumbled Harrison.

"Fantastic!" The bitterness of the moment was evident in Jennings' voice. "The front cover of *The Canadian Family*, plus eight pages. If bullshit was a dollar a ton we'd both be millionaires for that one. I should never have let you talk me into it. They should give you the byline." Jennings swung his chair until his back was to Harrison.

Harrison smarted under the verbal abuse. There was no other man he'd allow to talk to him in such a manner, but he had no defense. Jennings held the trump card for the moment. "Is that all?" he asked with a resigned sigh.

"Not quite. See Marcie on your way out. She has something for you."

"What?"

"Your ticket and itinerary. If you'd been here on time you could have worked on it with her. You'd better get moving." Jennings looked at his watch and smiled slightly. "Your plane leaves in less than four hours."

Harrison's face blanched. "To where?"

Jennings leaned back in his chair and entwined his fingers. "Halifax, then Moncton, Summerside, Fredericton, Saint John, Truro and St. John's." Harrison did not miss the tone of pleasure as Jennings rattled off the Maritime cities. "You're going to be a busy man for the next three weeks."

"You've got to be kidding," replied Harrison in a jesting

tone. "I can't leave Ottawa with all this shit hitting the fan."

"I'm through kidding, or haven't you noticed. I intend to call an election early in September and your assignment for the next two months is to organize party rallies and dinners to stir up the troops and raise money."

"Send somebody else, Chris. You need me to run interference."

"I need you in the Maritimes and that's it. By the way, don't fill your social calendar until after the election. Once you've covered the east you can begin in Quebec, Ontario and the west."

"You're full of surprises," snorted Harrison.

"One thing more. You'd better do a job with the party because there won't be any second chance."

"If that's a threat, Chris, I don't like it."

"It's no threat. It's a statement." Jennings would have enjoyed nothing better than to have fired Harrison on the spot, but he was astute enough to realize that he needed his administrative skills to fight the election. Under normal circumstances he would have made things much easier for Harrison by sending him out with a pre-election team. He had no intention of making things easier. He also had no intention of handing Cairns another opportunity to make political gains through the dismissal of his trusted advisor. He was boxed in on all sides, but he still controlled the box.

Harrison didn't reply. He rose slowly and walked quickly out of the office. A droplet of perspiration trickled down his forehead and glistened like a bead on the bridge of his nose.

11

James Cairns ran an index finger around his collar. It came away moist. The caucus room seemed to be overly oppressive but he was quick to accept that the stress of the moment could be a contributing factor to his discomfort. It had not been an easy caucus. While the chairman tried to work through the minor items on the agenda first, everyone realized that Cairns' television performance was going to be the major focus of the day.

Cairns was barely paying attention to a backbencher's pleadings for support in opposing a proposed change in tariffs as they applied to the shoe manufacturing industry. His threats of tabling a private member's bill were greeted with mild chortles. The legislation he opposed was not a popular one to oppose and the political climate was not right for crusading, no matter how just the cause. To the relief of all listening the speaker realized the futility of continuing and, with a disgusted and resigned grunt, sat down.

The Chairman nodded toward a raised hand. "If Mr. Cairns would be so kind, I would be grateful to hear an assessment of his appearance on television last night." Cairns was slightly taken aback that the speaker was Alistair Coleman, the Member for Vancouver East. Coleman was the last one Cairns expected to raise a thorny question. He could count on the fingers of one hand the number of times Coleman had spoken out either in caucus or the House. A hard worker in committee, he was not particularly high-profile but he was a loyal party member.

Cairns pushed back his chair and stood with hands on hips in a characteristic pose. It emulated Sir Winston Churchill at his fighting best. "I have nothing further to add at this time." Cairns was purposely using a disparaging tone hoping it would diminish the weight of the question. "I am sure you will agree that I revealed nothing more than what you are all privy to. We have had frank discussion on the question of patronage and payoffs within government and the bureaucracy. My views are clear."

"You were specific last night," interjected Coleman in a rare outburst of firm comment.

Cairns nodded. "Of course. We all know that the Prime Minister and his government are in a precarious position when it comes to defending the Bonnaventure sales. The relaxation of safeguards didn't go over well with the voters who care."

"That's old news. What about payoffs?" interjected an unidentified voice from the rear of the room.

Cairns bristled. "I make no apology for what I said on television last night. I am, as I stated, preparing a formal statement for the House. I shall advise this caucus of its contents prior to rising." Cairns sat down and slowly crossed his legs.

"The floor is open," said the Chairman.

Cairns was not surprised by who rose first. Grenville Nolan was an impressive man. By profession he was a corporation lawyer and prior to entering politics sat on numerous bank, industrial and commercial boards. Tough, uncompromising and politically ruthless, he was not universally liked within or without the party, but he was respected. His power came from high level contacts and influence, especially within the banking community. Publicly Cairns presented a friendly face when in his company. Privately neither man liked the other.

"I am quite sure I speak on behalf of this caucus," began Nolan in a pompous tone, "when I say it would have been greatly appreciated had we all had prior information as to the substance of your statement on television instead of receiving the shock of the year in prime time."

A current of controlled laughter filled the room. Grenville Nolan had scored decisively once more. While the statement was simply a summation of what the majority of members felt, his caustic delivery was carefully calculated. It was a golden opportunity to goad Cairns and he was never a man to pass up an opportunity. Should the question of a leadership review gain momentum the first one to declare his intention to challenge Cairns would be the Honorable Member from St. Mark's. Groundwork was being laid.

Cairns licked his lips. The possibilities of the next few moments had to be weighed carefully. He could conveniently throw all blame for what he had said upon Winston Morrant. It would be a convenient out to plead pressure of the moment. But to do so would be admitting weakness. He had taken great pains to perpetuate his image as a man of controlled reason and to imply that he could be shaken by a television interviewer would be tantamount to admitting that at a time of crisis he would panic and throw reason to the wind. It would be regarded as a minor manifestation of the 'Chappaquiddick Syndrome'. To tell the truth was nearly as dangerous.

Cairns cleared his throat. There was no mucus to clear. The

oppressive silence was slightly broken as he forced a series of deep throated hacks. "I regret that you were all taken by surprise." Cairns looked around the room and smiled as warmly as he could manage. "Had there been time to brief this caucus prior to going on-air with Mr. Morrant, I most certainly would have done so. Unfortunately there was not. Television as you are all well aware is immediate and one does not always have the luxury of time to do what one would like to do. I have always been a great admirer of those who can seize the moment and grasp the victory. I feel I have won a major battle for all of us by putting the Prime Minister off balance and on the defensive. If you were taken by surprise, imagine how the Prime Minister reacted."

Heartier laughter greeted this aside than Nolan's. Cairns was pleased that he had at least evened the score. "I have in my possession documented proof that will support my statement last night. When the full details are made public, which will be in a matter of days, I believe the government will fall and we shall once again lead this nation with responsibility and honesty." The room erupted in solid clapping and cries of "hear! hear!" Cairns looked at the caucus Chairman and nodded.

"If there is no other business, I declare this meeting closed. Thank you, ladies and gentlemen," intoned the Chairman.

Cairns quickly picked up his briefcase and, with a set smile on his face, left the caucus room. He headed down the hall toward his office with brisk steps.

Grenville Nolan took off his glasses and held them up to the light for inspection.

"What do you think, Grenville?" asked a backbencher.

Satisfied that both lenses were clean he replaced the glasses and turned to look at his questioner. "What I think at this point really doesn't matter but since you asked I have to say that our leader is a crafty bastard. He knew what he was doing last night. He also knew what he was doing a few moments ago. He is a man of balloons and smokescreens. Very clever. He may have the moment, but I shall have the day. Oh yes, I shall have the day."

Jennings looked across the House at the one empty seat in the front row of the opposition. Momentarily, he expected the rear curtains to part and Cairns enter with the flourish that had become his trademark and the subject of countless political cartoons. He admired Cairns' showmanship. He added a dash of color to the House by timing his entrances perfectly. For a brief moment all eyes would be on him. It was not done out of personal conceit, although he was, at times, a vain man. Rather, it was expediency. Few politicians had his panache or ability to play to the gallery while still maintaining an aura of creditability. Being the centre of attraction in the House kept his media profile high. At times he appeared to be obsessed with his profile, an obsession that became more apparent as election fever increased.

Jennings found it curious that today, of all days, Cairns was conspicuous by his absence. All sitting members were in their places and the atmosphere tingled with excitement and anticipation. The press and public galleries were packed and many strained for a better look. The stage was set and the players, less one, were in their places waiting for the confrontation.

Jennings looked at his watch and hunched forward in his seat. It was 2:38 and the one-hour afternoon Question Period was progressing far better than he had dared to hope. The first twenty minutes were taken up by members rising to speak "on matters of urgency". Another twenty-two minutes and he could relax until tomorrow. By then he might have additional information that could defuse Cairns' attack if and when it came.

For one of the few times in memory Cole Harrison's grapevine had let him down. Reluctantly, and with some embarrassment, he could find out nothing more than was common knowledge on Parliament Hill. Cairns and his caucus met behind closed doors. Security was tighter than usual and not even Harrison, with all his connections, could penetrate it. Instead of reporting his failure directly to Jennings he typed up a brief memo and asked Marcie Peckman to get it to the Prime Minister before he entered the House. He told Marcie that he was late for an appointment. She knew he was lying.

Cairns' absence told Jennings that Cairns had just launched another of his celebrated trial balloons. If so, there would be no snapping nor nibbling at the bait. It would not be the first time Cairns had grabbed media attention by shotgunning without substantiation. If the allegations were groundless, the RCMP, still smarting from some of his attacks in the House, would salivate at the prospect of proving Cairns wrong and seeing him held up to public ridicule.

Godfrey Lang, financial critic in Cairns' shadow cabinet was on his feet. A ponderous man, with a pontifical air, he was able to raise the hackles of government by merely rising to his feet. He was considered to be an embittered, mean-spirited man by the more generous. The less generous were quick to label him a son-of-a-bitch.

"Mr. Speaker, if I may be allowed to address the House without being shouted down before I put the question . . ."

"The House is giving you a message," called a voice from the government backbench.

The speaker rose to his feet. Three parliamentary pages popped up in front of him like rising pistons. "Order please," he intoned. "Let the Honorable member speak." The moment the Speaker sat down the pages dropped to their sitting positions at the foot of his chair.

Lang sighed and feigned exasperation. It was with great difficulty that he hid his pleasure. He was getting under the skin of government and enjoying it immensely. This was his moment of glory and he was playing it to the hilt. He was also playing to the bank of television cameras which were lined up behind the Hansard reporters and in front of the press. To be the star of Question Period guaranteed being seen by the constituents when the cable companies replayed the day's session in the early evening. Lang was not above seizing an opportunity to grandstand.

Lang's overblown rhetoric ate up valuable minutes, and as Malcolm Dewer, the Minister of Finance, rose to reply, Jennings signalled to him to stretch out the response. The 'parliamentary stall' worked to perfection.

Jennings glanced at his watch. It was three-and-a-half minutes to the hour. There would not be enough time for much more than a brief supplementary. Jennings knew that Cairns still held the focus of attention. Everyone would be questioning his absence.

Following the introductory handshake and polite conversation,

RCMP Commissioner John Chambers positioned himself comfortably in one of the two armchairs facing Jennings' desk in the study at 24 Sussex Drive.

"Thank you for coming at such short notice, Commissioner."

"My pleasure, Prime Minister."

"This conversation is for these four walls only. Agreed?"

"Agreed."

"I am sure you are well aware of what Mr. Cairns had to say on television regarding the sale of the Bonnaventure reactors to China. I am confident that you accept the fact that I have to dismiss his allegations totally out-of-hand until I am faced with hard, irrefutable proof of malfeasance."

"Of course, sir."

"However," Jennings leaned forward in his chair and fixed Chambers with a firm stare. "I have to consider the possibility that just perhaps someone in my government, party or a member of the civil service might have transgressed. I cannot run the risk of having *prima facie* evidence dictate the future. I must know whether there are grounds for Mr. Cairns' allegations or if he is just making mischief in order to embarrass the government. This is where I need your counsel and valued expertise."

Chambers placed both arms on the arms of the chair, entwined his fingers, and leaned forward. "My department is at your service, sir. What can we do?"

"You can instigate an immediate and thorough investigation of the Bonnaventures sales to China."

"Under what terms of reference?"

"*Carte blanche.*" Chambers smiled. "But," continued Jennings, "with one proviso. It has to be in the strictest of confidence with no one being privy to the investigation or the results but me. Do you accept?"

"Indeed, sir."

"I have instructed the Ministers of Science and Technology, Industry and Commerce, External Affairs, and Energy, as well as the Solicitor General to begin an immediate investigation into their own departments and report back to me at the earliest date. I shall make this fact public but I do not intend announcing that you are also conducting an investigation at my personal request."

"May I ask why not, Prime Minister?"

"There's no other way to resolve this problem, Commissioner. You've been around politicians long enough to accept the fact that cover-up is a way of life if it can be done without danger of exposure. I've been in politics long enough not to trust even those closest to this office. Every man has his price. I just want to find out if someone has settled on a figure."

Chambers looked away for a minute in deep thought. Of all the Prime Ministers he had served under he respected Jennings above all others. He accepted the fact that he was a political creature but he was a political creature with conscience. "Have you considered the possibility that my men just might turn up something questionable?"

"Of course I have, Commissioner. That was my first consideration."

"Will you act upon it if I bring in a negative report?"

"You have my word. If Mr. Cairns is speaking the truth, and God knows I pray he isn't, I shall see that due process of the law is carried out to the letter."

"You mentioned that every man has his price. Do you suspect anyone in government?

Jennings slowly shook his head. "No, but everyone needs money. It's no secret that Mr. Gravelle, the Solicitor General, is hard pressed to make ends meet. He married a young woman and is still supporting his first wife and six children under the age of fifteen. I know Lucien and I can say that until proven otherwise he is a man of the highest integrity. I can also say the same thing about Mr. Brian Beacom. All you have to do is read the financial pages to realize that his tugboat company is teetering on the verge of bankruptcy. Through no fault of his own he's wrestling with a financial disaster. I tried to get the Chinese to allow a search of their coastline for some missing barges but the area they were lost in is militarily sensitive and there was nothing I could do. Mr. Beacom needs an influx of capital in the worst way, but again I defend his integrity. I could go on."

"Well taken, Prime Minister. It's not unlike an Agatha Christie mystery where everyone including the butler is a suspect."

"No, Commissioner, it's not like an Agatha Christie mystery. We have to assume that no crime has been committed. That's your job."

Chambers nodded his head. "Agreed. I shall report back to you the moment I have anything definite one way or the other."

Jennings stood up and reached across the desk. The two men shook hands warmly.

12

With a sigh, Adam Sutton butted his fourth cigarette in the glass ashtray and began to push the other three butts into a straight line. The foyer of the Chinese Embassy was devoid of any basic comfort for guests. Two straight-backed chairs, separated by a small end table, and a glass ashtray comprised the furnishings.

Sutton ran an index finger around his limp collar and stretched his neck. He was uncomfortably hot and not in a particularly good frame of mind. The harassing he had endured from his peers at the Press Club the previous evening had given him a sleepless night.

The questions were mild and veiled at first. They centered around general working conditions as they related to filing stories and editorial control. As the evening wore on and the drinking became serious he was asked point blank if he still felt he was a good Canadian by selling his talents to what was once a hostile nation, a nation dedicated to the overthrow of the Canadian way of life.

It took all of Sutton's emotional control not to explode. The question was put by what he considered to be a bleeding heart liberal and a journalist who had championed the cause of civil rights to the utmost, including the right of child pornography if there was mutual consent. Stomping out of the Press Club, Sutton walked the streets for over an hour then sat up until nearly dawn trying to rationalize his position and come to terms with continuing on as Ottawa correspondent.

Money was the criteria. Peking had upped the ante to nearly twice the going rate for the right man. After years honing his craft, many times on subsistence wages, it was an attractive offer. Sutton convinced himself that it was not his responsibility to adjudicate on what nation was friendly and what nation was not. That was the role of government. The People's Republic of China was deemed to be a friendly nation, with full diplomatic recognition, so why shouldn't he make the most of the opportunity. His red-necked colleagues didn't stop drinking their rum and cokes just because Coca-Cola beat out Pepsi-Cola for the Chinese market.

The door at the end of the foyer opened and Lao Chengtu beckoned to Sutton. He did not speak as Sutton followed him into his office. Closing the door, Lao said, "Sorry to have kept you waiting. I never enjoy sitting in reception areas. They remind me of my schoolhood days and the times I spent sitting outside the principal's office." Sutton didn't comment. He handed Lao a brown manila envelope. "How many words?" asked Lao as he pulled out the pages and arranged them neatly on his desk.

"Just over 1,200," replied Sutton. Lao picked up the pages. "I did two versions. I thought it might be useful to submit one version for internal consumption and one for the international wire services."

Lao nodded. "You're catching on very quickly, my friend. I don't have to tell you that while Xinhua does a competent job for China and the Far East it is light years behind the West. We need all the help we can get. You did well to consider two versions. Peking will be pleased. It is always preferable to write for your audience and in most instances you will have two audiences."

"You don't have to apologize for Xinhua. Just ask any correspondent who covered Viet Nam. Their coverage was good, once you compensated for the bias. More than one story was based on a Xinhua feature."

"What do you mean, bias?"

Sutton squirmed slightly in his chair. Now was not the time to offend someone who had the power to make or break you. "Viet Nam was covered from two perspectives. Let's face it, the

72

West had one and so did China. There was bullshit pouring out of both sides."

Lao nodded. "Accepted, but when it comes to making the bullship readable the West beats us hands down. We have a lot to learn. We're not unlike the Arabs vis-à-vis the Israelis when it comes to sophistication in the fine art of propaganda. When was the last time you saw a Xinhua byline?"

"Not too long ago, as a matter of fact. It was an excellent roundup story on 'The Trail Of The Centaur' in Peking."

"I agree it was a very good story but when did you last see a Xinhua feature on something not relating to China or the Far East? American Press, Tass, Reuters, even Canadian Press are picked up internationally. Very seldom Xinhua. That will change."

"It won't take long for Xinhua to meet Western standards," said Sutton encouragingly.

"How long do you think it will take Xinhua to *set* the standards?" asked Lao.

"About as long as it will take China to overtake the Soviet Union and become number one."

"I wonder. Let me see what you have written then we'll talk. Smoke if you like." Lao pushed an ashtray toward Sutton.

The only sound in the room was the flipping of pages. Sutton inhaled deeply and looked intently at Lao for any indication of pleasure or displeasure. Lao's expression did not change. On a couple of occasions he went back to earlier pages then flipped forward.

Finally, after an agonizing fifteen minutes he jogged the sheets into a neat pile and laid them on the desk. "Excellent! My compliments. A well constructed story. It should receive wide circulation within my country. You have handled the entire question with great detail and detail is something we Chinese not only admire but demand. Your contacts are most impressive. How well do you know Mr. Brian Beacom?"

Sutton exhaled a lungful of smoke. "I can't say I know him personally, but I think I have an 'in' with him."

"An 'in'?"

Sutton was momentarily taken aback by Lao's question. "About five years ago, when I was, shall we say, slightly strapped for cash, I accepted an assignment from the editor of 'Maritime

Canada,' to write a feature on Beacom and his tugboat company. I heartily dislike doing trade press stories because they are nothing more than glorified puffs. However, this one was different. I spent two days with Beacom and came up with a pretty good piece. Beacom remembered me and that got me past his secretary. That's my 'in'."

"I see," said Lao with a broad smile.

"That's all there is to it."

"Don't limit yourself, my friend. When one can get in to see the Chairman of the Strategy Committee and a close advisor to the Prime Minister it is a remarkable achievement. I'm impressed." Sutton shrugged. He found the moment awkward. "Can he be relied upon?"

"In what way?"

"In what he says."

"He's no more or no less reliable than any bureaucrat, politician or party hack. He's playing a game and playing it very well."

Lao nodded approval. "Would he be above feeding false information to serve his own ends?"

Sutton laughed. "You've got to be kidding? No one in that bunch on Parliament Hill is above serving his own ends."

"You sound cynical."

"When you've been around as long as I have, cynicism becomes a way of life. It's an incurable disease."

"I assume you quoted Mr. Beacom verbatim. I'd hate to think that you took license with what he had to say."

"There's no editorializing with Beacom's quotes. Every word is exactly as he gave it to me. I have it all in my notes. Do you want to see them?"

"Of course not. I trust your professionalism." Lao smiled in a slightly patronizing manner. "One can't be too cautious when dealing with politicians, can one?"

"I can understand your reservations. I'd be the same if I were in your place."

"Splendid. It's nice to know we agree. What about my reservations regarding Mr. Beacom being so outspoken. Do you share them?"

"Normally I'd say yes, but not in the case of Beacom. He's a very high-profile party functionary and wields a lot of power with the P.M. Just consider how often senators speak out, and not too many have the political clout of Beacom."

Lao flipped through the sheaf of pages. "Ah, here it is. 'I get weary trying to answer outrageous and unfounded attacks upon the Government of Canada, especially when they are voiced by the Leader of the Opposition who in my opinion should know better. The Prime Minister has always championed good relations between Canada and The People's Republic of China. To cause a slur upon the integrity of Canadian civil servants and their counterparts in China is beneath comment.'" Lao smiled broadly. "Strong words, but necessary ones."

Lao stood up and extended his hand. "Congratulations. An excellent beginning for what I am confident will be a long and mutually beneficial relationship. Are you receiving any negative reaction from your fellow journalists for accepting the job?"

"Why do you ask?"

"It's expected and predictable. Mr. McBride found solace in alcohol. I hope you don't follow the same route."

"Don't worry about me. I'm not Tom McBride."

Lao nodded. "What do you plan for your next article?"

"I thought you'd assign it."

"When there's something specific we want you to write we'll assign it. For the meantime we'd like to have your suggestions. After all, you Canadians know the reader and what makes news and what doesn't make news much better than we Chinese do."

Sutton sensed a slightly patronizing tone in Lao's voice. "I'd like to do something positive on what China is doing with the Bonnaventures."

"Why the Bonnaventures?"

"Because they are in the news and because they interest me."

"They are certainly in the news, thanks to Mr. Cairns."

"I'll need some help if the story's to have a snowball's chance of being picked up."

"Such as?"

"Cleared information that I can use, plus deep background which will give me a solid foundation. Could you get me a rundown on some of the more glamorous programs that have been successful?"

"Be specific."

"Medicine, agriculture, science, communications, safety. Everyone's interested in the safety of nuclear reactors. What are your controls like? Are they more stringent than ours? If they are I have my hook. I'm looking for something to get my teeth into. I want something that will interest and satisfy the most demanding reader in both our nations. If I can write authoritatively about what China is doing in the light of Pakistan, China will come up smelling like roses."

Lao stroked his chin. He had a satisified look on his face. "You won't be able to write about China using the Bonnaventures for military purposes, because we're not. We have totally dedicated them to peaceful purposes."

"I accept that. It should be said in a positive manner. By simply stating irrefutable facts your message will come across with strength. Just thank God you're not trying to whitewash Pakistan. It's no secret that Canada has sold Pakistan vital components to help it enrich plutonium. I just read a report that Pakistan hopes to test a nuclear weapon before too long. Evidently it fears India, West Pakistan and China."

"We have no designs upon Pakistan."

"So you tell me."

"We are well aware of what Pakistan is planning. We keep a guarded eye upon our neighbours," said Lao icily.

"I'll just bet you do. Anyway, if you agree I'll go to work on my story and see how it shapes up. It wouldn't hurt if I could get some direct quotes from India or Pakistan. I don't hold out much hope of even getting them to speak to me but it's worth a try. Even if I don't I could always mention that I tried but they wouldn't talk. That would be just as damning as some nonstatement. Just think how China would look in the story. The reader would see how open your country has become. It would certainly counteract much of the bad press about China being a closed society.

Lao smiled broadly. "Excellent! Excellent! Give me a couple of days and I'll have more material than you can use. Don't forget to write positively about Canada's co-operation and participation."

"I won't. I'll give you a good story."

"I have no doubt about that, my friend."

Lao saw Sutton to the front door and shook hands. As Sutton

walked down the embassy steps he began to mentally compose the letter of resignation he would write to the Secretary of the Press Club. He was no longer uncomfortably hot.

Cindy Morris leaned across the table and refilled Kevin Ingram's glass with wine. He looked at her without speaking. He was a man at peace. For the first time in recent memory the pendulum of life had swung in his direction. His feature on Canadian/Sino relations had won him the accolades of his peers and the congratulations of his editor, which was a rarity. Dominion Press was never singled out as an organization that congratulated let alone even recognized good work. It was general policy to treat all good work as the norm and anything less as totally unacceptable. Ingram's story was pinned to the newsroom bulletin board. In the margin was the notation "excellent".

"You're looking very self-satisfied," mocked Cindy as she raised her glass in salute. "I suppose you think that the violation of my body would be suitable reward."

"Believe it or not I had not given your body any thought up to now. But since you mention it. . . . You know, I knew I had the makings of a good one but I never expected it to be picked up to the extent it was. I just saw a list of papers that picked it up. *Vancouver Sun, Edmonton Journal, Winnipeg Free Press, Sudbury Star, Globe and Mail, Kingston Whig-Standard . . .*"

Cindy held up her hand. "Spare me the glory list. I read your story and you have my congratulations and my body. What more can I offer?"

Ingram smiled. "I needed that story, Cindy. I was beginning to believe that I was washed up."

"Don't be stupid. You're good. I've always known that you're good. I remember the first time I saw your byline. It was on the exposé of babies for sale. I just hope they didn't suck you in. You can't trust those Chinese. They're as slippery as the Soviets."

"Don't be racist."

"I'm not. For the past thirty years they haven't had a good word to say about the West, now they're all filled with the milk of human kindness. I don't trust them." Ingram drained the remaining drops of liquid from his glass and passed it across the table. "You've had enough."

"Fill the damn glass. I'm just beginning."

"Might as well. You'll fall asleep and leave me alone."

"That's what you think. Wine makes me horny as hell, or haven't you noticed?" Cindy smiled and filled his glass to the brim. "Do you remember me telling you about Adam Sutton?" Cindy nodded. "He is in the same position I was before this story. The guys at the Press Club have been giving him a pretty hard time. I gave him some of my background notes and I hope he rubs their collective noses in a good feature."

"What are you sharing your hard work for? Let him get his own story."

"Just like a bloody woman. No compassion."

"Don't give it away. Become a hooker and sell it."

Ingram reached across the table and gently rubbed the back of Cindy's hand. "There's method in my madness. He has the inside track at the Chinese Embassy and if I give him one or two crumbs he'll be grateful. You never know he might come through and I could top what I just did. In this business it helps to have the odd person owe you one."

"What's next?"

"Haven't the vaguest. I was thinking about an in-depth feature on sex over thirty."

"Where did you plan to do your research?" Ingram nodded his head in the direction of the bedroom door. "That's what I thought. No imagination. Take the easy way out. Don't put any effort into your research."

"You'll rue the day you said that. You've just issued a challenge that a virile man such as I cannot walk away from."

"Well start walking toward the sink. I'm not leaving this mess to clean up in the morning." Cindy began to collect the dirty dishes. While she waited for the sink to fill with hot water Ingram put a record on the stereo and began humming along with the soft romantic music.

"Are you serious about not knowing what story you'll work on next?" she asked as she began to wash the dishes and place them in the drying rack.

Ingram nodded. "I'm serious. This is always a problem. You come up with a winner and the next day they ask you 'what's next'. Any suggestions?"

"Forget it. It's not your type."

Ingram was intrigued. "Come on. You never know."

"I saw something at the Summons Bureau that was a bit unusual. Diane Jennings got a summons."

"So she got a summons. What's so unusual about that?"

"Why would the wife of the Prime Minister be driving around Ottawa in a five- or six-year-old car after midnight?"

"You must be mistaken. The Prime Minister's wife doesn't drive five- or six-year-old cars near midnight. She has a chauffeur with an RCMP security officer. With all the political kidnappings they wouldn't let her out on her own to roam around at that time of night."

"I'm telling you it was her. We ran the driver's license number through the computer. It was hers. The only fun we have in the summons office is to watch for the names of prominent people. You'd be surprised how many M.P.'s get nailed for impaired. You'd also be surprised how many try and talk the cop out of issuing a summons. I guess they don't want to have to explain where they were going or coming from."

"Was she loaded?"

Cindy shook her head. "It wasn't serious. Speeding, failing to yield or something like that. I can't remember."

Ingram's curiosity was stimulated. "Could you find out who the arresting officer was?"

"I suppose so. Why?"

"I'd like to talk to him. It may be nothing but again you never know."

"I could get in trouble. It's against the law for anyone to give out that type of information."

"Who'd know?"

"What would you say to the cop?"

Ingram shrugged his shoulders. "I don't know. I'd probably tell him that I had heard from reliable sources that he busted the P.M.'s wife and if he doesn't tell me everything he knows I'll print his name and badge number. I wouldn't use undue force or threats."

"Charming," snorted Cindy as she pulled the stopper out of the sink and watched the water swirl down the drain. "Where do you suggest I apply for a job after I'm fired without references?"

"Don't worry. No one will know where I got my lead. What I need is the precise time, location and charge. Can you do it?"

"I suppose so. What kind of story are you planning to write?"

"I haven't got the vaguest, probably no story. I'm just curious."

"I'm taking a big chance. If you do anything and our manager thinks that one of us gave out classified information there'll be hell to pay."

"I don't have to reveal my sources. Anyway, if I do the story I'll write it in such a way that no one will connect me to you. Who knows you're sleeping with Canada's foremost investigative reporter?"

"Absolutely no one. A few of my friends suspect I'm having an affair with a hack writer who is basically insecure."

Ingram flicked the tea towel at her as she bent over the kitchen counter. She jumped. "What's in it for me?"

"You'll receive payment in advance." Ingram took her hand and led her to the bedroom.

13

The Tom McBride story was well known in Ottawa press circles. A veteran journalist with a sound reputation, he shocked his colleagues by accepting an offer to become Ottawa press correspondent for Xinhua. His acceptance was just slightly more startling than Xinhua's active recruitment within the press corps.

It is customary for foreign governments to handle their press requirements through experienced nationals with full press accreditation. Generally, they report to a bureau chief who in turn works closely with the press attaché at the embassy or directly under the ambassador. With minor exceptions, and those being Third World or emerging nations, the majority of Far and Near Eastern nations have a long and continuous history of co-operation with the Western press. They are experienced in how to gather news, write it in acceptable style and disseminate it. Because of China's more than twenty years of isolation behind the bamboo curtain there was a dearth of journalists capable of taking on the duties of Ottawa correspondent. It would take months or years to restructure the curriculum for journalism students, and most pre-revolutionary journalists had either been purged or were dead.

What Peking was desperately looking for was a Lao Chengtu within their media. None was to be found. Recruitment was the only answer. The danger of this approach was apparent. To find someone acceptable with ideological sympathies would be almost impossible. An avowed Maoist, of which there were many in the Canadian leftist community, could not be considered. To have a modicum of acceptability with the Canadian press the successful candidate should not be in Peking's camp. It would be difficult enough without having the added burden of resentment and suspicion because of political bias.

It was decided that the incentive would be monetary. Enough would be offered to entice the financially embarrassed or the avaricious. Tom McBride was the former.

Under normal circumstances a nation which lacks in one area will very often turn to a neutral nation or a closely aligned nation for mutual cooperation. Had relations between Peking and Moscow been on a better footing this route would have most likely been followed. Instead of McBride, Tass or Pravda would have been feeding Xinhua until they could take over for themselves.

McBride did a creditable job in the face of monumental obstacles. Immediately upon the announcement of his acceptance he became anathema to many of his former press friends. Questions were raised over drinks. Speculation was rampant that McBride had sold out his principles.

The opposition initially made McBride dig in and work with a vengeance, but the pressures began to have a telling affect. His drinking pattern changed from social to serious, his circle of friends narrowed to the point of non-existence, he began to deteriorate physically.

The honest, hardworking, uncompromising, foundation upon

which McBride had built his reputation began to crumble as he privately questioned his motivation. His day-to-day working pattern became a love-hate relationship with the Chinese. Once he could no longer rationalize why he, an avowed capitalist, was being held personally responsible for the slanted propaganda from Peking, he quit. It was a messy resignation culminating with a twelve-day drinking marathon. During a final fit of anger and remorse he attacked a Chinese waiter and threw a chair through a restaurant window. He was arrested for drunk and disorderly conduct and served his 30-day sentence on weekends.

When he finished his term he disappeared.

The Ottawa Valley hamlet of Haley's Station was set in a picturesque rolling landscape between Renfrew and Cobden. It hadn't changed much since the lumber barons of the early 20th century roamed from North Bay to Ottawa raping the forests of their hard timber. Small lakes dotted the area and the only visitors were cottage owners from as far away as upper New York State who found the tranquility an ideal refuge from the pressures of a fast-paced life.

A one-bedroom cottage with split pine siding nestled between two larger cottages on the south shore of Garden Lake. For the past two summers it had been empty. It's owner, Graham Morgan of Waterdown, New York, had been unable to spend his treasured vacations at the lake because his wife suffered from Parkinson's disease and couldn't travel. Concerned that the cottage might fall into disrepair, he decided to rent it to a responsible individual who would at least cut the grass and give it the semblance of being lived in. He was also concerned that if it remained empty it would fall victim to the thieves who looked for just such a prize. The rental price was very attractive. Two days after the ad appeared in the Ottawa paper Morgan and Tom McBride struck a bargain.

The emotional impact of McBride's resignation from Xinhau was profound. His drinking increased with his depression and his physical condition deteriorated even more. The once hard frame became bloated by an extra thirty pounds of mostly beer fat and small red veins streaked across his cheeks under watery blue eyes.

Except for periodic visits to Beaudry's combined service station and general store in Haley's for groceries or to Renfrew for his drinking supplies, McBride hardly left the cottage and spoke to no one. With icy politeness he responded to greetings or waves from the neighbouring cottages, but they diminished and he was left to his solitude.

The afternoon sun made McBride blink as he stumbled out of the cottage with a beer can in one hand and portable radio in the other. He made his way to the white Cape Cod chair he had positioned on the small dock the second day after he arrived. Settling himself as comfortably as possible, he pulled the tab on the can and threw it in the water. He watched as it slowly glided to the bottom to join a growing collection of tabs which glistened in the two-and-a-half foot depth. A boat with a lone fisherman caught his eye. It was about three hundred feet from shore and once he focused on it he became intrigued as the rod started to bob. A good-sized black bass was lifted out of the water and thumped on the boat's bottom. Looking at his watch, he positioned the radio on his knees and turned it on for the four o'clock news from CHOV Pembroke. He adjusted the dial and volume.

". . . confrontation between Prime Minister Jennings and James Cairns, Leader of the Opposition, over allegations of misconduct surrounding the sale of nuclear reactors to China appears to be coming to a head.

"Mr. Cairns commented for the first time upon his absence in the House of Commons' Question Period for the past eight days. The mystery surrounding his apparent reluctance to face the Prime Minister was heightened by his statement that he would not be panicked by the Prime Minister into making a premature disclosure. He said he would face the Prime Minister and Parliament when the time was right.

"The Prime Minister was unavailable for comment but a party spokesman, Brian Beacom, called Mr. Cairns' statement one of the most vicious and shameful smears upon the government and civil servants in the history of Canada."

McBride instantly recognized Beacom's voice and turned up the volume.

"'The Leader of the Opposition is duty bound to come forward and either substantiate his wild and fanciful claims or retract them with full apology. Again, speaking personally, I say that nothing less will satisfy Parliament and the Canadian people.

"The damage this situation is doing to Canada's international reputation could be reflected in possible loss of trade with other countries. It's no secret that a number of Bonnaventure contracts are pending. No one could expect countries such as Bulgaria and Portugal to continue negotiations until this matter is settled once and for all. I'd like to know what Mr. Cairns will say if and when jobs are lost because of his irresponsible charges.'

"Mr. Beacom was also questioned on his reaction to the Dominion Press story on Canadian-Chinese relations and the effect the current controversy might have on future relations.

"'I would prefer not to dignify such fabrication with a response,' said Beacom.

"'My colleagues have recommended to the Prime Minister that he write the strongest letter of protest possible to Mr. Ingram's publisher and a letter of apology to Ambassador Wu. We should show our Chinese friends that we will not stand for such breaches of bad manners. Mr. Cairns' allegations are totally unfounded; Mr. Ingram's story is 99 per cent conjecture. And those who were directly involved with the sale of the Bonnaventure Reactors to The People's Republic of China, on both sides, are honest, hard working men and women. They are not crooks. Canadians do not deal under the table and I am convinced that neither do the Chinese.'

"Russell Crozier of Forrester's Falls died this morning in Renfrew Hospital. . . . "

McBride turned off the radio. He tilted his head back, drained the remaining mouthful of beer from the can and closed his eyes. Sitting bolt upright, he closed his right fist and pounded it into his open palm. "No! No!" he mumbled and ran to the cottage with faltering steps.

With muffled oaths, he pulled out a battered suitcase from under the bed and snapped the locks. On the bottom of not too neatly folded clothes was a brown manilla envelope. He dumped the contents on the kitchen table and rummaged through them. Newspaper clippings about the sale of nuclear reactors, yellow copy sheets, and an item from a Panamanian newspaper

84

about a fire in the government records office scattered across the table. Stuffing a clipping in his pocket, he hurried out of the cottage and set out for Haley's Station to make a phone call.

At the moment the cottage door slammed shut the fisherman had another solid bite.

14

Luncheon at 24 Sussex Drive with Dr. Emmett Rogers was low key and productive. Jennings found the head of Atomic Power of Canada relaxed and candid. Their discussion had ranged from up-dates on current projects to plans for future research. Jennings had purposely avoided any mention of China or the Bonnaventures until both were comfortably settled in his study.

Copeland refilled their glasses, quietly turned and left the room. Jennings waited until the door was securely closed before turning to his guest. "Well, Dr. Rogers."

Rogers sipped his sherry and looked intently into Jennings' eyes. He felt slightly off-guard. The luncheon was excellent and the conversation pleasant, but he was under no illusion that there was still something left unsaid. Nothing they had discussed warranted a private luncheon. Everything he had told Jennings could have been obtained with a phone call or by written request. It was an awkward moment. Rogers was not certain what to say next.

"How's the hunting and fishing up your way? I understand you're quite a sportsman?" asked Jennings.

"Last fall wasn't exactly a banner year for deer or duck," replied Rogers with a look of relief mingled with surprise. "For the first time in years I didn't get a deer. I hunt with three other colleagues and we had to be satisfied with just a quarter each but we enjoyed the time together. If my friend hadn't got off a lucky shot we'd just be remembering the taste of venison. Fishing's another story. Just a great season. I have a couple of secret spots in the upper valley that never let me down. I always get my limit of pike and bass. I'm flattered you know of my love for the outdoors."

"I like to know as much as possible about those I work with and have confidence in," replied Jennings in a matter-of-fact tone. He didn't tell Rogers that an up-dated card file was kept on anyone who had business with the Prime Minister.

"Are you a hunter or fisherman, sir?"

"Never fired a gun in anger or for sport but I do enjoy wetting a line now and then. I used to get the odd opportunity when all I had to worry about was representing Renfrew/Bonnachere, but that is all in the distant past."

"A real pity, sir. There's nothing like the tranquility of a calm stretch of water with the bass or pike rising to the bait. If you ever do find yourself free for a day it would be my pleasure to be your Ottawa Valley guide. I'd be more than pleased to show you two places known to no one but me. You'd fill the boat. I don't make the offer lightly. A true fisherman would rather see his wife and daughters violated than share his secret places," Rogers chuckled.

Jennings smiled politely. "Thank you. I just may be giving you a call some day." He had no inclination to comment on the violation of a wife. Jennings leaned forward. "Dr. Rogers, what was the reaction in Chalk River to Mr. Cairns' allegations?"

The abrupt change of subject made Rogers pause. "Ottawa Valley folk don't take kindly to people speaking out-of-turn unless they can back up what they say with facts. He lost votes and you gained them."

"Well, that's something," said Jennings. "Do you think the charges could have substance?"

"I was involved with the sale of the Bonnaventures right from the beginning. I can honestly say without reservation that all negotiations and agreements were carried out to the letter of the law. I was most insistent about this. I instructed those at all levels that the prescribed procedures must be followed even at the expense of delivery dates. I would have no qualms or objections to a full audit of all documentation. In fact, I would welcome it."

Jennings relaxed in his chair and sipped his sherry. "I am pleased to hear you speak so positively, Dr. Rogers. I was sure this would be the case. As far as financial irregularities go, I think Cairns got caught by a rumor. He's a desperate man who thinks he can keep his party together and ensure his own survival by smearing the government. I consider that question closed. The charge that the reactors are being used for military purposes must also be closed. I have something to ask of you."

Being a past master in the fine art of executive stroking, Rogers immediately recognized the timing. The invitation, private luncheon, cordial conversation and sherries were just preludes to the moment. He was about to find out the real reason why the Prime Minister of Canada would spend nearly two and a half hours of his valuable day with him.

"What I am about to tell you is in the strictest confidence. Once it has been made public you are quite free to discuss it with the exception of the substance of our conversation today. Agreed?"

"Agreed."

"Mrs. Jennings and I have been formally invited by Chairman Hu to visit China. For the sake of speed, it would be a working holiday without the full trappings of a state visit."

"May I ask if you are accepting?"

"I have given a conditional acceptance pending timing and itinerary. I think I should go but it would be difficult if Mr. Cairns was still keeping the pot boiling. Peking has made a suggestion as a means of counter-balancing the negative press Mr. Cairns has generated. This is where you come in. Would you be agreeable to co-operate with Peking in the dissemination of positive stories concerning the peaceful accomplishments of the Bonnaventures and the interchange of technology between our scientific community and theirs?"

Rogers reached for the decanter and filled his glass. Momentarily embarrassed, he extended the decanter towards Jennings. The offer was accepted. "Who would write the articles?"

"They'd be assigned to a Canadian journalist named Adam Sutton."

"Sutton?" asked Rogers as he furrowed his brow.

"Yes, do you know him?"

"Not personally, but there is a request on my desk for an interview with him."

"I told them I approved of the idea and Ambassador Wu Tai Shan advised me that he was assigning the project immediately. I would see and approve any copy before it is released to the press. I want you to cut the red tape and encourage your colleagues to co-operate."

"How far do we go?"

"Just short of sensitive and confidential material. I have no intention of giving away the cookie jar along with the cookies. What they will be looking for is our input into some of their more exciting programs – breakthroughs in medicine, agronomy, forestry and the like. In other words, they will expect to take the major share of the credit. I want what we give them carefully monitored and controlled. If they have done something on their own so be it, but I want to make certain that Canada and A.P.C. get full credit for the Bonnaventure and our technology. It could be beneficial for future sales and I don't have to tell you what a few more Bonnaventure sales would mean to your budget and future research. It would also help repair any damage to Canada's reputation, to say nothing of re-establishing confidence in Canada's ability to conduct business in an honest and forthright manner."

"It wouldn't do China's image any harm either," interjected Rogers.

"Precisely. Peking is following this situation very closely. The Chinese pride themselves on their honesty in business and I'm sure they look upon these allegations as a direct affront. Any positive support would in effect help them save face both at home and abroad. This has to be the underlying motivation in inviting us to participate."

Rogers carefully placed his glass on the coffee table coaster. "May I be candid, Prime Minister?"

Jennings nodded.

"You have my wholehearted endorsement and co-operation; that goes without saying. But I have a request to make."

"By all means."

88

"It has to do with Mr. Brian Beacom."

"Indeed," replied Jennings with a quizzical look.

"It's very delicate, sir. But, I feel it is necessary that the question be raised if we are going to be closely aligned in the future."

"By all means raise it," replied Jennings. "I want our relationship to be completely candid at all times."

Rogers cleared his throat and wiped his mouth with a large, white linen handkerchief. "Has Mr. Beacom personally taken on the mantel of official party or government spokesman?"

"Nobody personally decides to be government or party spokesman!" The edge to Jennings' voice was obvious. "When something has to be said I say it or delegate a Minister. I'm surprised you'd ask such a question."

"No offense intended, but you'll have to admit that Mr. Beacom has been speaking out to the press with increasing frequency. I'm sure it hasn't escaped your attention that whenever he's quoted he is closely identified with the government.

"I won't debate that point and it is well taken. There is a very sound reason why he has become high profile. It was the consensus of my advisors that now is not the time for anyone in government to be speaking out on the utterances of Mr. Cairns. I am awaiting his pleasure and if he dares open up the question again I shall speak out, but not until then."

It was an awkward moment. Rogers appeared to be at a loss for words. Sensing his difficulty, Jennings smiled and said, "Come, Doctor, what is really bothering you? Whatever we say will not go beyond this room. When you leave I want to be assured that you have had all your questions answered."

"Thank you," replied Rogers with great relief. "It's Mr. Beacom's references to the Bonnaventures and China. To put it bluntly, I and my colleagues would have much preferred if nothing had been said."

"The less said the better?"

"Precisely."

"It had to be said. I have no intention of allowing Mr. Cairns to smear my government, party or the civil service."

"Isn't there room for concern?"

"In what way?"

"You've had more experience with the press than I have, but I'm sure you'll agree that a skilful interviewer or reporter can back you into a corner. I shudder at some of the close calls I've had."

"I can't ever remember you being put on the spot."

"Pure luck, Prime Minister. Pure luck."

"Beacom can handle himself. He has the largest collection of metaphors on Parliament Hill and whenever he gets in a tight corner he trots one out. By the time the reporter figures out what he's said the interview is over." Jennings smiled at the thought.

"Admirable quality. I only ask one thing."

"Ask it."

"Would you give me your assurance that nothing concerning A.P.C. or the Bonnaventures will be released to the press without first being cleared through me?"

"That's a tall order."

"Only as tall as Brian Beacom, sir."

"There's no way any of us can hope to control the Chinese. We can only hope for the best and co-operate as much as possible. Only Beacom," mused Jennings. "I'll speak to him personally tomorrow. He'll comply."

"I learnt something years ago. We used to call it P.Y.A.A.T."

"P.Y.A.A.T?" repeated Jennings.

"Protect your ass at all times."

Jennings smiled broadly. "Dr. Rogers, we're going to get along famously."

"Thank you, Prime Minister. I'm sure we are."

Jennings reached for the decanter. "One for the road?"

15

Kevin Ingram scratched out a cigarette butt in the nearly over-flowing ashtray and immediately lit a fresh one. He was totally oblivious to the clatter of typewriters and teletypes which were mingled with the undercurrent of raised voices and ringing telephones in the editorial room of Dominion Press.

For the past two hours Ingram had been absorbed in writing a memo to his managing editor. Finally, after a number of rewrites, he settled back in his chair to read it. He wanted to be absolutely certain that the content was factual and not an over-statement of the situation.

TO: RGW
FROM: KEVIN INGRAM
SUBJECT: CHINA STORY

I just had a phone call from Tom McBride and I think it's worth a followup. From the little that he said I think he could put me on to some deep background which could be the basis of another China story.

Initially I was skeptical. He sounded as though he had been drinking but he was quite lucid. His past problems are well known and initially I thought he might be simply trying to create mischief and do a number on his old employer, the Chinese. He seems obsessed with, as he puts it, 'setting the record straight'. Just what record he's referring to remains to be seen but he did say that Beacom was 'full of shit' shafting me on the air and that my piece only erred by leaving huge holes in the story.

It's no secret that his departure as Ottawa Correspondent for Xinhua was acrimonious. It is also no secret that Lao Chengtu would rather forget that he or the Ottawa Embassy had ever laid eyes on McBride. This was confirmed when I brought up McBride's name to Lao during the interview I had with him. There's no question McBride is *persona non grata* with Peking.

The more I talked to him, and it was less than a four-minute conversation, the more convinced I was that he's sincere. What his motivation is I'm not certain. It could be money. I assume he's experiencing the shorts but with his background he certainly knows that sound information can be translated into ready cash. In his defense, he didn't mention money. I just raise the question.

He's holed up in a cottage halfway between Renfrew and Cobden. He may be paranoid. He's in hiding and he swore me to secrecy before he'd tell me where to find him. What or whom he fears I don't know but I can speculate. It may be a wild goose chase but again I may hit paydirt.

I tried to draw him out but he wouldn't budge. All he would tell me is that there is more to Cairns' allegations of a payoff between Peking and someone high up on Parliament Hill than meets the eye.

I suggest that I meet with him. If I come up empty I can always do a piece on "Whatever happened to . . . "

There is no connection but it's worth mentioning. I got a tip that Diane Jennings was busted for a minor traffic violation. While there is nothing questionable about the P.M.'s wife getting a ticket it is curious that it was nearly midnight and she was driving her own car. Why wasn't she using the chauffeur at that time of night? I'd also like to know where she was coming from or where she was going. Where were the Mounties? Even if a direct request was made for no security they are duty bound to protect the P.M. and his immediate family. If for no other reason than personal curiosity I'd like to dig deeper. It could make a good human interest story. Please comment.

It was 11:20 a.m. when Ingram attempted to get past Robert Warner's secretary and deliver his memo personally but to no avail. Nothing, including assassinations or disasters, interrupted the weekly editorial meeting. To do so would incur the monumental wrath of the managing editor.

Hoping to speed up the system, Ingram settled for a compromise. He left his memo with Warner's secretary with explicit instructions to give it to him personally at the earliest possible moment.

By the time Ingram returned from lunch a reply was in his mail slot.

TO: KEVIN INGRAM
FROM: RGW
SUBJECT: CHINA STORY – JENNINGS

The idea sounds interesting and could be promising but I have some reservations.

1) While I respect McBride as a journalist I have grave doubts about his ability to reason with balance in light of what he's gone through. I agree that the question of revenge has to be seriously considered. It is a strong possibility.

2) On the other hand, he could have information that is genuine and he could be offering it as a means of salving his conscience if he is as filled with remorse as he told everyone within earshot he was at the time of the blowup with the Chinese. This possibility cannot be overlooked and should be confirmed if possible before proceeding.

3) The other consideration is money. Agreed, he could be pushed to the financial wall and is casting around to see what the market will bear. We have no assurance that just because he offers us something he hasn't offered it to the competition or even to the Chinese as a buy back. This must be ascertained.

4) Depending upon what he is offering and assuming that the motivation is either number 2 or 3 I suggest you proceed with caution. If number 2 is the case find out what he has and stall until you've cleared with me. Should it simply be a barter situation offer $2M if he can supply genuine proof which will stand up in a major feature. He'll know what he has to give without us telling him. Be prepared to negotiate either up or down from that figure based upon your evaluation of the material. If he's live don't let him off the hook for the sake of a few dollars.

5) Would consider the Jennings matter as secondary. Could be nothing more than a filler. Follow it up if you have the time but suggest you give McBride top priority.

6) Regardless of what you come up with we'll need three sources before anything's run. We are not prepared to risk a suit because of innuendo or speculation. This policy cannot be broken regardless of the story.
I await your report. Good luck.

Kevin Ingram would have enjoyed the two-hour drive from Ottawa more if he had been clear on why Tom McBride had called and insisted that they meet rather than talk on the telephone. Curiosity alone was enough motivation. Coupled with the possibility of a tie-in with the Chinese story, which was slowly becoming an obsession, it was irresistible.

Rounding a bend on Highway 17, he took notice of the road sign for Haley's Station and saw the yellow Shell sign hanging in front of Beaudry's combined service station and general store. He slowed down, pulled the car off the highway and stopped. With less than half a pack of cigarettes left he wanted to replenish his supply. If his visit was to be an extended one he had no intention of running out. The bell attached to the top of the front door by a supple band of metal announced his entrance. The only greeting he received was from a large black Lab which thumped the floor with its tail and closed its eyes slowly when satisfied that he was friendly.

"Day," said a voice in the unique Ottawa Valley accent that set its residents apart from any other region in Canada. Ingram looked around for the body accompanying the voice. Slowly, a shock of white hair rose from below the counter. "Day," repeated the man as he straightened up.

"Good day," responded Ingram. "Could I have a king-sized Rothman's please?"

"No Rothman's. The order's late."

"What have you got."

"What do you want? They're all the same. Can't tell one from another. Smoke a pipe myself."

"Du Maurier will be fine. Better make that two."

Stirling Beaudry reached for the cigarettes. "Just passing through?" Ingram was a people watcher and Beaudry fascinated him. His lower jaw gave the appearance of being unhinged and flopped as he spoke. Ingram suspected that it was probably due to a congenital defect or the lack of dental care.

"Visiting a friend who's staying at Garden Lake. If his directions were right it's not too far."

Beaudry nodded. "About a mile." He jerked his head. "It's off The Queen's Line."

"So I understand."

Beaudry's curiosity was on a par with Ingram's. There was very little he missed and finding out where strangers were coming from or going to was his hobby. It livened up the near sedentary existence of living in a community of less than a hundred residents.

"Has he been at the lake long?"

Ingram shook his head. "No. He just rented a cottage for a few weeks' vacation."

"Might know him. Know most of the cottagers. They come in here for gas and groceries and to use the phone. What's his name?"

"McBride. Tom McBride."

Beaudry furrowed his brow and pushed his glasses up on his nose. "McBride, McBride, don't mind the name. Who's cottage did he rent?"

"He said that if I got lost I should ask directions to the Duff cottage."

"Duff! Why didn't you say so. It's not Duff's now. They were from Ottawa. You from Ottawa?" Ingram nodded. "Harold Duff was his name. Big man, over six foot. Worked for Ontario Hydro. Ever run into him?"

"Don't think so."

"Died eight years ago. Fine man. His wife sold the cottage to a couple from the States. A lot of Americans own cottages around here. Fine people once you get to know them. A bit loud, but well meaning." Ingram picked up his cigarettes. Without offending the man he wanted to be on his way. He didn't want to be burdened with the geneology of a cottage he would probably never visit again. "The Duff cottage. I can point you right to it. Turn right at the next road, that's The Queen's Line. Follow it across the railway track and turn right at the second road. It will take you to the Garden Lake. Duff's cottage is the third one on the right at the end of the road. Can't miss it. Your friend is a popular man."

Ingram stopped at the door and turned around. "Why?"

"You're the second person lately to ask directions to Duff's cottage."

Ingram decided to fish. "Was it a tall man, just today?"

"No, no. Coupla days ago. And he was an oriental. Couldn't

tell if he was Chinese or Japanese. They all look the same to me. Funny little man. I told him how to get there and he got in his car and headed back to Renfrew. Never even said thanks. Couldn't figure him out. Why ask directions then go back the way you came? They're strange people, eh? Don't get many around here."

Ingram opened the door. "Thank you."

"Just up the highway, turn right . . . " The closing door and the jingling of the bell drowned out Beaudry's repeated directions.

16

James Cairns drummed the top of his desk impatiently and glared at his executive assistant, Garfield Logan. "What exactly are you saying?"

"It's not me. I'm just a spear carrier passing along what I was asked to pass along."

The mid-afternoon sunshine was pouring through the windows of Cairns' parliamentary office and the golden rays accentuated the flush of Cairns' cheeks. Logan fished out his handkerchief and coughed into it in an effort to clear his throat. "He told me to tell you that you can't stall any longer. You're putting the party in a bad light by avoiding the question period."

"Am I now? What makes him think he's the expert? I'll orchestrate my own timing. And why didn't he tell me personally? God knows he's had every opportunity, especially in caucus. He's the first one on his feet."

"I ran into him in the parking lot," replied Logan defensively.

"I do not appreciate getting messages second hand and you can tell Grenville Nolan that. If he has anything to say about party business he can say it to my face."

Logan pulled at the end of his nose. "While you mightn't appreciate the source you have to admit that he's only saying what most of the members are either saying or thinking. They all want this matter resolved so they can get on with planning for the election." Cairns thumped his desk. "You could be facing a vote of non-confidence within the party. Some are steamed enough to call for a leadership review on the question."

"Not this close to an election." countered Cairns. "They'll give Jennings the election on a golden platter. If there is a party revolt we might as well mail in the win."

"Beat Nolan at his own game." encouraged Logan. "Nail Jennings with whatever it is you have. And let caucus in on what you know. You have to trust them." Cairns shook his head. "Some are saying that you haven't anything."

"To hell with them. I know what I'm doing and I know what I've got."

"Give them something. You owe them that much. Their political futures are hanging on this issue. If you can't come across it will cost the party votes and credibility. I don't have to tell you that a number of ridings are so close any loss in votes could spell a disaster. That's the message I'm getting."

"It'll make them work all the harder. It's about time some of the party prima donnas realized that they can't ride in on my coat-tails," snorted Cairns.

"Be that as it may, you can't expect them to sit back and take the backwash without getting bitchy."

Cairns was on the verge of reminding Logan that he was the party leader and his boss. Their relationship was totally different to that of Harrison and Jennings. Unlike Harrison, who was the acknowledged power behind Jennings, Logan had little or no authority. But Logan's uncle was Senator Humphrey Ross, the most powerful Senator and most influential fund raiser within the party. While he never leaned on the executive on behalf of his nephew, it was generally accepted that anything negative would not be taken kindly. The thought crossed Cairns' mind that Logan might be subtly relaying a message from his uncle rather than from Grenville Nolan, though Nolan was not above using Logan; he'd use anybody to serve his own purposes and had done so on many occasions.

Cairns found Logan more of a challenge than a threat. He did not fear him but he respected his connections and experience. The Senator was another matter. He needed Ross' support for the election. Ross was not above sacrificing an election to either oust an undesirable or await the infusion of new blood for another assault on power. He had done it in the past and Cairns had no illusions about him repeating history if he thought it best for the party.

"Did anyone else voice Nolan's point of view?" asked Cairns.

"No," responded Logan casually, "Nolan was the only one who came directly to me, but I understand that there are rumblings. They say you could nail Jennings' hide to the barn door by speaking up and they can't understand why you don't."

Cairns eyed Logan carefully. "You don't think I have anything, do you?"

Logan was taken aback by the bluntness of Cairns' statement. "I never said that."

"You implied it. If you thought I had something you would never have relayed Nolan's comments to me. You'd have shut him up."

Logan was in a mild state of shock. He wasn't used to having Cairns come on so strong and he had to admit to himself that Cairns was right. He resented Cairns placing him in a position of weakness and giving him nothing to counter the criticism. His job was to protect the leader and run interference with opposition whenever it surfaced. To do his job properly he had to be privy to everything that was going on. He wasn't. The lack of communication between him and Cairns was seriously eroding his position. "It sure would have helped if I knew exactly what your position is."

"In other words you'd have liked to have rammed something down Nolan's throat."

"Exactly. It's no secret that Nolan is eyeing your job. He still thinks that if he had been leader he'd be Prime Minister instead of a member of the shadow cabinet. He's an ambitious man and he's building support within the party. He's getting ready to give you a run for your money."

"Let him. I can take Grenville Nolan with both hands tied behind my back," retorted Cairns confidently.

"Up to now I'd agree with you, but you've weakened your position. You can't continue to function like a one-man band and get away with it. Your support in caucus is now open to question, as I'm sure you realize."

"I realize nothing of the kind!" bristled Cairns. "I'll take this party into the election and by God I'll win. Where do you stand on the matter?" Cairns was enjoying the moment. He watched Logan's jowls quiver slightly. For a man in his early forties Logan was quickly going to physical seed. The paunch, jowls and receding hairline made him look ten years older.

"Are you asking for a loyalty oath?" demanded Logan.

"Just asking the question."

"If I didn't support you without reservation my resignation would be on your desk. I'm surprised you ask such a question."

"It's a reasonable one considering the circumstances."

"My answer should be obvious."

Cairns placed both hands on his desk and crossed them. "I realize these are trying times but the stakes are high. I haven't even told my wife the full story."

"I'm not your wife!" Logans' eyes flashed. "I'm your executive assistant and should be the one, if the only one, to know the full story."

Cairns reached in his pocket and took out a ring of keys. Logan watched him carefully as he opened a locked drawer in his desk and took out a blue folder. He made no attempt to open the folder. "You see this? There is enough in this file to not only win the election, but to finish Jennings once and for all. There is also more than enough to bring criminal charges and Royal Commissions."

"Release it then."

"I can't. I have to wait for one more piece to fall into place. The puzzle is just about complete but I have to wait."

"How long?"

"Very soon. If I gave out what I have I couldn't do anything more than speculate. I need hard irrefutable proof and until I get it I can't move." Logan shook his head in frustration. "I accept the fact that there are rumblings within the party. If I was in their position I'd be bitching too. But we're all in this together and we'll just have to stick together."

"Could you tell them that much?"

"I could but what good would it do. They'd only get steamed up and press. There'd be a path beaten to my door of party faithful demanding that they be taken into my confidence. If I turned them down, which I'd have to do, they'd start a ground-swell and neither I nor God Himself could stem it. I can't take the chance. It's better that we leave the question open and let them speculate. Nobody's going to pull the trigger. They have their own futures to consider."

"You have a point, but it's going to be hell until you open up."

"Granted," replied Cairns. "I want you to do something for me."

"What?"

"Did Nolan mention anybody else when he tackled you in the parking lot?"

"I don't follow you."

"Did he say he was speaking on behalf of any other member of caucus or was he just fishing for himself?"

"He never mentioned anyone. As I told you, he just said caucus was concerned."

"Good. That's what I thought. He's out for number one. Get back to Nolan. Make it look casual. Tell him that you and I have had a very confidential talk and that you relayed his concern. Tell him that I am sympathetic to his position and that I will be briefing him personally on the situation at the earliest possible moment. Tell him that it's all a matter of timing, that to be premature would not only be ill advised but disastrous. Without making an issue of it casually mention that I have enough to win the election and leave it at that. He'll buy it. Nolan is one of the shrewdest men I know. If he can smell victory he won't care where it comes from. He'll wait because he knows he'll be in cabinet if we win. He wants Finance and I intend to give it to him. He'll also be Deputy Prime Minister. We don't have to like one another personally to work in harmony. We did it in the last House when we were in power and we'll do it again. I respect his abilities and I know that respect is reciprocated."

Logan relaxed in his chair. "I'll do my best. Will I be included in the briefing?"

"Of course. We're going to win. I need you to win. I need

100

your support, and your counsel," said Cairns confidently. It was the closest he had ever come to executively stroking Logan. "By the way, how's your uncle?"

TO: R.G.W.
FROM: KEVIN INGRAM
SUBJECT: PROGRESS REPORT – McBRIDE

It would appear that my trip to see McBride was an exercise in futility but, and it's a big "but", I think I'm on to something. When I arrived at the cottage McBride was nowhere to be seen and the cottage was closed up tighter than a drum. The shutters were even secured over the windows. I asked at the neighbouring cottage and they couldn't tell me anything. Evidently McBride kept to himself and didn't make any attempt at being friendly. I was just about to leave when I decided to try and get into the cottage and see if he left anything for me. I slipped the lock with a credit card and found McBride on the bed. He was barely alive. With the help of a neighbour I got him into the car and to Renfrew Hospital. Dr. David Ferguson diagnosed a massive stroke and he's in intensive care. As soon as he's able to stand the trip they want to move him to Ottawa Civic for neurological testing by a specialist. The prognosis is not encouraging. He is totally paralyzed down the right side and cannot communicate even by blinking his eyes. I called Dr. Ferguson this morning and he said there is a slight improvement but his condition is guarded.

What makes me think that I might be on to something are two unrelated things. First: when I stopped for cigarettes at a gas station in Haley's I was questioned by the owner. Initially I put it down to nothing more than curiosity until he told me I was the second person to inquire directions to McBride's cottage. The first was a Chinese who instead of following directions turned around and headed back to Renfrew. Second: when I went back to the cottage to get McBride's belongings and take them to the hospital I found a letter from a woman who wanted McBride to use his influence to trace a long lost relative in China. She wrote to McBride care of the Chinese Embassy in Ottawa. She made a point of saying that she had lost his Ottawa address but remembered that he said he once worked for the Embassy and was taking the chance of them forwarding the letter to him. The letter was innocuous enough, but it means that in spite of McBride's insistence that keep his whereabouts secret the Chinese certainly knew where he was. If they wanted to they could get to him and shut him up if they feared he was on to anything that they were concerned about. The inquiry about directions to his cottage by a Chinese can hardly be coincidental.

I went through McBride's effects and included in them was his contact book with some interesting names and numbers, including James Cairns' home telephone with an asterisk beside it. The number was in old writing but the asterisk was fresh. I would like to keep on this story and see where it leads.

TO: KEVIN INGRAM
FROM: RGW
SUBJECT: McBRIDE

Agree with progress report. Keep on the story. There are a few points I'd like to make.

1) It's too early to let your imagination run wild. Follow up on the points you've made but keep an open mind. We can't afford to get the Chinese riled up unless we have concrete information to go on.
2) How competent is this Renfrew doctor? Is he anything more than just a G.P. making an easy and convenient diagnosis?
3) Has McBride had any medical history that would lead one to suspect a stroke?
4) Have you tried to track down this mysterious Chinese? Might be worth a check on Renfrew motels and hotels to see if anyone like him checked in. If they are up to something it would be reasonable to assume that they'd want to keep an eye on McBride.
5) The reference to Cairns is interesting. Might be an idea to quietly try and get to him and see his reaction when McBride's name comes up. You have a logical reason for contacting him re: the Bonnaventures.
6) Find out who's looking after McBride's hospital and medical bills. Even if he has O.H.I.P. there will be additional specialists' bills. Offer to underwrite them as a friend. Don't bring Dominion into the picture at this point.

I'll approve any expense within reason. It might obligate McBride to some extent if he recovers and will talk.

7) Find out from an independent source the cause and effects of a stroke. Have you considered the possibility that it is not a stroke? See if you can get a medical report from the admitting doctor and have it evaluated. Should it not be a stroke find out what it is. Contact the neurologist as soon as he's moved to Ottawa Civic.

8) If necessary secure the services of someone to keep an eye on McBride while he's in Renfrew Hospital. See if we can find out if anybody is showing undue concern and who they are.

9) If this proves out to be explainable you could do a personality piece on the fall of McBride.

10) Anything more on the Diane Jennings traffic violation? Keep me informed.

17

The top of Christopher Jennings' desk was covered with papers and a map of The People's Republic of China. He was deeply engrossed in tracing with his finger the tour he was planning to make and did not notice the flashing light on his telephone. Finally it caught his eye and he reached for the receiver.

"Mrs. Jennings is on line two, sir" said Marcie Peckman.

Jennings pressed the button. "Diane."

"Sorry it took me so long to get back to you. I was in the garden with the girls."

"That's alright. I won't be able to make it for dinner tonight so go ahead without me."

"If that's all you wanted you could have left a message," replied Diane testily.

"There's something else. I'm going to have a busy six or

seven weeks gearing up for the election and this China trip. I won't be able to spend much time with you and the girls. I was thinking that it might be a good idea for the three of you to go up to Harrington Lake for two or three weeks."

"I don't want to spend two or three weeks at Harrington Lake. I'd go out of my mind."

"No you wouldn't," defended Jennings. "It's summer and there's plenty to do."

"I'd sooner visit Mom and Dad in Loganville. They haven't seen the girls for a while."

"You're not taking the girls to the Maritimes without me," snapped Jennings. The thought of Diane and Harrison being in the same province flashed through Jennings' mind. They'd probably schemed to get together, he thought, and he wasn't about to convenience them. "You're going to Harrington and that's final. Marcie's advised the staff to expect you tomorrow afternoon so please be ready to leave. I'll see you before you go."

"Chris," breathed Diane. "I don't want to go."

"I'm sorry, Diane, all the arrangements have been made. I'll come up on the weekend after I get back from Victoria. I'm speaking to the Empire Club."

"Don't bother," replied Diane churlishly. "I'd have to introduce you to your daughters and it could be embarrassing."

"Let's not quarrel. I have a lot on my mind."

"You have two daughters who need a father."

Jennings switched the receiver to his other ear. "I'll tell Marcie you'll be ready and I'll say goodbye tomorrow morning," he said ignoring her gibe. The telephone clicked and Jennings replaced the dead receiver in its cradle.

Diane stared blankly for a minute then stomped out of the library and was hurrying up the stairs when a voice called out, "Mrs. Jennings."

Turning, she saw the cook at the foot of the stairs. "Yes," she replied.

"How many for dinner?"

"Three, Ada. The Prime Minister is delayed and won't be joining us."

"Very good. Shall I prepare a heavy lunch before we leave for Harrington tomorrow?"

Diane wheeled around on the stairs. Her eyes flashed in anger. "How do you know I'm going to Harrington Lake?"

Ada Scholtz had been cook at Sussex Drive for four prime ministers and was well insulated from the complex personalities of those who assumed residence. Stiffening her spine, she replied in a firm voice, "The Prime Minister advised me during breakfast. I have made all the necessary arrangements and, with your permission, I would like to submit the menus for the next week once we arrive."

"Thank you, Ada. That will be fine," replied Diane in a softer tone. She walked to her bedroom. The moment the door was closed she picked up the phone and dialed.

"Prime Minister's office," answered Marcie Peckman.

"Hello, Marcie. It's me again."

"Mrs. Jennings," replied Marcie. "You've just missed the Prime Minister. He had to go to a . . . "

"It was you I wanted. Do you happen to know where Cole Harrison is tonight? Do you happen to have his itinerary?"

Marcie pulled a file out of her desk drawer and leafed through the contents. "Unless he was delayed in Moncton he's scheduled to check into the Chateau Halifax for the next two days."

"Chateau Halifax. Thank you, Marcie."

"You won't be able to reach him until well after eleven, Halifax time. His Moncton flight isn't due in until ten twenty-three and knowing Cole," Marcie chuckled, "he'll have a planning meeting underway in his room fifteen minutes after he checks in. That man does more business in hotel rooms than in his office." Diane smiled at the comment. "I could get a message to him. He calls in every day between nine and ten in the morning."

"Not to worry, Marcie. It's not important. I just wanted to know where he was if something came up." Diane was not very convincing.

"Very good, Mrs. Jennings."

"Marcie," said Diane in a patronizing tone. "Thank you for making all the Harrington Lake arrangements. You're so efficient."

"Not at all, Mrs. Jennings. That's what I'm here for. Any time."

Diane hung up the phone and looked at her watch. It was 4:20. With an exasperated sigh she walked to the closet and began selecting dresses and sports clothes that she would need at Harrington Lake. Following dinner and the customary quiet hour she spent with the children before putting them to bed, she returned to her room and finished packing. The television set in the corner was turned on but she paid little or no attention until she heard Ed McMahon's booming voice. It was 11:30, and time suddenly became important. She sat motionless on the edge of the bed, then reached for the phone and dialed the operator, station-to-station to the Chateau Halifax.

"Mr. Cole Harrison's room, please," said Diane. It took the operator a moment to make the connection.

A woman's voice answered. She sounded sleepy. "Hello."

Diane did not answer.

"Hello," repeated the voice in a firmer tone. "Who is this?"

Diane hung up the phone without answering. She waited half an hour then called again. This time Harrison answered.

"Hello."

"Cole."

"Diane," Harrison's voice became noticeably excited. "Where are you?"

"At Sussex Drive, but only for tonight."

"What do you mean only for tonight?"

"Chris is making me take the girls up to Harrington Lake for two or three weeks, maybe longer."

"I'm not surprised. He's banishing us both and putting as much distance as possible between us."

"I don't want to go."

"Do you have any choice?"

"No. I have no say any more."

"Welcome to the club."

"How are things going?"

"From early morning to late at night. I just threw the last party member out of my room two minutes before you called. You couldn't have timed it better."

"What were you doing?" asked Diane. She was desperately hoping for an explanation as to why a woman answered his phone. If she asked him a straightforward question and he was innocent it would put him on the defensive. If he was guilty she wasn't sure if her emotions could stand another pounding.

106

Harrison laughed. "Having an orgy with wild women, booze and pot."

"Don't make jokes, Cole. I'm fresh out of laughter."

Harrison sensed her fragile mood. "I've been having my moments too. Chris knew what he was doing when he gave me this assignment. These Maritimers are the touchiest bunch of bastards I've ever met. You have to handle them with kid gloves. Do you know Addison Harrop?"

"Sure, he's from Truro. He's a big fund raiser."

"He was the one I had to practically throw out. He's mad as hell over the election and I had to get him calmed down."

"What's his problem?"

"He's just blowing smoke over the timing. He may be politically astute but he's sure dumb when it comes to anything else."

"What do you mean?"

"He's shacking up with a girl young enough to be his daughter. You know the type – great body but no brains. She always talks in a breathless whisper. I had to tell her to sit in the bedroom and watch television. She was on the bloody phone all night, probably drumming up business." Diane breathed a sigh of relief. "Is Chris still going to Victoria?"

"Yes. He'll be away until the weekend. Why?"

"How about getting together in Perth Thursday night. Could you get away without your security tail?"

"Thursday," said Diane with excitement. "How can you get back?"

"Easy. I tell a few lies, catch the afternoon plane to Ottawa, rent a car and . . . "

"And what?"

"And its just you and me for a few beautiful hours. What do you say?"

"I say yes, darling."

"O.K. Unless the plane's delayed I could be in Perth by six-thirty. I'll make the reservations under the name of Mr. and Mrs. Coleman Williams at the Eastview Motel. Plan to get there around seven."

"I'll be there."

"I'll be in Moncton Thursday morning. If for any reason you can't make it call me at 225-6614. That's the riding headquarters. I'll be there all morning." Diane scribbled the number down on her telephone pad and repeated it back. Her eyes were dancing with anticipation. "Be well rested. I don't want you tired."

"Cole, I love you. I'll be counting the days."

Diane was too excited to sleep. She switched on the television set and settled comfortably in bed to watch the late night movie. It was 'Brief Encounter' with Trevor Howard and Celia Johnson.

18

Dr. Chester Wainwright's credentials were impressive. As Chief of Neurology at the Ottawa Civic Hospital there was a constant demand on his time. If he wasn't consulting he was looking after a heavy case load and, whenever he could find the time, he lectured to medical students and wrote widely acclaimed papers which he presented at medical symposiums across the country and abroad. The inordinate pressure under which he worked necessitated a facade of brusqueness. If he were not interested in the patient or individual seeking his counsel he would dismiss both with nothing more than a curt "No time" or, on occasion, impolite indifference. Should he become intrigued he would throw himself into a case with a passion. He was intrigued by Tom McBride.

His Ottawa Civic office was comfortable and bright, the brightness accentuated by the warming sunlight pouring through the venetian blind covering the window behind him. Kevin Ingram faced Wainwright across his desk. It had taken six days of constant calling to secure an appointment. Eight days earlier McBride had been transferred from the Renfrew Hospital. He was still unconscious.

"Mr. Ingram," began Dr. Wainwright in his finest lecturing tone, "there are a couple of things I would like to make abundantly clear before we proceed. First, I do not normally involve myself with routine stroke cases. There are many fine doctors on staff who are more than competent to look after such patients. The last thing they need is me puttering around and getting in the way. Since Mr. McBride is not a classic stroke patient I was asked to look in. Second, I would like to clearly establish my terms-of-reference so that we will have no misunderstandings in the future. If you agree to my conditions and abide by them we shall have no problems. Breach the guidelines and that will be the end of any co-operation or communication."

"I understand, Doctor," acknowledged Ingram.

"It is my practice to never discuss a patient with a third person unless it is at the specific request of the next-of-kin and only then with reluctance. More times than not I refuse, but Mr. McBride's situation is extenuating." Wainwright leafed through a small pile of papers and pulled out a letter written on Dominion Press letterhead. "I have a letter from Mr. Robert Warner, your Managing Editor. He has outlined his concerns for Mr. McBride and assures me that to the best of his knowledge Mr. McBride has no living relative who can speak on his behalf and has nominated you to act for him."

"That's correct."

"Mr. Warner goes on to say that because of Dominion's high regard for Mr. McBride, all his expenses, over and above his O.H.I.P. coverage, will be underwritten. Generous. Most generous indeed."

"Tom is a remarkable man and colleague. We all feel keenly about what has happened to him and want to do everything possible not only to ensure his complete recovery but get him back on his feet as quickly as possible."

"Do you do this for all your colleagues who have fallen on hard times?"

"No. In fact I've never heard of it being done before."

"Why Mr. McBride?"

"Because he has contributed to our profession and because we like to think we have a heart. Wouldn't you do the same for one of yours?"

"Well taken, Mr. Ingram." His voice remained skeptical. "If I do agree to your request for a full discussion will you assure me of total confidentiality?"

"Of course."

"Will anything concerning Mr. McBride's condition appear in the press?"

"Only what you release for publication."

"What has appeared so far?"

"Nothing more than the fact that Tom has had a serious medical problem and is currently under treatment."

"I'd be pleased to see a copy. I understand," said Wainwright as he flipped open a medical chart, "that you were the one to find Mr. McBride. Would you mind filling me in on precisely how you found him."

Ingram carefully detailed what had happened, omitting the reasons for his visit to the cottage.

"When you found him did he give any response whatsoever?"

Ingram shook his head. "He was completely unconscious and appeared to be breathing with great difficulty."

"Was there any sign of vomiting?"

"Saliva was oozing from his lips and it had a strong odor."

"Did it smell like vomit?"

"Yes. I suppose you could say it did. It wasn't like vomit as I remember. It was frothy. I don't recall seeing any regurgitated food. Frankly, I didn't inspect him too carefully. I wiped his chin but didn't bother with his shirt, which was quite damp."

"Did you notice if his bladder had emptied or if his bowels had evacuated?"

Ingram shook his head. "Not particularly, but come to think of it there was quite a heavy odor. I couldn't lift him myself. I had to get a neighboring cottager to help. We wrapped him in a blanket and got him to hospital as quickly as possible. I was sure he was dying."

"He probably was and you probably saved his life by your quick action. Did Mr. McBride drink to excess?"

"Without question, especially lately. He's been under a lot of professional strain."

"What does he drink?"

"Beer mostly but I noticed a number of empty vodka bottles around the cottage. He wasn't the neatest of housekeepers."

"Did he have what you'd consider good eating habits?"

"I don't know how to answer that because I don't know what he's been doing the last little while. When I knew him he was a man who enjoyed his food, sometimes to what I would consider excess."

"In other words he was a glutton."

"I suppose you could put it that way."

Wainwright made notes as Ingram talked. "I assume he travelled extensively during his career?"

"He did. He's covered most of the hot spots over the years – Viet Nam, Korea, the Middle East, South America."

"Was he a promiscuous man?"

Ingram smiled slightly. "How should I know?"

"I assume that if he was normal with normal drives he would seek out female companionship. Did he frequent houses of prostitution?"

"Never with me. But I suppose it's safe to assume that he has paid for it on occasion. Unless you're made of strong stuff something has to give when you're on assignment for four to six months."

Wainwright drew his pen horizontally across the page. Ingram strained to see what he had underlined but couldn't. Wainwright tapped his pen on the top of the desk and mused to himself, "Hard drinker, hard liver, possibly promiscuous, poor eating habits."

"I wish I could be of more help, Doctor, but he was basically a very private man. Most journalists are."

"You've been of enormous help, Mr. Ingram. You are filling in a number of blank areas."

Ingram was uncomfortable with Wainwright's long silences. "Dr. Ferguson in Renfrew was not very optimistic about Tom's chances. He told me that the prognosis for anyone suffering what he termed a 'massive stroke' was not promising. At best he could be a vegetable for the rest of his life, unable to communicate. But you said he wasn't a classic stroke case. Don't you think he's had a stroke?"

"All the classic symptoms of a cerebral vascular accident are in evidence. He's had a left side accident and exhibits severe weakness. His speech is certainly affected or will be if and when he regains total consciousness. He has experienced a great deal of damage. The paralysis extends down his right side. His peripheral vision will be affected and he will be bound to suffer intellectual and emotional problems as well. However, at the moment the cause is more important than the damage. We can identify the damage but we can't identify the cause."

"I'm afraid I don't quite follow you, Doctor."

"A stroke can be caused by a number of things, such as a local infection within the brain tissue or a bacterial infection in the heart that causes clots to form which ultimately embolize in the brain." Ingram made a face and shook his head. "I'm just beginning, Mr. Ingram. It could be the result of an aneurysm. If your friend was born with a weak spot in the main artery of the brain he was living with a stroke that was looking for a time to happen. Another possibility that we can't overlook is syphilis. If he was ever infected the possibility of it damaging the walls of the brain arteries is very great. I'd like to know if he ever had meningitis. If he had there is a strong possibility that the brain arteries were narrowed and a clot was formed. He could be suffering from leukemia and not know it or encephalitis, which is a non-generalized infection of the brain. It can cause symptoms that look like a stroke. So you see, Mr. Ingram, we have our work cut out for ourselves."

"Trial and error, Doctor?"

Wainwright nodded. "If we're fortunate one of the tests will come up positive and we can go on from there. We'll do our best for your friend. The reason I am taking a personal interest in this case is the slight possibility that we might stumble across something we haven't seen before. In doing so we might be able to help future sufferers. I know this sounds noble but there is always something new or something medical science has not acknowledged."

"What is the bottom line, Doctor? What do you suspect?"

"Did Mr. McBride ever use drugs?" asked Wainwright without directly answering Ingram's question.

"Prescription or illegal?"

"Either."

"I have no idea. I do know that he once wrote extensively about the drug trade and usage of drugs in the Far East. As a matter of fact he won a press award for the series. If I remember correctly it had to do with the use of marijuana, cocaine and heroin by the American forces in Viet Nam and how the drug dealers of Saigon kept the supply line open to the States and Canada."

"Could you get me a copy of those articles?"

"They'd be in the morgue files."

"I'd appreciate it. It might help."

"Anything else, Doctor?"

"Do you still have access to Mr. McBride's cottage?"

"I took his key after I got him to hospital so I could go back and get his personal effects. I still have it."

"How very convenient," smiled Wainwright. Ingram returned the smile. "Could you go back and do a bit of detective work for me? It might help your friend."

"Of course. What would you like?"

"I want to know if he was taking any prescription drugs. Scout around and see if there is a bottle or vial. If I could have a chat with the prescribing physician it would be most helpful. While you're there look for anything that he might have eaten or drank. Whatever you find put it in a plastic bag and bring it back to me."

"What do you suspect?"

"Nothing, absolutely nothing, at the moment. I'd like to have a clear picture as to your friend's eating and drinking habits. That's all. Since I can't ask him you'll have to take his place. It will be some time before he'll be able to communicate even at a very basic level."

"The cottage is no problem. His sex life is another matter."

"You're an experienced reporter. If anybody can dig things up it should be someone with your capabilities. By the way, I enjoyed your story on the reactor sales to China. A well researched article. I'll bet it caused some sleepless nights on the Hill."

Ingram accepted the compliment. "I'm surprised you had time to read it, Doctor."

"I have more interests than just bedpans and rectal thermometers," replied Wainwright with a wry smile. "Anything new to report?"

"Nothing that I can discuss at the moment. That story is not dead by any means."

"Thought as much. Now," said Wainwright, "I have to be off.

113

I'm already half an hour late for rounds. Be sure to keep in touch. My nurse can always get me on the pager. If you come across any of McBride's next-of-kin it would be wise to have them come and visit him as soon as possible."

Ingram stiffened. "You mean he's dying?"

"I mean precisely what I said, Mr. Ingram. If anyone in the family wants to see him they shouldn't procrastinate."

Ingram followed Wainwright out of the office. With a curt nod he walked quickly down the corridor. The tails of his white coat billowed behind him.

The pressure on James Cairns was beginning to tell. A man of enormous energy, he prided himself on being able to function at a high level with only four or five hours of sleep a night. Disciplined, he planned his activities carefully and tried to make every working minute productive.

The Morrant interview was fresh in his mind as he parked his car in the driveway of Senator Humphrey Ross' Rockcliffe home and walked up to the front door.

Ross opened the door on the second knock and with a broad smile extended his hand. "Jim, delighted to see you. Come in. Let me take your coat."

Thank you, Senator," replied Cairns as he struggled with the right sleeve which had become caught on the buttons of his suit jacket.

Ross took the coat and hung it up in the hall closet. "A pleasant day, Jim. Looks like we're going to get a spell of good weather for a change." Cairns followed Ross into the graciously appointed livingroom and sat down in the highback chair that was offered. "I thought we could have a chat over a drink before dinner, Jim. What's your pleasure?" Ross lifted the top of a large ornate Spanish globe and inspected the well-stocked bar. "I usually enjoy a rye and water before dinner."

Cairns smiled acceptance.

Ross seated himself comfortably in a well-used lazyboy and raised his glass. "Here's to our party and here's to success in the election." Cairns acknowledged the toast. "Garfield tells me that you're being kept on the run."

It was the first time that Ross had ever mentioned his nephew in conversation. Cairns was on the defensive. He wasn't sure if it was just small talk or a deliberate indication that Ross was being kept totally informed and wanted him to be aware of the fact. Cairns leaned toward the latter.

"It's a busy time, Humphrey. I am accepting bookings to appear at a number of nomination meetings in key ridings."

"Good. It always helps the candidate to have the leader appear and give his benediction." Ross smiled.

"How do you view our chances, Humphrey?"

"How do you view them?" asked Ross rhetorically.

Cairns shifted in his chair. The liquid in his glass swished from side to side. "Nationally we're in good shape. I can't see us having any problem retaining our base and I'm optimistic about our chances at eating away at the Conservative and NDP blocks in Ontario and Quebec."

"What about the west?"

"I was going to ask you about the west. Since you just returned from Saskatchewan and Alberta, how do you see it?"

"Questionable. I'm concerned," said Ross frowning.

"We've always been questionable in the west but this time I feel confident. We'll make significant inroads."

Ross drained his glass and stood up. "A refill?"

Cairns emptied his glass. Neither man spoke until Ross was seated again.

"We've never had a better election to fight. I'm sure you'll agree. Jennings is in serious trouble on employment, inflation and the economy. I just saw the most recent Information Canada statistics. The G.N.P. is slipping badly. I intend to hammer him on it. My major point will be raising the question of the competence of his government. Jennings is ripe for plucking."

"No question," Ross' eyes narrowed. "You'd have it in the bag if it weren't for one serious question that has to be resolved and resolved immediately."

"What's that?"

"The Bonnaventures."

Cairns knew the question would be raised and was slightly relieved that it had been brought up so early in their conversation.

"I intend to update you on the matter this evening."

"Splendid."

"The Bonnaventure question will ensure us victory."

"I'm pleased you're so confident. Up to now it has raised problems. As I see it, the creditability of the party, and you in particular, is being severely challenged."

"Are you speaking from first-hand knowledge?"

"I am." The friendly tone in Ross' voice disappeared.

"I'm most interested in your views."

For the next five minutes Cairns did not speak. He listened carefully as Ross outlined his personal concerns and those of the party members he met on his trip. Nothing he said surprised Cairns until he ended by saying, "To win this election the party needs a significant infusion of campaign funds and they are not coming in to any degree until this problem is resolved to everyone's satisfaction."

"We're in better financial shape than we were before the last campaign and we'll be offering a stronger slate of candidates," defended Cairns.

"I'm very encouraged by the new blood coming into the party and I agree it will be the strongest slate yet, but the last time we weren't fighting creditability. This time we are. I don't have to remind you that last time we lost and if you expect to remain as leader we have to win and win handsomely. A squeaker won't do you a bit of good."

"Are you questioning my leadership, Senator?"

"You might say so. If I don't there will be others. It's tradition to change leaders after two defeats. All parties follow that practice and I for one support it. It's soul-destroying to have a loyal and dedicated contributor tell you that he is more than willing not only to match previous contributions but increase them provided the Bonnaventure question is put to rest."

"What did you tell them?"

"What can I tell them? I'm in the dark as much as anybody. All I can say is to have patience, trust you as leader, and have confidence in how you are handling the situation. It is a very weak offering but I've been provided with nothing more. I'm looking forward to what you have to say and am pleased we finally got together."

"Have you canvassed the other senators on the question?"

"Not formally. I've had numerous conversations plus an extended meeting with Gavin Edmunds. Personally, he has the greatest confidence in your leadership but as party president he is deeply concerned. I assume he has conveyed his feelings to you?"

Cairns nodded.

"Are you in a position to bring me into your confidence?"

Cairns realized his back was to the wall. If he rejected Ross' request it would seriously erode his creditability. He could not lose Ross if he were to survive. "Of course I can bring you into my confidence and do so willingly. But, I must insist that what I'm about to tell you is for your ears only until the appropriate moment. Timing will have to have the utmost priority if success is to be assured."

"Of course."

Cairns chose his words carefully. What he told Ross was approximately a word-for-word rehash of what he had told Logan, though he carefully embellished one or two points to feed Ross slightly more information. It would enhance his position should Ross compare notes, which he most certainly would do. It was important that Ross feel he was privy to more information than his nephew. Ross listened with an intensity that marked his political career. He weighed every word, phrase and nuance. Cairns spoke slowly.

When finished Ross stood up and walked toward the globe. "I don't usually allow myself more than two evening drinks but this calls for a third. Join me?"

"Thanks, but no. I have a stack of reports to wade through when I get home. I'm still nursing my second."

Ross refilled his glass and sat down. "Let me recap. I don't want to misinterpret or conject. What you are saying is that you have irrefutable proof that person or persons yet to be named have had their fingers in the national till." Cairns nodded. "These individuals are bureaucrats and possibly Members?" Cairns nodded again. "What about Jennings? You haven't mentioned the Prime Minister."

"I have neither heard nor seen anything that indicates Jennings is personally involved, but the executive responsibility is on his shoulders. Regardless of the fact that I do not personally like or respect the man, I would defend his honesty." There was a note of disappointment in Cairns' voice.

"Quite, quite. I feel the same way," Ross admitted. "While I have serious doubts about his abilities to govern the nation, I too respect him as an honest man. The bottom line, as I see it, will be proof that cannot be challenged either in the House or in the courts, if criminal charges are laid."

"You have my personal assurance that charges will be laid when I table what I have. You can depend on it, Humphrey. You can depend on it."

19

Dr. Emmett Rogers tamped down the tobacco in the bowl of his pipe and cleared his throat. "Gentlemen, if you please," he said, "we have a full agenda."

The seven other men seated around the table in conference room "B" in Atomic Power of Canada's Chalk River complex were a study in dress. Extremes were represented from Dr. Roger's conservative grey pinstripe suit complete with vest to Dr. Louis Panzica's corduroy pants and turtle neck sweater.

"Damn," muttered Panzica as he violently shook an inexpensive plastic lighter and thumbed the wheel. All he got for his effort was a small spark with no flame.

"Here," said a disgruntled voice from across the table. A package of matches flew toward him. "With Emmett's pipe and your cigars we'll all be lucky if we don't get lung cancer before this meeting adjourns."

Panzica laughed as he relit the respectable butt jutting clenched between his teeth.

"I'd be grateful for your input on the question of safety guidelines on reactor sales," began Rogers. "The Minister's after me for the benefit of our counsel. The question will be asked in the House so I think we should have our little say." A hand was raised at the end of the table. Rogers nodded. "Fred."

Dr. Frederick Campeau, one of A.P.C.'s senior scientists, was as well liked as he was respected. A mild mannered man, his patience and restraint were renowned. Many times, meetings would have disintegrated into bedlam if it hadn't been for his calming presence. This was especially true when it came to budgets. Each man in the room represented a division of A.P.C., and each man was jealous of his kingdom.

"Wouldn't we just be going over old ground, Emmett. Our views on the question are well known to the Minister."

"Agreed, but here's a new wrinkle." Rogers' comment immediately grabbed the interest of those assembled. Opening a file folder, he extracted a paper and adjusted his glasses. "I won't read this in its entirety because we are all familiar with the debate but there is one paragraph that disturbs me. I know it is causing the Minister concern. Let me quote. The writer is Jack McAndrews, editor of the *Canadian Scientist.* 'There are strong pressures to lower safety standards and non-proliferation controls imposed on overseas buyers of nuclear reactors in order to increase sales. There should be the constant fear of world stability and world peace in doing so. What is needed is a groundswell of public opinion – letter campaigns, demonstrations . . .'. Loud murmuring filled the room.

"Does McAndrews single out A.P.C.?" asked Panzica.

Rogers shook his head. "No, but we're certainly one of the targets, of that you can be sure."

"I don't know what the rest of you think," said Panzica as he looked around the table, "but personally I'm getting a bit weary of all this sniping by hacks like McAndrews. Our controls will stand up against those of any other nation."

"Agreed," responded Rogers. "But try and convince the antinuclear lobby of that fact. This is the sort of ammunition they welcome."

"Tell the Minister to ignore McAndrews," suggested a slight balding man.

"He would if he could, Charles, but he can't. McAndrews goes on to say that 'the perils attendant on nuclear-weapon proliferation are so great that some governments must take a firm stand, including Canada.' What he is saying in effect is that we're letting our standards drop in order to be more competitive in the world market."

"Does he single out the Bonnaventures?" asked Campeau.

"No. If he did we could defend from a stronger positon. He makes blanket statements and damns by implication."

"The answer's simple. We defend with the truth," said Campeau in quiet terms. "The Chinese are making great strides with the Bonnaventures. From what I've seen they are not only meeting our guidelines they are exceeding them."

"Would you all be in agreement if I tabled this question and held off reporting to the Minister until we have had time to think this matter through and then make our recommendations?" asked Rogers.

Unanimous agreement was received.

"This brings me to the next item on the agenda. A direct request has been received from the Ottawa Embassy of the People's Republic of China for joint co-operation on the preparation of articles highlighting the use of the Bonnaventures in China. Would any of you object to being interviewed for such a series, conditional upon my approval of the questions asked and the information provided?"

Panzica removed the stub of his cigar and wiped the back of a hand across his mouth. "Would these articles be for the scientific community?"

"No," replied Rogers. "It's my understanding they would be basically written for the general public."

Panzica pulled at his chin. "Basically written. In other words they'd be journalistic pap."

Campeau laughed out loud. "You are not giving the average reader much credibility, to say nothing of the journalist."

"Not at all. If all we want is to wave the Maple Leaf and say 'look at us we're great and because we're great the Chinese are great', I suppose there is no problem. We could use a bit of good press for a change. On the other hand, if the Chinese want to hog all the glory for themselves we should tell them to go to hell and go back to building junks."

Rogers tapped the table with his pencil. "As I see it the request is very straightforward. The Chinese want to put their best foot forward to the world. All they want to do is as simply as possible say 'here's what we're doing in such fields as medicine, agronomy, marine biology, etc. and we couldn't have done it without the

Bonnaventures which were designed and built by Canadians'. I can't see anything devious in the request. It would be a great selling tool for other nations if they can see what China has accomplished, especially when it is China saying it and not us."

"Do you think anybody is going to believe the Chinese any more than they believe us?" asked Panzica in a pejorative tone.

Campeau stiffened in his chair. "Until proven otherwise I accept that the request is being made in a spirit of mutual co-operation. We have nothing to lose. They can't include anything we don't give them. If they did we could raise holy hell."

"A lot of good that would do us once the damage was done," snorted Panzica.

"You'd question a rerun of the Last Supper with the original cast," said Campeau with a chuckle. Laughter filled the room.

"You might be impressed with the Chinese, Fred, but I don't share your enthusiasm. If you recall, I spent four weeks in China three years ago on that trade mission. I have never been pumped so hard in all my life. It was all take and very little give."

"That's three years ago, Lou. Times have changed. Put yourself in their position. If they crossed us up we'd slap the lid on any further support. I don't have to remind you that the contract we signed with them includes an ongoing up-grading of the Bonnaventures in both hardware and software. No, I don't think they'll be foolish enough to jeopardize a long term relationship by playing games. They are desperately trying to bring their technology into the 20th century. I don't have to remind anyone here that there is a lot of money riding on our future with China."

"Well taken, Fred," interjected Rogers. "I should mention again that the one condition I insisted upon was in seeing and approving any story that might be written. I'll go one step further. I will approve nothing until I've checked it out with each division head concerned. I suggest we invite their writer in and take it from there."

"Who will it be?" asked Panzica.

"Adam Sutton."

"Never heard of him."

"He's the Canadian correspondent for Xinhau, the Chinese Press Agency. He's requested a meeting. I don't know his credentials but I shall certainly find them out before we proceed. I assume he's qualified otherwise he wouldn't be assigned."

"It makes sense to have a non-Chinese doing their writing," said Campeau.

"That was my initial reaction. We'll proceed slowly, gentlemen. We'll not give a commitment until we know for certain we're on firm ground. Do I have your agreement to proceed on that basis?"

Rogers looked around the table. All hands were raised. Panzica's was the last to go up.

With great delicacy and panache Ambassador Wu Tai Shan sipped his tea and savored the amber liquid with obvious relish. The atmosphere in his embassy office was tranquil. No one spoke. All waited patiently for the Ambassador to begin the meeting. Adam Sutton sat between First Secretary Yuan Tzu and Lao Chengtu. Following the lead of his companions, Sutton sipped his tea and accepted the almond cookie offered by the secretary. It crumbled in his mouth the moment he took a bite.

The Ambassador was in good humor and his contented smile set the tone for what was to come. Yuan and Lao appeared at ease but Sutton was uncomfortable. This was his first informal meeting with Wu and he wanted the meeting to go well. Remuneration notwithstanding, there was the question of professional pride. He was well aware of the comments that were being made at the press club. While no one held him responsible for McBride's fall from grace it was the general consensus that if the job broke a man such as McBride it would totally destroy him. There were the critics to silence. The only way to silence them was by turning out copy that could not be ignored.

"A most pleasant tea, Mr. Sutton," said Wu as he held out his cup in the direction of the secretary who was seated beside his desk. Without speaking she bowed slightly and poured. Wu nodded toward the other three men who were serviced in order of importance: Yuan first, Lao second and Sutton third. The almond cookies were offered again.

"Very pleasant, Excellency. A special blend from China?"

Wu smiled broadly. "It comes from a small shop in Toronto's Chinatown. The cookies are from an Italian bakery in Bell's Corners. It's an excellent blend. It's Taiwanese." Wu looked at Lao. "Would it not be ironic if we were enjoying tea that your uncle exported?"

"Ironic indeed," replied Lao softly.

Sutton frowned.

"Puzzled Mr. Sutton? Quite simple. When the Great Revolution took place many of our people remained loyal to Chaing Kai-shek and went with him to what was then called Formosa. Comrade Lao's uncle was one of them. Today he is one of Taipei's more prosperous tea exporters."

"Sounds like quite a story. It would appear that both did extremely well under two opposing systems. The uncle's a successful businessman under the free enterprise system and his nephew equally successful in the diplomatic corps of a Communist state."

Wu chuckled. "You should have Comrade Lao tell you his story sometime. It would make a good novel. Ever thought of writing a book?"

"Every journalist thinks about writing a book. Someday, perhaps," said Sutton. He was beginning to feel more at ease. Wu's small talk was disarming. He was amazed at his excellent English.

"I understand from Comrade Lao that you are very thorough."

"I try to be, Excellency. When you write fiction you have license but I'm not writing fiction so I have to make certain that my facts are right."

"I understand that you have confirmed a meeting with Dr. Rogers at Atomic Power."

"I meet with him Wednesday at three."

"Do you feel confident?"

"One is never confident when dealing with scientists. The majority distrust journalists. They run a pretty closed operation and only talk within their scientific community."

"Be prepared for controls and restrictions. They are to be expected."

"I'm sure everything I do will be monitored, checked and double checked. Even if I am only given the most basic of information I can do a creditable story. There is so much that hasn't been told, anything will be virtually newsworthy. I must say that my friend here, " Sutton indicated toward Lao, "has been more than helpful. I'm impressed with the research material he's supplied. It's making my job so much easier. I think Dr. Rogers will be surprised with my background."

"I'm sure he will, Mr. Sutton. Comrade Lao is always most thorough. If he had elected to go with his uncle, he'd be a capitalist millionaire by now instead of sacrificing material considerations for the higher ideals of Marxism and socialism."

Yuan Tzu recrossed his legs. He had remained silent following his reserved greeting when Sutton was first introduced at the beginning of the meeting. His eyes followed from speaker to speaker with intensity.

Wu was impressed with Sutton. He liked his no nonsense approach to polite conversation and his candor.

"More tea, gentlemen?" asked Wu.

All three accepted. To refuse would have been impolite.

"I understand Mr. McBride is unwell," said Wu casually.

Sutton glanced at Lao. The glance was not returned. "I'm sorry to hear that. He's had more than his share of setbacks in recent months."

"Do you know him well?"

"No. I've met him on occasion but I can't say I ever knew him well. He is a very private person and does not encourage friendship."

"A very able man. We were sorry to lose him."

"He's certainly well respected within the media. What's wrong with him?"

"I was hoping you could tell us. What have you heard, Comrade?"

"Very little, Excellency," said Lao. "All I know is that he is reported to be in the Ottawa Civic and is quite sick."

"We should find out and offer our help if needed. Regardless of the circumstances surrounding his departure from employment we must be charitable. Do you think you could find out for us, Mr. Sutton?"

"I could ask around the Press Club. It must have been quite sudden. The last I heard was that he'd left Ottawa and no one appeared to know where he'd gone."

"See what you can do, Mr. Sutton. Try the hospital as well. It would be better if the inquiry came from you rather than from us directly. Curious minds might jump to the wrong conclusions."

Sutton felt uneasy. He was hired as a journalist not a messenger boy. Now, he thought, might be the time to establish his position.

"If you find out that Mr. McBride is in financial difficulties we would be pleased to help, anonymously of course. True charity never boasts."

"I don't believe I was ... " Sutton suddenly gasped in mid-word.

Wu looked concerned. "What's wrong?"

"Nothing," said Sutton as he rubbed his ankle.

"My apologies," said Lao. "I crossed my legs and accidently cracked Mr. Sutton on the ankle. I do apologize."

"You were saying, Mr. Sutton?"

Sutton pursed his lips. There were two questions he wanted answered before he made his stand. How did Ambassador Wu know about McBride's sudden and apparently little known illness, and was Lao's kick accidental or a not too subtle warning to keep his mouth shut and do what he was told without complaining?

"Nothing, Excellency. I shall do my best."

"Splendid," replied Wu with an almost upper-class British accent. "I trust your meeting with Dr. Rogers goes well and I wait expectantly for your report."

The more Wu talked the more amazed Sutton became. When he first met him following his appointment as Xinhua correspondent their conversation was stilted. It appeared that Wu's vocabulary was limited and he was constantly grasping for the correct word or phrase. On more than one occasion Lao would whisper in his ear apparently giving him the correct word. Sutton now realized this was merely role playing and a very convenient ploy when assessing an individual or situation.

"I shall report back the moment I return, Ambassador."

Wu stood up. It signaled the end of the meeting. "This has been most pleasant, Mr. Sutton. We shall meet again."

Lao and Yuan bowed. Sutton nodded and smiled.

20

Tom McBride was not a pretty sight as he lay motionless in his hospital bed. His partial plate had been removed and the upper lip fell flaccid into the opening. It moved slightly with each breath. His color was pallid and irregular beads of sweat glistened on his forehead. The left eye was tightly closed and the right one half closed adding to the grotesqueness of his features which were framed by the grey flecked stubble of his beard.

Kevin Ingram stood beside the bed and gently touched his arm. "Tom." he said in a quiet voice. There was no flicker of recognition. "Tom," he repeated as he gently shook the limp arm.

The door to the hospital room opened quietly and Dr. Chester Wainwright entered. "You're wasting your time," he said. "Even if your friend can hear you he's incapable of responding."

Ingram turned quickly to face Wainwright.

"My nurse told me you were here."

"My God, to end up like this," said Ingram as he glanced at McBride.

"I've seen worse. How did you make out at the cottage?"

Ingram bent down and picked up a small overnight flight bag. "I brought you everything I could lay my hands on. I hope it helps."

Wainwright took the bag and pulled the zipper. The stench of decaying food filled the room. "This is ripe," said Wainwright as he rummaged through the contents.

"You told me to bring anything I could find that might indicate what Tom had been eating or drinking."

Wainwright pulled out a soiled plate. The remains of pork and beans had solidified. "Good. What else is here?"

"A couple of beer cans, a bottle of gin with a few ounces left, half a loaf of stale bread, a couple of mouldy oranges and three slices of bologna that are as green as grass."

"Certainly not cordon bleu. I thought you said he enjoyed food?"

"I thought he did too. Is it just garbage or can you find out anything?"

"I'll know better after I've seen the results of the analyses. They may shed some light."

"Isn't it a stroke?"

"As I told you I never make a firm diagnosis until all possibilities have been investigated."

"What about your tests?"

"We've ruled out a local infection, bacterial infection and an aneurysm. We're working on the others."

"How is he?"

"Guarded. It's too early to tell."

"Will he die?"

"Possibly. We all have to die sometime."

"Can he hear us talking right now?"

"He could but I doubt it. I wouldn't be discussing his condition if I thought for a moment that he was conscious. He isn't. When he is conscious there'll be no conversations of this type conducted in his presence. This is a classic mistake that is often made with stroke patients. I've seen many devastated by what was said around their bed when relatives or friends assumed that just because they couldn't speak they couldn't hear or understand."

"I thought you said you weren't satisfied it was a stroke?"

"I'm not. I only use stroke as an example."

"Being realistic, how soon do you think I could get some intelligent response from him?"

"Why the necessity of getting intelligent response as you term it?"

"I want to talk to him. It's important," replied Ingram emphatically. "He's my friend."

"He has a number of friends. He's a fortunate man."

Ingram's spine stiffened. "What friends?"

Wainwright shrugged. "I have no idea. The floor supervisor told me that a man inquired about his condition earlier this afternoon. He told her to get anything Mr. McBride might need or request and he'd look after the cost. Not too often I have a patient with such generous friends."

"Who was he?"

Wainwright shrugged. "I have no idea. Ask the floor supervisor. He may have left a name or number."

"Was he oriental?"

"She could tell you. I didn't see him."

"Did he get in to see Tom?"

"No. I've restricted visitors to you or verified next-of-kin. I don't want a stream of people in and out until I know what his problem is and can begin treatment. Speaking of relatives, any luck?"

"No, I went through his effects but couldn't find anything. I even checked his passport to see who he listed in case of accident or death."

"Who was it?"

"The secretary of the Ottawa Press Club. That appears to be his closest next-of-kin. He was surprised that Tom had put his name down."

"Where is his passport?"

"I have it at my place. As soon as he's functioning I'll get everything to him."

"Could I have a look at it? It would give me an idea of where he's been recently. There are new strains of tropical diseases we've never even heard about coming to light. It's a long shot."

"There is also a new strain of syphilis coming out of the Phillippines that's harder to treat than herpes. Correct?"

"You're well informed," said Wainwright. "I'm impressed."

"I did a story on V.D. You think Tom is syphilitic, don't you?"

"If he is you'll be the first to know. Any luck with the ladies?"

"I asked around at the Press Club and talked to his former landlord. Nobody ever remembers seeing him with a woman socially."

"Is he celibate?"

"I can't imagine it at his age. His isn't that old."

"Is he gay?"

"You've got to be joking," said Ingram with a laugh.

"I'm not a frivolous man, Mr. Ingram," snapped Wainwright.

"I never joke about one of my patients. I ask you again is he gay or bisexual?"

"From what I've seen of him I'd have to say he was totally heterosexual, but how can you tell these days?"

"Precisely. If I knew for certain he only went to bed with women it could save a lot of time."

"Do you think you're on to something."

"This is one of the most damnable cases I've come up against in years. It's also one of the most intriguing. When I first examined him I was ready to confirm the initial diagnosis of a massive stroke but something doesn't fit and I can't put my finger on it."

"If it's any help I'll dig around some more. He worked for the *Vancouver Sun* a few years back and I have a friend still with the paper. He'll certainly remember him. I'll give him a call."

"Another generous offer. I'm being submerged in beneficence. Don't you have any work to do?"

"Of course."

"How can you devote so much time to Mr. McBride? I can understand your concern but don't you have a boss?"

"This is part of my work. Warner assigned me to looking after Tom's needs and when your Managing Editor speaks you jump."

"Ah, so that explains why you didn't hesitate at going all the way back to the cottage to dig around in garbage."

Ingram shoved both hands in his pockets and glanced over at the motionless McBride. Wainwright was pressing. To give too little information might create a barrier. He had no doubts about Wainwright being trustworthy but until he found out what McBride wanted to tell him he had to be cautious. "He's also a colleague. He'd do the same for me."

"Somehow I doubt that. Do you appreciate candor, Mr. Ingram?"

"I always have."

"Splendid. Let's stop playing games and be perfectly honest. That man in the bed is more than just a colleague. He's part of some puzzle. What that puzzle is only concerns me because I assume I am also part of it to some degree. I never like working

129

in a vacuum. If we are to continue you'll have to take me into your confidence to the same degree I've taken you into mine."

"If it were up to me I'd fill you in on what I've got so far but I can't until I check with somebody first. I can tell you this much. My interest in McBride goes beyond charity. He is the key to what might be the biggest story of the decade. This is why I have to speak to him and hopefully keep him from speaking to anyone else."

"Is this a police matter?"

"Not at this point. It could be, though, especially if you find that McBride's person was violated in any manner." Wainwright smiled. "Initially I couldn't understand why you were so interested in what Tom had been eating or drinking, then it hit me. You suspect some foreign substance such as a drug. Correct?"

"Suspect is probably too strong a verb at this point. Let's say I'm curious. For example, if he suffered from abnormal heart rate problems which were sufficient to place him under the care of a doctor he could be taking biquin durules. It's a prescription drug but it has to be handled carefully. Some of its side effects are convulsions, disturbed vision and color perception, fever, localized edema, coma apprehension, even death."

"Were those symptoms present when you first examined him?"

"Some. He was also experiencing respiratory distress and rapid heartbeat. His chart indicated that upon admittance to Renfrew Hospital he had acute diarrhea. That is why I asked you if his bowels had evacuated. I wanted to know at what point the diarrhea began. But don't jump to premature conclusions. I never said he was drugged. He certainly exhibits classic stroke symptoms."

"How soon will you know for sure?"

"I'll have everything you brought from the cottage run through the lab as quickly as possible. So where do we stand?"

"Well," Ingram paused, "I have to talk to someone first and if I get approval I'll fill you in completely. Until then I can't say any more. Will you go along with me?"

Wainwright slowly nodded his head. "I have no other choice, do I? My prime concern is for my patient. I assume you want him isolated until further notice."

"Is that a problem?"

"No. I'll order him restricted. Should bonafide relatives turn up I'll have to allow them in."

"Would you do this for me?" Ingram took out a card and wrote on the back. "Here are my office and home telephone numbers. Will you call me if anybody tries to get in or if his condition changes?"

"Certainly. Are you going to look into who the would be benefactor is?"

"You bet. I want to talk to the floor supervisor before I leave."

Wainwright stiffened slightly as he heard his name being paged. "I have to go."

Ingram extended his hand. "Thank you, Doctor. I appreciate your co-operation.

"I just hope that this all works out for everyone's benefit, especially his."

Both men looked at McBride's rigid form. The only sign of life was a slight heaving of the bedcovers as he breathed and the tremor of his lip as air was expelled from his lungs.

21

Cole Harrison looked at his watch and carefully parted the drapes covering the front window of Unit 17 in the Eastview Motel on Highway 7 on the outskirts of Perth. It was 7:15 and the sun's rays were beginning to slant from the west.

The "no vacancy" sign was flashing over the office door and only five parking spaces were unoccupied. He wondered how many guests were on legitimate business and how many were on one night stands.

Hearing a car pull up and a door slam Harrison parted the

drapes again. A weary looking man struggled to pull a battered suitcase out of the trunk and walked slowly to the door of Unit 16. Harrison flopped on the bed and listened. The sound of muffled footsteps was followed by the flushing of the toilet and the running of water in the sink. He made a mental note to make certain that he turned the television set on when he and Diane were in bed. It would mask the sound of their love-making which at times was exuberant and vocal.

Rolling to one side, he looked at his watch again. It was 7:30. He swung his legs over the side of the bed, sat for a moment then quickly walked to his over-night bag and took out a bottle of Mumm's Champagne. It was warm to the touch. Mumbling a curse because he couldn't find an ice bucket he turned on the cold water tap in the sink and let it run at full force. The running water drowned out all extraneous sound. Testing the water with his hand, he reduced the flow and gently placed the bottle under the tap. He thought he heard a slight tapping on the door and listened for a moment as he slowly revolved the bottle. The tapping became more incessant.

"Were you hiding a woman under the bed?" asked Diane as she quickly entered the room and waited for him to close the door and secure it with the lock and night chain.

"I was in the bathroom chilling the champagne. I couldn't hear anything with the water running."

"A likely story," replied Diane as she dropped her small bag and put her arms tightly around his neck.

"That's more like it," mumbled Harrison as he kissed her passionately and began to gently massage the small of her back.

Diane felt his rising hardness against her and responded with her body, at the same time kicking off her shoes. Harrison slipped his hand between their bodies and cupped her left breast. He could feel the firmness. They walked to the bed. As Diane lay down, Harrison stood above her and admired her body. He removed her dress. The time at the Lake had changed her flesh to bronze, with subtle lines of pink marking the borders between the tanned skin and the white circles around her breasts and the whiteness of her abdomen and buttocks. He lifted her legs from under the knees and reached up to remove her panties. He lowered her legs, spread them apart and began kissing her golden skin. He began at her calves and moved up slowly, one eye always on the feast of black and white that awaited him at the end of the journey. She held his head in her hands as his tongue moved over her.

The strain of separation had not dulled their passion. It was an hour before they could lie on the bed without caressing each other's body, without needing to feel the sensation of the other being warm and near and loving.

Suddenly, Diane turned cold and distant.

"What's the matter?" asked Harrison in surprise.

"I feel like a whore."

"Come on," said Harrison in a soothing voice. "We've been through this before. You're not a whore; you're a beautiful and desirable woman and I love you very much."

"I love you but . . ."

"But what?"

"I want more than just this," Diane patted the bed.

"We have more. We have each other." Harrison stood over her and looked down into her upturned face.

Diane shook her head. "No we haven't. All we have are one night stands in crummy motel rooms. You call this having something? My God, you'd get a two-bit hooker complaining!"

Harrison was well aware of Diane's mood swings and up to now he'd been able to control them. A gentle touch, an overt caress or a direct assault upon her body usually worked. This time he was not certain. He had never seen her like this before. She appeared to be teetering on the verge of hysterics.

"Let's have a glass of champagne," he suggested. Diane shook her head. "Come on," coaxed Harrison. "It'll pick up your spirits and we can talk." He didn't wait for a response. He walked quickly to the bathroom and returned with the bottle and two glasses covered in plastic.

"Not exactly the *Chez Gatineau* but it'll probably taste just as good." The cork popped and the amber liquid flowed out of the top and down the neck.

"It's still warm," protested Diane.

"There is just one thing worse than lukewarm champagne and that's no champagne," said Harrison with a smile as he generously filled the glasses.

Diane sat rigid on the edge of the bed and accepted the glass.

"Here's to us," said Harrison raising his glass and clinking hers. He sat down on the bed beside her.

Both locked eyes as they sipped the champagne. Neither spoke. A gulf was widening between them which was painful.

Harrison drained his glass and reached for the bottle which was on the floor.

"Warm champagne has a real kick," said Diane. "You don't want to get bagged so early in the evening."

"I'm alright," replied Harrison as he refilled his glass nearly to the brim.

"What are we going to drink for the rest of the night?"

Harrison smiled at her positive statement. "I can get some more. There's a liquor store just off the main street. What do you say I get a couple of bottles more and something to eat? What do you want, a pizza, chicken or Chinese food?"

"Surprise me."

Harrison tilted his head back and emptied the glass. Jumping to his feet he made a mock appearance of running for the door. Her melancholy mood and tone returned as quickly as it had left.

As Harrison reached the door, he turned and said, "I love you. I really do."

"So do I," was the response.

It took Harrison nearly three-quarters of an hour to do his shopping. First he bought three bottles of a medium-priced Canadian champagne from the liquor store. Next a picnic package in the Beamish 5 and 10. It contained six paper plates, six napkins, six plastic spoons, knives and forks. The selection in the florist store was limited. He purchased the remaining half-dozen red roses. The card read "Everything's coming up roses. I love you." Service at the take out counter of the House of Chiu was infuriating slow. By the time he drove back to the motel the streets lights were on. Parking in one of the two remaining spaces, he hurriedly gathered up his parcels and walked quickly to Unit 17. With his toe he kicked at the door. There was no answer. He kicked again. Juggling the parcels, he opened the door. The lights were off inside the room.

"Are you asleep?" he called out softly as he closed the door with his foot. There was no reply. "Diane," he said in a raised voice. The flushing of a toilet in the next unit was the only response. Stumbling toward the dark shadow that was the bed, he laid the parcels down and turned on the night table light. The first thing that caught his eye was a piece of white paper on the pillow. It had a line sketch of the Eastview Motel at the top. Underneath, in Diane's familiar handwriting, was a short message.

Cole:

I need some time to think things out. Tonight just won't work. If I want to see you again I'll get in touch. Please don't call me. I think I love you but I'm not sure. I have to be sure.

Sorry,
Diane

22

The afternoon was bright, sunny and ideal for the Governor General's garden party. The beautiful setting of Government House added to the relaxed atmosphere as the Ottawa diplomatic community mingled on an informal basis.

RCMP Sergeant Ken Mackie, resplendent in full dress uniform, stood under the canopy and surveyed the courtyard. He felt uncomfortable in the heavy scarlet coat. While the three stripes on the sleeve of his tunic identified him as a sergeant, his official rank was Inspector, attached to "A" Operation-Security Screening. He conveniently dropped in rank when not wanting to draw undue attention.

The winding driveway in front of the main entrance was filled with black and silver-grey limousines. The uniformed chauffeurs stood in clusters, smoking and exchanging embassy gossip. Half-way down the line, sandwiched between the British

Ambassador's Rolls-Royce and the German Ambassador's Mercedes-Benz, was the Lincoln Continental of Soviet Ambassador Vladimir Kulik. The hood was suddenly raised, and all that could be seen was the lower portion of the chauffeur's body as he leaned into the engine.

Mackie noticed the raised hood and walked across the lawn. He stood motionless on the opposite side of the car and said loudly, but pleasantly, "Problems?"

The Soviet chauffeur raised his voice. "I noticed one cylinder missing slightly and I want to make certain it is nothing more than a loose or disconnected spark plug wire. I can get along very well without having his Excellency discourse on the poor quality of American automobiles."

Mackie smiled. "What's on your mind, Colonel?" he said quietly.

Nikolai Volsky was officially accredited as Senior Chauffeur for the Soviet Embassy but he was known by the RCMP Security Service to be a KGB officer. Both men jealously guarded each nation's interests, but they had profound respect for one another and had, on occasion, exchanged information their superiors wished transmitted to senior officials without going through diplomatic channels or putting it on the official record.

"Good afternoon, Inspector," replied Volsky in a subdued voice. "Why is your government considering a move which could rupture relations between our two countries?"

"I didn't know we were. Be more specific."

"We have it on good authority that Canada is on the verge of selling condensers, resisters and components to The People's Republic of China for the Bonnaventure nuclear reactors."

"I don't think that's any secret, and why would the Soviet Union worry about such a small matter? All reactors use condensers and resisters."

"Not the type I'm referring to," said Volsky as he deliberately removed a spark plug cable.

"What type are you referring to?"

"Components for a US-made converter. It's a complex piece of equipment that can be used to enrich plutonium to weapons grade or provide electricity for precise manufacture of nuclear weapons."

Mackie stood up and arched his back. The clusters of chauffeurs had not changed or moved. "I don't suppose you are in a position to substantiate your concern?"

Volsky handed Mackie a folded piece of paper listing the components. On the bottom of the paper was the question. "Doesn't this contravene Canada's export restrictions for nuclear reactors?"

Volsky replaced the cable and walked to the front of the car. Reaching up, he made ready to slam the hood. "All clear, Sergeant?" he said in a raised voice. Mackie stood back. Volsky pulled the hood down. "Thank you for your help. I'll get it seen to by a mechanic in the morning."

"Any time," replied Mackie. He began walking toward the front entrance and his assigned post.

The weeks that followed Jennings' return from British Columbia were busy and productive. Parliament was in recess for the summer, and to Jennings' relief the Bonnaventure matter appeared to be forgotten or set aside. Jennings was not lulled into a sense of false security. He didn't trust Cairns and fully expected him to once again be the master of timing. When it came he would be ready, but he hoped it wouldn't come until he could submerge Cairns and his party in their own mire.

Jennings shoved his reading glasses up on the bridge of his nose and reached for the ever present cup of coffee that Marcie Peckman had placed on the corner of his office desk. Taking a long slow drink he shoved a pile of letters across the desk. "What did you do, advise every program co-ordinator to write in requesting me to speak?"

"You're a very popular speaker, Prime Minister," replied Marcie as she leaned forward in her chair and reached for the stack of letters.

"I'm cheap too. Not only do I speak for nothing, they don't even have to pay my expenses. I've indicated the couple that interest me and the ones that should be turned over to the appropriate Ministers. Attach a memo from me requesting that they accept in my place and send the rest the usual perfunctory letter of thanks and regrets."

"The Ministers will love you for that."

"Gives them something to do besides sleeping in the House." Jennings smiled. "What's next?"

"Commissioner Chambers is cooling his heels and Cole called from Sept Isles."

"What's he want?"

"Probably to see how you want him to respond to the cartoon in the Toronto *Express*. Have you seen it?"

Jennings made a face. "I've seen it. I assume everybody in the country has seen it."

"You have to admit it is clever, Prime Minister."

Jennings opened the top drawer of his desk and removed the torn-out editorial page of the Toronto *Express*. The editorial was a hard-hitting denouncement of security for the Prime Minister and his family. It pointed out that in a day of international terrorism and political kidnappings the wife of the Prime Minister should not be allowed to drive alone, in a private car without RCMP officers covering her every move. It criticized Jennings for allowing her to do so and raised the question of whether or not she did so without Jennings' knowledge. To the right of the editorial was a Carl Olsen political cartoon. Olsen had drawn a devastating caricature of Diane standing beside her car with a grinning Ottawa traffic cop behind her. The caption read "DID YOU JUST PINCH ME, OFFICER?"

For a fleeting moment Jennings started to grin, then his features hardened. "I don't find my wife being held up to public ridicule humorous. Olsen's had his knife into me more than once and I can live with it. But I won't tolerate him taking swipes at my family."

Marcie realized she had spoken out-of-turn. "I'm sorry, Prime Minister."

"It's all right. I understand. Politicians, and especially Prime Ministers, are fair game and I accept it. One would expect, however, that members of the family would be immune."

"Shall I send in Commissioner Chambers?"

Jennings nodded. He didn't raise his head. His eyes were riveted on the cartoon. John Chambers entered the office. "Prime Minister," he said and sat down in the chair Marcie Peckman had just vacated.

"Commissioner," replied Jennings. "Sorry to keep you waiting. I had some pressing business." The newspaper page slithered across the desk. Chambers took a deep breath. "Where was my wife's security officer when this happened?" demanded Jennings.

"I've asked for a full report from the Inspector in charge of the detail."

"That doesn't answer my question."

Chambers was a direct man who insisted on direct answers to his questions, and his credo for himself and all ranks was excellence; nothing else was acceptable. The fact that his force had been openly criticized and vilified in both the House and press over the last decade rankled. His explicit orders were for a low profile and strict adherance to the law by all ranks.

He instigated an internal investigation half an hour after the first edition of the *Express* landed on his desk. A phone call to the Deputy Chief of the Ottawa Police Department provided the details of the summons and a verbal explanation that the officer was only carrying out his duty. He did not know he was summonsing the Prime Minister's wife until the summons had been written out. A call to the summons bureau shed no further light other than the director refusing to accept the fact that someone in the department had breached rules and regulations by revealing that the offense had taken place. An investigation was promised.

Chambers was willing to apprise Jennings of the facts up to that point but was reluctant to reveal the report of the security officer who said that Diane had dismissed him early in the evening. She claimed that she would be retiring early and there was no point in him staying on as she did not plan to leave Sussex Drive until mid-morning of the next day.

He felt that if the Prime Minister pressed for a full report he would have no recourse but to request a meeting with Diane and face her with the officer's statement. Not knowing her side of what could be nothing more than a personal matter, he hesitated to pursue the matter further unless ordered to do so by Jennings. "I regret, Prime Minister, that until I have all the facts I can tell you nothing more. I assume you have spoken to Mrs. Jennings?"

"She told me that she retired early but couldn't sleep so decided to take a drive," lied Jennings.

"Neither you nor any member of your family should venture out without security officers. These are violent times. My department is put in a precarious position when breaches of security occur, but we must have full co-operation if we are to do our job."

"Agreed, Commissioner. I assure you it will never happen again."

"Thank you. May I make a suggestion?"

"Please do."

"The damage this incident has done, if indeed there has been any real damage, will be forgotten within a day. I suggest that since it was just a minor error in judgement we should let the matter rest. If word gets out to the press that I have launched an internal investigation they will have a field day. There is a segment of the press that enjoys nothing more than seeing the force embarrassed. I venture that Mr. Olsen would take his pointed pen in hand once more and I shudder to contemplate what the results would be. This cartoon, while disturbing, had its humorous touch. The next one could be vicious."

"I was contemplating that very course, Commissioner. I appreciate your counsel. The matter is closed."

Chambers exhaled a lungful of air in relief. "I give you my personal assurance that such a thing will never happen again. We shall reassess our security procedures and tighten up wherever necessary. You and your family will be protected around-the-clock. There will be no lapses, of that I assure you."

Jennings returned the cartoon and editorial to his top drawer. "Further business, Commissioner?"

Chambers placed his attaché case on his knee and snapped the locks open. "I have a preliminary report on the Bonnaventure sales to The People's Republic of China."

"Good!" enthused Jennings. "It couldn't have come at a more opportune time."

"It's only interim, but I felt it was comprehensive enough to provide you with the background you requested. A more detailed analysis of the investigation will be prepared and forwarded to you at the earliest possible moment."

Jennings took the folder. Stamped across the lower left corner was "CONFIDENTIAL". Diagonally in the upper right was "FOR YOUR EYES ONLY."

"Perhaps it would save valuable time if I covered the highlights and then you could read in detail at your leisure."

"Please do."

"I placed two of my best men on it," began Chambers in a slow methodical voice. "They are chartered accountants and auditing experts and only used on financial investigations of the highest order. They were personally briefed by me. No one else in the department was brought into the picture. Because of the delicate nature of the assignment I did not inform them that the request came from you. As far as they are concerned I and I alone ordered it."

"Excellent!" responded Jennings.

"Their assignment was to audit a number of foreign contracts, of which the Bonnaventure was just one."

"Which contracts did they look into?"

Chambers flipped open his file and ran a finger down the index page. "The Saudi Arabian communications network, the 170-kilometer highway in Haiti, the filtration plant in Chad and the hydro-electric plant in Nepal."

"I congratulate you, Commissioner."

"My men," he continued, "turned up a number of interesting items which I am sure you will want to look into. For instance the Winnipeg contractor supplying heavy equipment for the construction of the four-lane highway running along the coast from Port au Prince to the coastal town of Jeremie is also a part owner of the new hotel complex which just happens to be on the beach at Jeremie. The original contract was for the highway to run inland on the island as a means of opening up rural Haiti. From what we were able to find, the change in direction was ordered by President Jean Claude Duvallier. The president also has an interest in the resort complex."

"Were we advised of the change in direction?"

"To the best of our knowledge, no."

"Interesting. I'd like you to follow it up. Cairns was the one to spearhead that project when he was Prime Minister." Jennings immediately grasped the possibilities of making political yardage by using it against Cairns in the election. Even if there was an acceptable explanation, the very fact of raising the question would be sufficient to put him on the defensive.

"What about the Bonnaventures, Commissioner?" asked Jennings.

Looking up, Chambers said," As far as the financial procedures are concerned, they're so clean they squeak. We've come up with absolutely nothing and believe me our investigation was thorough. All invoices, from the very first one, have been paid in full by the People's Republic of China. As a matter of record they've been paid to the cent. The only negative aspect I can see is in the slight delay in transferring funds from Hong Kong to Ottawa, but that is probably explainable."

"I don't follow."

"For some reason they were not transferred immediately, but that could be nothing more than paperwork. We all know how slow banking procedures can be at times."

"Have you checked the payment schedule for other foreign contracts?"

"Yes and that's why I don't think there is any problem. Nepal and Chad took as long if not longer, but that's explainable. The payments for both countries began with a local bank which transferred the monies to their European bank which in turn transferred them to a New York bank and then to Ottawa. The wheels of international banking revolve slowly."

"Based upon what you have uncovered, or better still not uncovered, would you say I'd be on safe ground to stand up in the House and categorically say that the Bonnaventure sales are clean?"

"Yes, Prime Minister," replied Chambers emphatically. "Absolutely clean. Do you intend to say that the investigation was conducted by my department?"

"Not unless I am pressed by the opposition. I'd prefer to keep them wondering. It will be enough that I am making the statement."

"Will you advise China?"

"Yes. I intend to request a meeting with Ambassador Wu before I speak out. It is a courtesy that I feel is owing them. Some time ago, I abruptly cancelled an appointment with Mr. Lao Chengtu, the Press . . ."

"Lao, sir?"

"You know him?"

"Of course. He's a complex man. We're keeping an eye on him."

"Why?"

"He's more mobile than we would like to see but we know

that he's quite a ladies' man. We like to keep tabs on who he is bedding down with."

Jennings smiled. "Find out what he's drinking. It may be a Chinese aphrodisiac and we can all benefit."

Chambers chuckled.

"Well, Commissioner, if that's all that's bothering you I'm relieved."

"A word of caution, sir. I wouldn't tell the Chinese too much."

Jennings looked surprised. "Explain."

"It's nothing we can put our finger on."

"Are you saying there are problems?"

"I've learned through bitter experience to never completely trust anyone from a foreign nation, especially those who represent a socialist or hard-line Communist country. They have their job to do and sometimes how they do it is not necessarily in the best interests of Canada."

"I've always found Ambassador Wu and his staff totally open and co-operative," countered Jennings in a defensive tone. "China needs Canada more than Canada needs China at the moment. I can't comprehend them putting themselves into a compromising situation. I accept what you say until proven otherwise. But that's your job, Commissioner. I admire your vigilance."

"I just make the point that a cautious stance does not necessarily indicate mistrust. It is merely prudent."

Jennings looked straight into Chambers' face. "There's something more, isn't there, Commissioner?"

Chambers returned the gaze. "Yes. Could I, with your permission, bring in Inspector Bullis? He's in the outer office. I would like him to give you the benefit of his evaluation on a situation which may be of importance. It concerns the Bonnaventures."

"By all means, Commissioner." Jennings buzzed Marcie Peckman and asked her to bring in Inspector Bullis. Bullis entered and after formal introductions took a chair beside Chambers.

"Inspector," ordered Chambers, "would you apprise the Prime Minister of the conversation Inspector Mackie had with Nikolai Volsky at the Governor General's garden party, and your assessment."

Bullis opened his notepad and cleared his throat. Jennings

listened intently and without interruption as the report of the conversation was given verbatim. Settling back in his chair, Jennings placed both hands together and chucked at his chin with his thumbs. "Can Volsky be trusted?"

"In this instance, yes. It's no secret that Russia fears China more than it does the United States and would do anything to embarrass them or limit their military capabilities."

"Any idea where Volsky got his information?"

"It certainly wasn't from China," interjected Chambers. "After the ideological split the Soviet spy network in China was totally broken and as far as we know it hasn't been re-established."

"Where would they get such information from if it wasn't from field agents?"

"Taiwan," replied Bullis emphatically. "Their spy system is very sophisticated."

Jennings recoiled in surprise. "I find that hard to accept. What do you base that assumption on?"

"I don't think there is any question, sir," continued Bullis. "It would serve Taiwan well to feed useful information to the Soviets, especially if they could use it against China. The world pays little heed to Taiwan but they listen to the Soviets. We've spoken to M15 in London and the CIA in Washington on the matter. Both concur. The CIA is most interested because of the fragile relations between Washington and Taipei. They've requested that they be kept informed and have offered full cooperation should they be of assistance. M15 made the same request and offer. Taiwan realizes that it will never return to the mainland as a victor in a war. They need someone else to fire the bullets. Until a few years ago they believed it would be the States but Nixon changed all that." Bullis spoke in measured tones. A big man with a ruddy, outdoors complexion and jutting jaw, he was no stranger to organizing his thoughts and expounding his theories in concise terms.

"If China and the Soviets square off against one another, and Taiwan believes that will just be a matter of time, the States will probably throw in with China. Unless there is a complete reversal of the current position there is no question that this will be the scenario. Since Washington has opted for Peking at Taipei's expense, they will have no choice but to turn to Russia for protection. Their uneasiness is also predicated on the new axis between China and Japan. In exchange for industrial and technical aid China is now selling oil from its northern wells to fuel Japan's industrial empire. This locks Japan in and will guarantee their support should hostilities break out. They need the oil and China will play on that need. When you consider the facts, sir, you can sympathize with Taiwan's feeling of isolation. At the very least they need a Superpower navy to keep their sea lanes open. They live by trade."

"What does it imply, Inspector?"

"We are not exactly certain, sir, but on the surface we have to come to the conclusion that there is a leak to the Soviets somewhere within the government or perhaps at Chalk River. There is no way that the Soviets could get such information unless there was."

Jennings placed both hands palms down on his desk. "Let me get this straight," he said solemnly. "You are telling me that there is a Taiwanese agent working in government or Chalk River. Is that correct?"

Both Chambers and Bullis nodded in unison. "There's no other answer. Someone is feeding information to the Soviets. It certainly isn't coming from Peking."

"Why couldn't it be Soviet agents? God knows we've had our share."

"We're not ruling that possibility out, Prime Minister," responded Chambers, "but on the evidence to date, we believe that the information is coming to them from outside their own system. If it was fresh intelligence I don't think they'd use Volsky. It would be official at the ambassadorial level or directly from Moscow to Ottawa."

"I want this to be a top priority investigation," ordered Jennings, "and I want to be kept informed the moment you have anything further."

"You can be assured of that, sir," replied Chambers. "The Soviets could be just mischief making; they've been known to do that on occasion and are past masters in the art. But I think not. The very fact that Volsky specifically mentioned the piece of equipment that can be used to enrich plutonium leads me to believe that it's a serious, well calculated offering. We've been given a message. Moscow is concerned and expects us to act."

Jennings shook his head. "Incredible." he said.

Chambers gave Bullis a shrewd sidelong look and asked, "Are we supplying China with components that could convert the Bonnaventures to military capabilities, sir?"

Jennings glared at Chambers. "Even if we were, and I'm not saying we are, I couldn't comment. You know that!"

"My apologies." Chambers studied Jennings' face. He was too experienced in interrogation not to be able to spot a raw nerve when it had been exposed.

Chambers rose and Bullis followed. "I shall be in constant touch, Prime Minister."

23

TO: R.G.W.
FROM: KEVIN INGRAM
SUBJECT: PROGRESS REPORT – McBRIDE

McBride's condition is still critical. He has not regained consciousness. Dr. Wainwright can give little or no encouragement. Even if he recovers, the possibility of him ever being able to communicate is questionable. On the other hand he could experience a full recovery at any time. There appears to be some question as to the diagnosis. The Renfrew doctor said it was a massive stroke but Wainwright isn't totally convinced. He suspects something more but is reluctant to say what it is until he has run all the tests possible on McBride and checked out the load of garbage (food and drink) that I brought back from the cottage. Personally, I think he suspects that McBride was drugged or something. There was one anonymous phone call to the Renfrew Hospital asking about his condition. No name was given and no record kept of who made the call. However there has been direct contact made at the Ottawa Civic. An open offer of financial assistance was made and I tracked it down. Adam Sutton who succeeded him as correspondent for Xinhau made the offer. When I spoke to him he just said that he did so out of conscience but I doubt it. He hasn't the financial resources to make such an offer. I tried to pump him but didn't get anywhere. It's my opinion that he's functioning as a third party and I'll lay odds the Chinese Embassy is behind it. Came up dry on who the Chinese was who requested directions to his cottage. Sutton denied any knowledge. Wainwright is co-operative but that co-operation will dry up if I don't fill him in on why we're so interested. He's given an ultimatum. If I level with him he'll do whatever we want as far as keeping McBride under wraps and giving me first access to him if and when he recovers. Do I have approval to do so? The more I get involved the more certain I am that I'm on to something pretty big. Request permission to be relieved of all assignments not directly involved with McBride. Regret that I was scooped on the Diane Jennings item. I have to admit Olsen's cartoon gave me my morning smile. I have no idea where they got the lead from. I thought I had the inside track.

TO: KEVIN INGRAM
FROM: R.G.W.
SUBJECT: McBRIDE

1) You are exclusively assigned to the McBride story until further notice.
2) It would appear that you have no choice but to bring Wainwright into the picture. Assuming that he can be trusted fill him in on what you know and what you suspect with the possible exception that there may be a tie-in to the Bonnaventure story. Keep that in reserve for the time being. Tell him that you are working on a personality piece. If he doesn't buy the personality piece then level with him. It's my opinion that he'll treat anything you say as privileged.
3) Don't close the door on Sutton. If he's following orders he could be invaluable. Suggest that you make a counter offer of splitting the costs, whatever they may be. It will be interesting to see if he takes the bait. If he doesn't it will be an indication that he is sincere. If he accepts make certain

that Wainwright restricts visits unless you are present. We don't want Sutton getting in without our knowledge and beating us to the gun.

4) Should it be discovered that McBride was drugged against his will it will become a police matter. Wainwright will have no recourse but to report it. If this happens, ask him to hold off until you contact me. I might want to have one of our lawyers present as you will be involved.

5) No problem re the Diane Jennings matter. You have bigger fish to catch. Agreed, it was a good cartoon.

The mood of the Liberal caucus was ugly. Members stood around the room in deep and somber conversations. No jokes were passed or Parliament Hill gossip exchanged. All conversation focused on the just released McCadden Public Opinion Poll which showed a drastic drop in public support for both the party and leader.

"You'd think we were attending a wake," observed a backbencher.

"If the poll is correct," replied another, "we might as well be because we'll be dead on election day. I just heard from my riding president. He's steaming and suggested that I cancel Cairns' appearance at my nomination meeting. He feels Cairns would be a liability and we'd be better to go it alone and take our chances."

Alistair Coleman elbowed his way through the room. Spotting Granville Nolan in animated conversation by the door, with a shadow cabinet colleague, he stood to the side until he caught his eye. Nolan excused himself and taking Coleman by the arm guided him to a vacant corner.

"I tried to call you at home this morning but just missed you," said Coleman.

"I wanted an early start. This is going to be a long day." Nolan noticed the clipping Coleman was holding in his hand. "Surprised?"

"Devastated! How in hell could such a thing happen just when we were beginning to roll toward the election? Look at it!" Coleman held up the clipping. "Nine percentage points below last time in public support and Jim is in third place behind Dalton Raynor. Can you imagine it, our leader trailing the leader of the NDP? Incredible."

Nolan rubbed a large hand across his mouth. "It's going to be a rough caucus. They're in a mean mood. I hope Cairns has some answers."

"Someone should demand an accounting," said Coleman. "Cairns owes us that much. Why don't you raise the question?"

"It would be better if you did." Nolan studied Coleman's face carefully as he planted the suggestion. "After all, the caucus won't forget the man who starts the ball rolling and gets this matter cleared up. I'll back you all the way, of course." Nolan glanced toward the opening door. "Here he is now."

Cairns entered to a smattering of polite applause and took his place at the table. Everyone hurried to sit down. The chairman waited for quiet then tapped the table with his pen. "If you please. We have a full agenda," said the chairman in an officious tone. Without looking up, Cairns opened his attaché case and placed a large manilla file on the table. He glanced at the chairman and nodded. "The meeting will come to order and we'll call upon our leader," intoned the chairman.

"Before we begin the business of the day," said Cairns, "I am sure we are all concerned about the results of the McCadden poll. I hasten to say that my views on the reliability of public opinion polls are well known. I place little or no faith in them. History has proven that far too often they are not representative. They are selective in their sampling and questionable in how they frame their questions."

Coleman raised his hand.

"Mr. Coleman," acknowledged the chairman.

Coleman lumbered to his feet and with an agitated kick pushed his chair back. "With all due respect I don't see how you can dismiss the results in such a cavalier manner."

"Dismiss them yes, cavalierly, no," countered Cairns. He was slightly taken aback by Coleman's aggressiveness. It was totally out of character. "I have nothing but profound respect for the power of the polls. Used properly they can be a great tool in swaying the swayable. But I say without reservation that this poll is totally inaccurate and not representative."

"Accepting your premise of inaccuracy it is nevertheless not only swaying the swayable, as you put it, but the committed as well."

"I'm sorry, Alistair, but I have to reject that statement. I acknowledge that a negative poll raises questions in some minds but those who know the truth and are loyal dismiss it out-of-hand. You're not ascribing much confidence to the loyal Liberal. I'm disturbed by your surprising negativism." A small bead of sweat glistened on Cairns' upper lip.

"I have the utmost confidence in Liberals, sir. The voter I'm concerned about is the uncommitted. In the last election we lost because we were incapable of garnering the majority of that voting block. This time it is predicted that the uncommitted vote will rise to close to thirty percent before the polls open. This isn't my prediction. I'm quoting from a memo the President of the Conservative party sent out to all riding presidents urging them to get busy and work like hell. Unless the Tories are stupid they'll not wait for the election to be announced; they'll be moving into high gear immediately. The McCadden results will be all the incentive they need."

"Possibly," said Cairns unwilling to yield ground. "But they are still off guard. They can't afford to jump the gun before they know what we're going to do. The advantage of time is on our side for the moment." Cairns spoke with supreme confidence. "With the platform we're going to present plus the slate of candidates we'll put forward we will not only win the lion's share of the uncommitted, we will win the election!"

Solid applause greeted his firm statement.

"I hasten to remind each and every one of you that Parliament has not been dissolved and the Prime Minister is not about to do so for some time yet. He has his China visit and unless I miss my guess he'll issue a formal invitation to the Chairman for a state visit to Canada. He'll want to greet the Chairman as Prime Minister in good standing and not as one going into an election."

Coleman exhaled a lungful of air and shifted from one foot to the other. "We'll be in worse shape than ever if that happens."

"You're continuing to be negative, Alistair."

"Not at all. I'm being realistic. If he comes back from China covered in glory and then pulls off the first Western visit by the

Chairman his public image will be so strong that God himself couldn't beat him at the polls."

"He'll need more than God to win," snapped Cairns. "He's in real trouble and I intend to compound that trouble."

"You keep telling us that but to date we've seen no evidence."

"You want evidence! I'll give you evidence." Cairns angrily flipped open the file in front of him. "What I have in this file is sufficient to bring the government down and re-establish this party as the champion of truth and honesty."

"Would I be out of order to ask for details?"

Cairns scanned the caucus. Most eyes were firmly fixed on his and did not blink. He fully accepted the fact that everyone was letting Coleman fire their bullets and were relieved that it was he who was taking the grave risk. He suspected that Nolan was the architect.

With an exaggerated motion he closed the file. "To do so, Alistair, would be inopportune and inadvisable. I have made my position crystal clear on the Bonnaventure question. When I have irrefutable evidence I shall stand up in the House, table it, and make an immediate motion of non-confidence. There will be no question of the NDP supporting the motion and unless I miss my guess we'll see a number of Tories joining in as well. This situation will rise like a stench in the nostrils of all sitting members who espouse truth and honesty. Personally, it would be much easier for me to open this file and reveal its contents. However there is such a thing as trust and confidence. This is what I am asking. I've led this party through deep waters in the past and I shall do so again."

The room exploded. Coleman attempted to continue but was drowned out. Realizing that instead of supporting him the members were rejecting his attempt to force Cairns into action, he sat down with a resigned sigh.

Cairns reached for a cigarette and slowly lit it. Exhaling a lungful of smoke, he peered through the haze and made a mental note of how the caucus thought – leaders were reacting. He was particularly interested in Nolan and Coleman who were sitting side by side in the first row. He fully expected Nolan to indicate sympathy or support, but it was not forthcoming. Instead Nolan was half-turned in his chair with his arm firmly placed over the rear of the chair of the backbencher to his right. He was doing all the talking and the man listened intently. Such a blatant rejection did not come as any great surprise. Nolan had a reputation for using people and when they ceased to be useful rejecting them. Cairns seriously doubted if Nolan knew the man's name much less his riding. It was no secret that Nolan remained aloof from the rank and file unless it served his own interests. As a senior member, former Cabinet Minister and self-appointed heir apparent to the leadership, he jealously guarded his inflated image.

The undercurrent of conversation died down when the chairman called for order. With the exception of a few furtive glances at Coleman, all eyes turned to Cairns.

"We are not fighting to win a battle; we are fighting to win a war," said Cairns emphatically. "I have never led this party down a blind alley. I have always tried to be forthright and candid. To cave in now would be the most serious political error of the decade. But, since it appears that my plan of action is in question, I put myself in your hands." Cairns stared at Coleman's bent head with eyes flashing. "If it is the consensus that I should make a statement on partial evidence I shall. What are your wishes?"

Chairs were kicked back. Two tumbled to the floor as the caucus rose to its feet with cries of "fight", "we're with you", and "carry on" intermingled with thunderous applause. Nolan was one of the most enthusiastic applauders. Coleman rose with great effort and returned Cairns' fixed stare.

24

Christopher Jennings enjoyed the beauty and tranquility of Harrington Lake, and the mild July breeze with the singing cicadas provided the ideal escape from the pressures of government which were mounting as he prepared for the up-coming election.

He was in a relaxed mood as he sat on a padded Cape Cod chair on the lawn and studied Commissioner Chambers' report. He did not notice Diane until she was standing in front of him.

"Am I interrupting?" she asked.

Jennings placed the report on his lap and closed it. "No. Want to join me?"

Diane sat down on a chaise lounge.

"Where are the girls?"

"They're playing with their Barbie dolls on the veranda." Diane disliked polite conversation at the best of times and felt awkward. "I'm glad you could get away for a couple of days. It's nice to have someone to talk to for a change besides the girls."

"I'm enjoying it. It will probably be the last couple of days I get this summer."

"How are the election plans coming along?"

"Slowly, but things will pick up."

"Are we still going to China?"

"As far as I know." Jennings was not making any conscious effort to keep the conversation flowing and Diane sensed the communications gap widening.

"You don't sound very excited."

"I'm passed getting excited by official visits and protocol. They're damn hard work. It's all part of the job."

"We're still going, aren't we?"

"That all depends on the election. I can't fight one from Peking."

"I thought everything was set."

"Nothing's set in politics. You should know that."

Jennings' coolness was infuriating. She felt like crying out "Damn you! I'm trying. You try too. Don't make me crawl." Fighting back her rising anger and frustration, she said, "I'm rather looking forward to the trip."

Jennings looked at her closely. "I find that hard to believe, especially after all the fuss you've made over attending official functions."

"I'm serious. I hope the election doesn't spoil things. I'd like to go with you."

"I would have thought you'd welcome an early election."

"I've never liked elections."

"Surely," said Jennings in a mocking tone, "you'll welcome this one. Just think of it. Once it's over you'll have your freedom and can begin to put your plans into effect."

"What plans?" asked Diane caustically.

"Your plans for a new life with Cole, my colleague, my confidant, my friend." Jennings spat out the word friend.

"I have no plans," mumbled Diane.

"No plans? One would expect you to be bursting with plans. It's not like you. You're so organized."

The dreaded moment had finally arrived. Many times Diane had pondered how she would react when Cole's name was finally brought into the conversation. She feared she would react badly. Being sensitive to his wife's mood swings, Jennings noticed the rush of color to her cheek and the moistening of lips with her tongue.

"I had hoped," Diane chose her words carefully and slowly, "that we just might be able to have a pleasant, civilized conversation without getting the knives out, but I see I am mistaken."

"What did I do?" asked Jennings in exaggerated wonderment.

"You spoiled it!" snapped Diane. Jennings shrugged. "That's right! You spoiled it with your goddamn sarcasm."

"My apologies. I was only trying to show an interest in you and our mutual friend. No, that's not entirely correct. The situation has changed. He's your friend." Jennings' pointed finger cut through the air in Diane's direction. "If this were an Elizabethan comedy, or better still a tragedy, it would be easier to define roles. He would be the cuckler and I'd be the cuckold."

"Don't, Chris. For God's sake, don't."

"Don't what, Diane? Speak your lover's name."

Jennings watched the tears begin to stream down Diane's cheeks. He wanted to reach out and gently wipe them away. He longed to tease her until she began to smile and then laugh, just like he used to do when they were young and in love. Her face was ashen and her deep blue eyes swam in pools of tears. Jennings ached to take her in his arms and tell her he loved her. He wanted to wipe the past from their memories and begin anew. He wanted her. Every sinew and fibre throbbed to possess her body. He could smell the gentle fragrance of her

Medallion perfume. Mentally he pictured her in the shower they used to share, lathering her body with the sensual strokes that aroused him to the very roots.

Like a giant hand erasing a beautiful picture, Cole Harrison flashed through his mind. All vicarious lusting evaporated. He was near blind with jealousy and hatred. He wanted to strike out and give hurt for hurt, anguish for anguish. The thought of Harrison possessing the body that was rightfully his cut through his mind like a blazing sword. Did she caress Cole the way she used to caress him, he thought? How did they make love? Did they experiment? Was it conventional?

"Would it do any good if I said I was sorry?"

"Would it change things?" Diane lowered her head. Her shoulders shook. "I asked you would it change things?" demanded Jennings.

"I don't know. God, I don't know."

"Let me know when you do," said Jennings caustically.

"Can't we talk?"

"What's there to talk about?"

"Us."

"Oh. I'd forgotten there was an 'us'."

Had Jennings made any move towards Diane, even the slightest gesture, she would have been in his arms. Both were proud, both were stubborn.

"There still could be an 'us'."

"Too bad we're both too Presbyterian for a *menage à trois*. That would solve all our problems, especially yours."

"Don't be stupid."

"Trusting, but never stupid, Diane. I'm serious. It's done all the time when one person cannot choose between two people they share. The only problem is my selfishness. I'm dedicated to self so it would never work. I'm sure Cole would be most agreeable, though, wouldn't he?"

Diane stood up. Her eyes were flashing. There was no sign of tears. "Bastard!" she said in a firm voice. "I'm not innocent, God knows, but neither are you. Have you ever considered that?" Diane's feet were firmly planted as she glared down at her husband.

"Every day."

"Thanks for nothing."

Jennings reached in his back pocket and took out his wallet. "By the way, have you seen this?" Diane took the folded newspaper clipping. "Go ahead; look at it. You made the Toronto papers. It's really quite a good likeness. I'm sure you can see the humor of it."

Diane looked at the cartoon then crumpled it in a small ball and threw it at Jennings' face. Without speaking, she spun on her heel and walked quickly toward the house. She was white with rage and fighting mad.

25

Dr. Emmett Rogers opened the door to his office and entered. Adam Sutton followed and sat in a comfortable chair facing the large oak desk which was piled high with papers, reference books and files.

"Now that you've seen our operation and have had a chat with some of our senior people what do you think?" Rogers swung from side to side in his swivel chair.

"Impressive. It's not what you show the public."

"Indeed it isn't. The public tours are very superficial."

"I had no idea that Atomic Power's facilities were so complex."

"Designing and building nuclear reactors is a very complex business, Mr. Sutton. You've only seen a portion of what we do here. There are a number of highly restricted areas that are out-of-bounds to anybody without top security clearance."

"Of course. I compliment you on what I've seen. It was more than I'd expected."

Rogers was impressed with Sutton. His questions were intelligent and his basic grasp of nuclear reactors was above average. He had either some experience in the field or had done his homework prior to the interviews. However, Rogers and his staff were guarded in what they said and showed him during the two-hour tour.

"Do you feel you have enough to begin writing?" he asked.

"More than sufficient. I'm sure there'll be points I'll need clarified and points that you'll want changed but on the whole I'm very satisfied."

"Are you clear on the approach you will be taking?"

"It will be very basic, Doctor. I'm not a technical writer. I shall look at the story through the eyes of the man and woman on the street."

"Pleased to hear you put it that way. I get so weary of some writers who try to impress with their expertise. Many times their facts are either totally wrong or out of context."

"I believe I know who I'm writing for and their level of comprehension. For example, if I write about a breakthrough in wheat genetics every mother and homemaker from Peking to Winnipeg will be interested, especially if the results mean a better wheat and a more nutritional bread for their table. They couldn't give a damn about circuitry, diodes or S.L.T. chips."

Rogers smiled approval. "We're on the same wavelength, Mr. Sutton. Too many times writers get carried away with their own brilliance. Most scientific articles are written in such a ponderous manner that comprehension is next to impossible even if you are at the Ph.D. level. How did you find our misanthropic Dr. Panzica?"

"Reserved, to say the least."

Rogers chuckled. "He didn't throw you out of his office did he?"

Sutton shook his head and grinned.

"That's an accomplishment. He's not an easy man to impress. If you don't believe me just ask Jack McAndrews of 'The Canadian Scientist'. To say their relationship is fragile is putting it mildly."

"I heard about that. Dr. Panzica said he would have thrown him out of his office bodily if he hadn't left on his own free will."

"I warned McAndrews but he wouldn't listen. He wanted to explain his story to Panzica."

"I read it and it wasn't that bad."

"Did you tell Panzica that?"

"I tried to but it didn't impress him. He sure has a thing about journalists."

Rogers chuckled and stroked his chin slowly. "Our Dr. Panzica is a man of minimal patience. He gave McAndrews an interview and felt he had been betrayed. When that happens his monumental temper comes surging to the surface. We laugh about it around here but at times it is frightening. Thank God he has been able to curb it for the most part. Now, when he feels he's ready to blow, he packs his bags and heads for the wilderness with his rods and guns."

"What's his problem?"

"Simple. He doesn't trust journalists and he has a passionate hatred of Communists. It goes back to his early days in Sicily. He can tell some hair raising stories about what the Italian Communists did to his village during and after the war. Couple that with the fact that you, as a journalist, are representing a Communist nation and you can see 'the problem' you're facing."

"I assure you I am not a Communist or even in their camp on a fringe ideological position. I am a professional journalist who was hired to carry out an assignment and I intend to do a professional job."

"Accepted. Did Panzica co-operate?"

"Yes. Once the ice was broken he was more than helpful. In fact he said that if I was determined to write he'd do everything possible to give me the necessary background and help wherever he could."

"You're smiling, Mr. Sutton," said Rogers in amazement.

"He finished up with what I'm sure was a dire warning. He told me that if my story was slanted, inaccurate or a pile of 'shit', as he succinctly put it, I'd better give him and Chalk River a wide berth."

"For Panzica that's being friendly," said Rogers. "Anything else I can do for you?"

Sutton closed his notebook. "Not at the moment. I appreciate your co-operation."

"May I be candid?" said Rogers as he leaned forward and placed both hands on his desk, palms down.

"Of course."

"Why?" asked Rogers solemnly.

"Why what?"

"Why are you working for China?"

"Why not? It's a job that interests me and they pay very well. I told you I am a professional, and in my business you have only one thing to sell and that's your ability to turn out acceptable copy."

"Doesn't it bother you that you are taking money from what could be politely termed an unfriendly nation?"

"Three or four years ago I'd agree, but not now. The People's Republic of China is a fully accredited nation with Canada. And, while I underline that I am not in their camp, they have every right to engage Canadians to work for them and any Canadian has the right to accept or reject. Would you be asking the question if I was in the heavy construction business and selling equipment to China? Or, would you have problems if I was churning out copy on behalf of the Soviet-built Lada cars which are being sold in Canada?"

"I can't quarrel with your argument but . . . "

"But what, Doctor?"

"Forget it," replied Rogers as he sat back in his chair.

"Do you have any problems building a Bonnaventure for China?"

"I'm not the one who sold them, the government did. I'm only following directives."

"Precisely. The only difference as I see it is that you are following orders and I'm exercising my rights under the capitalistic free enterprise system."

"Good argument. I just hope and pray that both of us don't regret the paths we have chosen to follow."

"In what way?"

"Wouldn't it be ironic if this were all part of some grand plan to take what we have done and turn it against our system?"

"You don't honestly believe that do you?"

"Stranger things have happened."

"Aren't you forgetting one thing? Unless we've been sold a bill of goods Canada has put some pretty stringent conditions on how the reactors will be used regardless of what country purchases them."

159

"Need I mention Pakistan? They feel threatened and want to get into the nuclear club and we all know how they are going about it in spite of what conditions Canada placed on the sale. What makes you think China wouldn't do that very thing?"

"They're already in the club. That's no secret."

"Granted, but if they could see a way to improve their capabilities by making use of the Bonnaventure's potential and were pressed, don't you think they'd reverse their policy if for no other reason than self-preservation?"

"I have no answer to that, but," Sutton straightened up in his chair and looked Rogers straight in the eye, "I have no intention of being a party to such a scenario. Should it ever happen I'd walk away from my assignment without giving it a second thought. What more can I say?"

"Nothing, Mr. Sutton. Absolutely nothing."

Rogers lapsed into silence and gently swung in his chair. He was encouraged by the openness of Sutton but still felt uneasy. All too many times he had seen altruistic individuals become trapped and their principles set aside for expediency.

"Let me ask you a question, seeing as how we are being so candid with one another. If you have such strong reservations, why co-operate? Why don't you just tell me that you don't want to be party to what I'm doing or simply tell me to get out?"

Rogers expected the question. He would prefer to level with Sutton and tell him that he was under orders from the Prime Minister. To do so would not only be a breach of trust but foolhardy. Sutton was a journalist and would either use such information publically or would, if the occasion arose, use it as a lever if the situation demanded it. This was not the time or place to shift responsibility from his office.

"I suppose you could say that I'm somewhat of a gambler. We've been burned a number of times in the press, especially by the anti-nuclear lobby. We have nothing to hide and would welcome some positive exposure to what we are trying to do for a change. Hopefully, you will aid us in meeting that goal."

"I'll do my very best."

26

Winston Morrant adjusted his tie and held his head sideways for a final touch of makeup. The television cameras were in position and the floor director, who was standing off-camera to the left of the news set, was taking final direction from the executive director through his headset.

"Thirty seconds, Winston," he called out.

Morrant nodded, shuffled the papers on the desk in front of him and straightened up in his chair. With a well practiced movement he looked directly into the lens of camera two as the seconds-to-air were being counted off.

"Eight, seven, six, five, four, three, two, one," called out the floor director as he held his right arm up with index finger extended.

A fanfare of trumpets blared from the studio speakers and the intro graphics came up on the screen. The director called for a slow dissolve to Morrant and for the pre-recorded voice-over introduction to begin.

"This is the Morrant Report," stated the sonorous voiced announcer, "with award-winning journalist and commentator Winston Morrant."

The floor director's arm dropped on cue and the red tally light blinked on.

"Good evening," began Morrant. "This has been quite an eventful day in the House of Commons, which just returned from its summer recess this afternoon." With practiced skill his eyes followed the teleprompter which kept pace with his delivery. There was little or no eye movement and only the most knowledgeable would be able to detect any as he read the well rehearsed copy.

"In an unexpected move this afternoon, Prime Minister Christopher Jennings called a snap election for November 10th. To say he took Mr. Cairns and his opposition members by surprise is the understatement of the year.

"If it is simply timing then I take my hat off to the Prime

161

Minister, but I suspect it goes much deeper. The Progressive Conservatives have not done too badly under Mr. Jennings. Granted the economy is in trouble, but what country isn't facing problems? Canada is doing as well or better than most. I could go down the list and not really hit on one single problem that is sufficient to suggest to me that Mr. Jennings should place his record prematurely on the line with the Canadian voter.

"Being charitable, it would appear that Mr. Cairns needs vindication far more than Mr. Jennings. The question of the Bonnaventure sales to the People's Republic of China keeps nagging. Mr. Cairns made a serious allegation of misconduct on 'Meet the Lawmakers' and to this day he has neither supported nor retracted those charges. Every day that goes by weakens his credibility and strengthens Mr. Jennings'.

"Yes, if I were in the Prime Minister's position I'd do precisely what he did this afternoon – seize the advantage and make the opposition come to me.

"Another issue, and an important one, was the Prime Minister's statement that he was postponing his second visit to China until after the election. He told the House of Commons that the postponement was with the full concurrence of Chairman Hu. Since the Norman Bethune nuclear power hydro generating station, which is being built near Hangzhou in Shejiang Province, has had it's official opening postponed until mid-October the timing is excellent. Chairman Hu has invited Canada's Prime Minister to officially open what will eventually be the largest hydro electric plant in the Far East. Much of the technology was generated through the Bonnaventure nuclear reactors so the tie-in is natural.

"It is too early to place bets on the outcome of the election but initially it would appear that Mr. Jennings is in the driver's seat. Mr. Cairns has to catch up and he also has to remove the shadow of lack-of-credibility that surrounds him. By preventing Mr. Cairns from having the freedom of the House of Commons, Mr. Jennings is forcing him to either put up or shut up without being able to hide behind parliamentary privilege.

"On the other hand, if Mr. Cairns indeed does have information or proof of wrong doing, then Mr. Jennings could be in trouble. Again, it's too early to tell. It's going to be an exciting and lively election."

Morrant caught the floor director's thirty-second cue to a commercial break.

"One final observation. I sincerely trust that both men do not underestimate Canadian voters. For the most part they are intelligent and well informed. They also have the ability to weigh the facts and decide for themselves. I'll be back in a moment with the rest of the news right after these messages."

Morrant sank back in his chair with a deep sigh as the make-up girl hurried on the set and began wiping his forehead and face with a powder puff.

Kevin Ingram grunted as he backed into a tight parking space in the visitors area of the Ottawa Civic Hospital. Cindy Morris was sitting beside him and turned to check the distance to the car on the right.

"You don't have to double check me," mumbled Ingram. "I'm quite capable of backing into a parking space."

Their relationship had never been at a higher pitch. Cindy had become genuinely interested in Tom McBride and Ingram's researching. They had even talked about getting married. Every night during dinner or many times after they had made love Cindy would insist on being brought up-to-date on the day's happenings.

Ingram opened his door but Cindy made no move to open hers. "What's the matter, aren't you coming?"

"Would you mind if I just stayed in the car and read my book," replied Cindy as she opened her purse and took out a paperback.

"It's up to you. I thought you wanted to see Tom."

"I'd rather not. From what you say he's not a pretty sight."

"Probably just as well. No sense getting you depressed so early in the evening. I shouldn't be too long."

The elevators and corridors of the Ottawa Civic Hospital were filled with visitors. Many carried flowers and just as many had worried looks on their faces. Nurses and interns clustered around the nursing stations and only interrupted their conversations when asked for directions to a room or to comment upon the condition of a patient.

Ingram walked quickly toward McBride's room. As he reached it he was surprised to see a uniformed policeman sitting on a chair beside the door. He was just about to push the door open when the officer stood up. "I'm sorry, sir, but no one is allowed in the room."

"I'm here at Dr. Wainwright's request," said Ingram.

"I'm sorry, sir. I have my orders. No one is allowed in the room."

Ingram stepped back and looked down the corridor. Chester Wainwright was hurrying towards him. "Hope I haven't kept you waiting," he said in a calm voice.

"What's this all about?" asked Ingram.

"It's all right, officer. I'll vouch for Mr. Ingram." The police officer nodded and sat down on the chair. Wainwright placed his hand on the door then pulled it back. "Thank you for coming on such short notice."

"What's the matter?"

"I want to show you something." Wainwright opened the door. Screens were around McBride's bed on all three sides. The venetian blind was closed and the only illumination came from the glow of the lamp on the night table. Ingram blinked and adjusted his eyes to the reduced lighting. Wainwright closed the door securely and walked towards the bed. As he pushed back the screen Ingram gasped. A white sheet was pulled up over McBride's head.

"I'm sorry. We did all we could possibly do."

"When?"

"About half an hour before I called you."

"Why?"

"I won't know until we've done an autopsy. He was doing fine and I was optimistic. It came completely without warning. I suspect his heart gave out but we'll be able to tell more after . . ."

Ingram swallowed hard. He abhorred death and dead bodies. The first and last time he had viewed a corpse was when he was twelve years old and his mother had insisted that he kiss the alabaster cheeks of his grandmother as she lay in her coffin. From that day onward he had steadfastly refused to attend funerals.

"Are you all right? Do you want to see him?" asked Wainwright as he started to lift the corner of the sheet.

"No!" replied Ingram emphatically. "I'd rather not."

Wainwright let the sheet fall. The outline of McBride's forehead, nose and chin were clearly visible in macabre relief.

"I don't believe it," said Ingram in hushed tones. "He wasn't that old."

"They never are, regardless of how old they are, when it happens like this."

"What about the lab tests?"

"I still haven't got the reports back. It's too early to tell."

"Why the police?" asked Ingram.

"I called them in because I suspect something."

"What have you told them?"

"Nothing more than I told you. I asked for a guard until he is moved to the morgue and I can supervise the autopsy. I've got a call in for the coroner and the staff pathologist. If there is anything irregular I want him protected until we've explored all avenues. It's not uncommon. It's my duty as a physician to inform the police if I feel there is just reason."

"Why not have him moved to the morgue?"

"I want some control. I don't want anybody touching his body until the autopsy."

"Then you do suspect foul play?"

"I never said that. I just want to assure myself that this is nothing more than a routine death," replied Wainwright defensively. "You sure you're all right?" Ingram's face was ashen. "You'd better sit down," said Wainwright as he reached for a chair. "Do you feel faint?"

"It's just the shock," replied Ingram as he slowly sat down. "Everything I've been working on died in that bed. I was so close."

Wainwright reached into his breast pocket and took out a folded piece of paper. "This may be something. He had a brief period of lucidity before he died and indicated that he wanted something to write on. It's not uncommon. It's like a light bulb glowing at its brightest just before it burns out." The color rushed back into Ingram's cheeks and he straightened up in the chair. Wainwright unfolded the piece of paper. "I can't make head nor tail of it. His hand was very unsteady and it was

165

impossible to help him because he couldn't speak above a grunt. Perhaps you can decipher it."

Ingram took the paper and studied it carefully. He frowned. "It's nothing more than a scrawl."

"You can pick out the odd letter," said Wainwright pointing.

"The letters and words all run into one another and most of the words trail off as though he couldn't control his hand or the pen. It doesn't make sense."

Wainwright pointed at the top word. "It looks like it could be your name. That's an 'I', at least it looks like an 'I'. It could be the beginning of Ingram."

"Possibly. Did Tom know he was dying?"

"He could have. It's hard to tell. He certainly made an effort to indicate that he wanted something to write on. He was extremely agitated and impatient."

"Were you with him?"

"Yes. I was called by the floor supervisor when he appeared to be regaining consciousness."

"Did anybody see him write?"

"His nurse held the paper."

"Will she tell anybody?"

"I doubt it. She'd have no reason to. It happens all the time with stroke patients."

"Would you mind if I took this with me and we kept it strictly between ourselves?"

"By all means."

"Thank you. Will you let me know the moment you have the autopsy results?"

"Of course. Do you want to attend? I could arrange it."

"Thanks, but no. I don't think I'd be up to it. I'll wait for your call."

Wainwright smiled slightly and extended his hand. "I'm sorry." Ingram shook Wainwright's hand warmly. Without saying anything further he wheeled on his heel and left the room.

The corridors and elevators were still filled with staff and visitors, but Ingram was oblivious to those around him. With a near run he left the hospital and headed towards the parked car. He started to gag and with great effort stopped his stomach from turning over. His face was again ashen. Droplets of sweat stood out on his forehead and began trickling down the side of his face.

Cindy did not look up from her book until she was startled by the sudden opening of the door. Ingram flopped in the seat beside her.

"My God!" she exclaimed. "What's the matter?"

Ingram gripped the steering wheel so tightly that his knuckles turned white. "He's dead! Tom's dead!"

27

Diane Jennings had a blinding headache. As she gently massaged her temples with her fingers she could feel the pulsation of the engorged arteries. Her mother had suffered from severe migraines and one of the triggers was excessive stress. Whenever they would have a bitter mother-daughter confrontation she would usually end up in her bed with violent nausea and at times virtually unable to speak. Diane had inherited the weakness. The last time she had suffered an attack was following her declaration of love for Cole Harrison.

The drapes in her private bedroom were drawn and she lay fully outstretched on the top of her bed staring up at the ceiling. The slightest movement of her head caused excrutiating flashes of pain which caused her eyes to fill with tears.

In the semi-darkness of her room the past two hours came flashing through her mind in a kaleidoscopic jumble of memories. With a supreme effort she forced herself to sort them out and begin with the telephone call to Harrison.

After eight rings Harrison answered. "Cole," said Diane hesitantly.

"Diane," replied Harrison as he recognized her voice.

"How are you?"

"Fine." Harrison's tone was neither warm nor indifferent. "It's good to hear from you. It's been a long time."

"Can you talk?"

"Sure."

"Are you by yourself?"

"Of course. Who do you think I have here?"

"You tell me."

"What's that supposed to mean?"

"I'm sorry . . . I have no right . . . ". Diane was jealous, even though she realized she had no right to be jealous. Biting her tongue, she took a deep breath.

"What is it, Diane?"

"I've got to talk to you."

"Is there anything left to say?"

"You can answer that better than me."

"I thought you said it all in your note," Harrison replied testily.

"I'm sorry. I realize it was a cruel thing to do but I couldn't stay with you. I had to have time to think things out."

"They've been thought out for us."

"What do you mean?"

"Chris has beaten us to the punch by calling the election."

"I don't understand."

"Simple. He's just bought time to get you back. He still loves you."

"How would you know?"

"Take my word for it. He's doing precisely what I'd have done if I were in his place. By cancelling the China trip and calling the election it will force you to be with him and if I know Chris he'll fight as hard to get you back as he will to win the election."

"You don't know that for sure. He hasn't said a kind word to me since I told him."

"Do you blame him?"

"Forget about Chris!" snapped Diane. "What about us? You sound like you want out of our relationship."

"Listen, Diane. If I thought there was a snowball's chance in hell of getting you I'd be in there fighting. But there comes a time when it's insanity to fight further. I'm in a no-win position."

"Thanks for nothing. You got what you wanted so now it's time to move on. Thanks a hell of a lot."

"Listen, Diane, it's not my doing. You were the one to call halt! Are you forgetting that it was you who walked out on me and not the other way around?"

"Oh sure, blame me," Diane's voice began rising. "Get what you want then to hell with it!"

"What's that supposed to mean?"

"You know goddamn well what I mean. All the cheap sex in cheaper motels. All the hollow words and promises. God, I'm beginning to sound like a letter to Ann Landers."

"Nobody twisted your arm. You liked it as much as I did."

"No, Cole. You liked it." Diane pulled at the cord to her telephone and, holding the phone in one hand and the receiver to her ear, she began to pace back and forth between the bed and the window. She wanted to hurt Harrison the way she had been hurt. She wanted to cut through his macho façade and rip open his monumental insecurity that was always just beneath the surface. She was crossing the fine line between love and hate and her detestation was surging through her body like fresh blood being pumped into her veins. "You're no better than a mongrel in heat; any bitch will do."

Harrison audibly sucked in his breath. "That's hitting pretty low."

"No lower than your crotch," replied Diane as she rapidly began to lose control of her emotions and vocabulary.

"What's this all proving, Diane? Why don't we stop before we destroy everything we had."

"We never had anything. You've just proved it. Do you want to know something? Chris is twice the man you are, in or out of bed. He could teach you lessons on how to really love a woman."

"You never complained," he countered weakly.

"I'll tell you something else. I never made love to you without shutting my eyes and fantasizing that it was Chris and not you. At least Chris doesn't bring two-bit whores to his bed."

"I've never paid for sex in my life and you know it."

"Why can't you be honest for once?"

"I am."

"Pardon me. I forgot I was talking to the greatest stud in Canada."

"Diane . . . " Harrison's voice trailed off.

"I'm surprised that you even remember my name with all the women that must be banging down your door to get you into bed."

"I told you I was a one-woman man."

"Then who was the woman who answered your phone in Halifax?"

"I explained all that. She was Addison Harrop's girlfriend."

"I'll bet."

"I don't have to give an accounting to you."

"That's the first honest thing you've said in months."

"I'm being honest. She was Harrop's girlfriend."

"I don't believe you. And I'm very sorry I interrupted your whoring. I mean, I know how long it takes you to get going again once you've been interrupted. You should have your friend give me a call and I'll be pleased to share my experiences and give her an evaluation of your sexual prowess. It won't take long. Tell her to give me a call when she has a couple of minutes."

The click on the line and the hollow sound signalled an end to the conversation. Cole Harrison had hung up.

28

Lao Chengtu paced back and forth in front of Wu Tai Shan's private office. His customary stoicism was not evident. Abruptly pushing up the left hand sleeve of his blazer, he depressed the button on his digital watch. It was 10:47. The door quietly opened. First Secretary Yuan Tzu bowed slightly and nodded for Lao to enter. Lao returned the bow. Wu was sitting behind his desk sipping a cup of tea. "Good evening, Comrade," he said as Lao bowed deeply. "Thank you for making yourself available at such short notice and at such a late hour. I understand from Comrade Yuan that you have some interesting news."

Lao sat down and stroked back both sides of his hair with open palms. "Tom McBride is dead."

Wu's eyes widened slightly. "How very unfortunate and unexpected. How did you come by this knowledge and when did it happen?"

"My contact within the Ottawa Civic Hospital called me late this afternoon. He passed away around four-thirty."

"You have such interesting contacts, Comrade. Is she pretty?" Lao replied with a knowing smile. "I trust she is being suitably rewarded for her services." Wu refilled his cup. "Won't you join me?" No one spoke as Yuan responded to Wu's glance and filled two cups. He passed one to Lao. The three men sipped in silence.

"Do you think your friend would be amenable to further service, Comrade?"

"If it were within her power I'm sure she would. She's been most willing and co-operative."

"Splendid." Wu glanced at the three-drawer steel file cabinet in the corner of his office. The bottom two drawers were secured by sturdy locks. The top drawer was slightly ajar. The open lock was on top of the cabinet.

Wu opened a green file folder on top of his desk and leafed through the contents. "This file is still incomplete, as it was found to be following the late Mr. McBride's departure. Being a thorough man who abhors incomplete files I would be grateful to retrieve the missing documents, return them and close the file."

The platitudes, smiles and the Ambassador's gracious demeanor did not lull Lao into a false sense of security. He knew full well that he was being held responsible for the missing documents. It was he who had recommended McBride. It was he who vouched for his reliability and it naturally followed that it was he who was being singled out to rectify the situation.

"I have," said Wu as he turned over a document, "the report of our Chief of Security. The locks on the file cabinet were deftly picked by an expert. The lack of scratches indicate a master's touch. If Mr. McBride were here I would sincerely compliment him. It is obvious that he was well trained by his masters whom I assume are the RCMP." Lao winced slightly. Running a well manicured finger down the page, Wu continued. "According to the security report the only opportunity Mr. McBride might have had to gain entrance to this office undetected was on the night of April 23rd when you and he were meeting in Comrade Yuan's office. You met that evening, is that correct?"

"That is correct, Excellency," replied Lao knowing full well that the question need not have been asked. It was asked however because Wu, in his precise manner, was emphasizing the point that there was no question in his mind where responsibility lay.

"If I may be permitted, Excellency, I gave a full statement to the Chief of Security on that very matter. Mr. McBride was not feeling well and asked if he might use the washroom. I saw him enter the downstairs washroom. I anticipated no problem. He entered the washroom, made use of the facilities and returned without deviating."

"Ah, yes, he went to the washroom. We all have to go to the washroom." Wu entwined his fingers and examined each fingernail in turn. He was pressing home a point. "You say he was not feeling well. What was his problem?"

Lao shook his head. "I don't believe he said what was bothering him. It is no secret that Mr. McBride drank to excess. It could have been the effects of his drinking, but I have no idea."

"Would you enlighten me once more on what happened after Mr. McBride asked permission to use the facilities? It's all here," Wu tapped the report, "but it is so much better to hear it first hand."

"I accompanied him into the hall, watched him enter the washroom and close the door. I returned to Comrade Yuan's office."

"What did you do while awaiting Mr. McBride's return?"

"I continued to proofread the draft of the story he was writing for us."

"Did you use Comrade Yuan's typewriter?" Lao nodded. "The noise of the typewriter would drown out the opening of a door and the flushing of a toilet would it not?"

Lao grudgingly admired Wu's interrogation techniques. He learned them well during his early years in intelligence. With skill he interjected seemingly innocuous questions that could prove damning if not answered to his satisfaction. "Comrade Yuan's typewriter is old and noisy," admitted Lao.

Wu nodded slightly at the confirmation of his statement. "We are in agreement. Mr. McBride had opportunity. When opportunity is confirmed it narrows down the suspect list, does it not?"

Lao sipped his tea. His hand was trembling slightly and he quickly put down the cup hoping that Wu did not notice. Wu noticed. "The question now is, did Mr. McBride seize the opportunity? Since he is not here to answer for himself we shall have to go on the assumption that he did. That being the case our Mr. McBride is the prime suspect. Where are the missing documents?"

Yuan glanced sideways at Lao. Yuan was a taciturn man. He never made overtures of friendship and privately distrusted Lao's easy outgoing manner which he considered to be the antithesis of that required for a representative of his country in a foreign nation. He coveted promotion within the diplomatic service and was determined to serve well and keep his record clean. "His last residence must be searched for a clue to where he has hidden them," Yuan finally said.

Lao cleared his throat. "If he took them and if he was operating under the direction of the RCMP, wouldn't he have turned the documents over?"

"As much as I'd like to think he was working as an agent for the RCMP, I somehow think not. The Canadian government doesn't usually enter into intelligence. They are more spied upon than spy. History has proven that. It's my consensus that Mr. McBride was working unilaterally for the purpose of feathering his own nest. First, he had no idea what the file cabinet contained. Second, he would be astute enough to realize that highly classified documents would be secured in the embassy safe and beyond his reach. And third, everything or most everything in the files is in Chinese. I seriously doubt if he realized what he came across. No," Wu placed both hands on his desk palms down and fixed Yuan and Lao with a penetrating stare, "he took whatever first came to hand in the hope that it would be of sufficient value to barter. It's unfortunate that he just happened to land upon a file that I was using, a file that unfortunately should never have been left in such a precarious place."

"How do you answer the skill that was employed in picking the lock?" asked Lao.

"He could very well have been trained by the RCMP even if he was not working with them. I have no problem in coming to that conclusion," Wu shrugged. "But that is not the problem. The problem we face is in getting the missing documents back. We can all imagine the serious repercussions between Peking and Ottawa if the wrong people become privy to such detailed analyses of how to improve the use of recovered plutonium for weapons. Those missing documents must not fall into the wrong hands. Our scientists feel they have come up with a new technique that will put China in the forefront. Can you fathom what those traitors in Taipei would do if they got their hands on that information?" The veins in Wu's neck stood out as he thumped the desk with a tightly closed fist. "Those documents must be found! I will accept no excuses. To fail will be to fail our leaders, our people and ourselves. Do I make myself perfectly clear?"

"Where do you suggest we begin, Excellency?"

"That is your problem, Comrade," replied Wu as he extended his index finger directly at Lao. "I would suggest that it might be an idea to begin with Mr. McBride's personal effects before they leave the hospital. This is why I asked if your friend would be in a position to help us. If the documents are not there, and I seriously doubt that they are, there may be something which could lead you to them such as a locker key, a postal box key or a registered letter slip. Anything!"

Lao and Yuan sat motionless as Wu rose and left his office without a further word.

Robert Warner swore loudly and threw a crumpled styrofoam coffee cup in the overflowing wastebasket in the corner of his

Dominion Press office. Half moons of sweat were visible every time he raised either arm. His shirt was wrinkled and matched the wrinkled trousers he hitched up from time-to-time. The wrinkles were the only thing that matched in his apparel. A stained and unstylish paisley tie hung from the open collar. Robert Warner was not a man who worried about style. He was more concerned with deadlines, keeping the editorial staff on their toes and in line. Seldom, if ever, did he brook any argument. He was Managing Editor and his word was law in the newsroom. The fact that the reverse was true in his own home was something that Warner put out of his mind and refused to acknowledge.

Placing a large photographer's magnifying glass on his desk, Warner lit a cigarette and straightened up. "Damned if I can make anything of this scrawl," he said through a haze of smoke.

Kevin Ingram picked up the magnifying glass and positioned it over the blowup of McBride's last attempt to communicate with the living. The staff photographer had taken great pains with the blowup, which was three times the original size, but skilled as he was he was unable to bring the writing into sharp relief. The letters and words ran into one another and at first glance made absolutely no sense. "Tom was trying to tell me something. I know it. It's here if only we can find it."

"You'll go blind if you don't let up. We've gone over his note for twenty minutes and what have we got?" asked Warner as he picked up a piece of double carbon yellow copy paper. "We can," he said adjusting his glasses, "definitely make out 'In', 'H' and either a 'Y', a 'K' or an 'X' and that's about all. The rest is illegible."

"I agree, Bob, but I'm going to keep at it until it makes sense. Let's put ourselves in Tom's position for a moment. He knew he was dying and probably realized that he'd been taken by person or persons unknown. He wanted to tell someone. He wanted to hit back even from the edge of the grave."

"Pure speculation," said Warner as he took a deep drag on his cigarette, "pure speculation. All you know is that McBride wanted to see you about something at his cottage and before you got there he had a stroke or something."

"It wasn't a stroke. Tom was murdered."

"Prove it!"

"Dr. Wainwright will do that for me. He's convinced that Tom was murdered. Why do you think he asked for a police guard?"

"To protect his ass."

"Protect his ass nothing. What's he got to protect?"

"He lost a patient that he probably feels he could have saved."

"Wainwright did all he could. I am sure of it. He has suspicions and it's his duty as a physician to report any suspicion of foul play to the police."

"Has he come up with anything that confirms those suspicions?"

"Nothing conclusive. The lab reports are not all in yet. He's sure that when they are they will confirm a foreign substance in Tom's body."

"I'm not being negative," said Warner as he butted his cigarette and lit another one, "but my hands are tied. I've backed you as long as I can. We're short staffed and I have to put you back on general assignment."

"You're pulling me off the story?" asked Ingram in amazement.

"I'm sorry. It was a great lead but let's face reality. It's dried up. There is nothing more to justify futher time being spent on it. It's dead and we might as well accept it. That," said Warner tapping the blowup, "was the last thread and it's cut."

Ingram bent low over Warner's desk and adjusted the magnifying glass. "What is that?" he asked.

Warner took the glass. "What?"

Ingram ran his finger under a word. "What's that look like?"

"Ren . . . " said Warner. "I can't make the rest of the word out."

"Look," said Ingram with excitement registering in his voice. "That word in the second line. Two of the letters are decipherable. "There's a 'c' and there's an 'o'. They're as plain as the nose on your face. Look at the balance of 'Ren'. It's not plain but I'll bet a month's pay the ending to 'Ren' is 'co'. Renco!"

Warner squinted and pushed his glasses securely up on his nose. "You could be right. Again, it could be the start of rencounter, which would fit in with your theory that he had unwelcome visitors to his cottage before you arrived."

"No." said Ingram. "It's a capital 'R'. It's the name of something."

Warner's interest was rekindled. "Let's go over this again carefully. We have a word or at least we think we have a word. Let's play some games. I accept that 'In' at the top means Ingram and that means the message is for you. Now what does 'H', 'Y', 'K' or 'X' stand for? Those letters are clear."

Ingram wrote the letters on the paper. "They could be initials. 'H' 'Y' doesn't ring a bell."

" 'H' 'K' doesn't either," breathed Warner. " 'H' 'K'. Shit! H.K. could be short for Hong Kong."

Ingram straightened up with a smile on his face. "Renco, Hong Kong. It could be a business, a hotel or nothing."

"Let's try and find out," said Warner in a firm tone. "Frankly I'm not expecting much. It's a long shot and will probably be nothing more than a waste of time but it's worth a chance. I'll contact our Hong Kong correspondent and see what he turns up. We may get lucky."

"Are you leaving me on the story?"

Warner dragged deeply on his cigarette. The end glowed intensely for a moment. Blowing a cloud of smoke out of the corner of his mouth, he looked straight into Ingram's eyes. "I don't know. I need you more on assignment than on tracking down something that might never prove to be a story."

"You wouldn't be contacting Hong Kong if you believed that."

"I'm just doing it to shut you up."

"Bullshit, Bob! If you believed that you'd be telling me to get my ass back into the editorial room and you know it."

Warner smiled slightly but tried to catch himself before Ingram noticed. "If I leave you on the story until I hear from Hong Kong have you enough to keep you busy?"

"Damn right."

29

In a matter of days following the dissolution of parliament, the election swung into high gear. Jennings and Cairns made no attempt to hide their personal animosity as they stumped the hustings seeking justification and votes.

Fueled by the media and the excitement of a personality oriented campaign the candidates followed the example of their leaders. Rhetoric liberally mixed with vitriol, which at times verged on libel, flowed from the political platforms. Partisan passions erupted as issues were dealt with in the same manner as personalities at the packed meetings which became the community highlight.

The endless meetings, coffee parties, mainstreeting, talk shows, handshaking and press conferences ran into one another in a succession of eighteen to twenty-hour days but few complained. It was the liveliest campaign in recent memory and the adrenalin flowed.

On points, Jennings took the early lead. He never missed an opportunity to flay Cairns on his creditability. Without exception he would dare his opponent to come forward and make a public statement on the Bonnaventure allegations. Cairns steadfastly refused to take up the challenge. He countered with damning charges of gross mismanagement on the government's behalf, citing its inability to sell Canada's surplus wheat on the world market for the past three years. He was not hesitant in pointing out that the last time a Canadian government did anything of significance for the wheat farmer was during his term in office. Cairns could do no wrong west of the Great Lakes and this strength was of serious concern to the Jennings' organization. The meetings were turning ugly and the heckling was becoming pointed and nasty.

"There'll be no more nights like tonight," Jennings told Harrison after a Brandon rally. "I have no intention of repeating myself at every whistle stop between here and the Rockies. I've called Diane and she's leaving tomorrow morning with the girls."

"She's what?" Harrison asked with amazement.

"You heard me! Diane's going to be on the platform at every meeting until we reach B.C. The girls will be with her. That should keep Cairns' gang in line. They won't be so vocal with a woman and children on the platform."

"I don't like it, Chris. It could backfire."

"I'd thought you'd be ecstatic. Didn't you hear me? I said Diane will be with us for the next ten days. You'll be able to see each other without being devious. We'll have a great time, just the three of us." Jennings paced back and forth. He did not look at Harrison as he spoke. "It's nice that we have so much in common," continued Jennings through clenched teeth.

Harrison swished the half-melted ice cubes and watched them bounce around in the glass. He wanted to say something but there was nothing to say. Jennings had every right to lash out. He would probably do the same thing if the roles were reversed. He realized it was the only way Jennings had to hit back.

"Looks like rain," said Jennings as he parted the curtains. "I hope it won't delay Diane's flight. You don't seem pleased. I'm surprised."

"It's not a good idea, Chris. These meetings are going to get hotter. I'm surprised that you want to put Diane and the girls in that kind of pressure cooker."

Jennings wheeled. His eyes flashed. "I'll put them in anything I damn well want to. She's still my wife and they're my daughters, or have you forgotten? Once she's yours you can do anything you like with her."

"It's over Chris. It's . . . "

Jennings held up his hand. "Spare me the details. I'm not interested in what's over or not over. Right now I'm fighting to win this election. If Diane and the girls can help me win I'll use them. Understood?"

"Understood," replied Harrison. "Don't you think it would clear the air if we talked this thing out?"

"No, I don't think it would clear the air. There's nothing to talk out. You and Diane have made your position abundantly clear. There's nothing more to say. She's due to arrive in Regina at 11:15 tomorrow morning. I want you to meet her. You'll have plenty of time to drive to Melville for tomorrow night's eight o'clock meeting."

"Couldn't someone else meet them? I have a pretty heavy schedule tomorrow."

"Cancel it! I want you to meet them and that's final."

"What about your appearances on radio and television?"

"I'm perfectly capable of appearing on a talk show and open line show without you holding my hand."

"I never suggested that you weren't, but it's always better if there is someone along to run interference."

"There's no further discussion. You'll meet them and that's final."

Harrison rose and walked to the door. "Is that all?"

"For the time being. I'll let you know when there's more." Jennings parted the drapes. Large drops of rain were beating against the window.

Kevin Ingram rushed across the editorial room and without knocking opened the door to Bob Warner's office. Warner looked up from his cluttered desk. "Where the hell have you been?" he demanded.

"I was at the Parliament Buildings. Luckily I called in for messages. What's up?"

"Look at the night letter that was just phoned in." Warner handed Ingram a typed sheet of paper.

> TO: Robert Warner
> Managing Editor
> DOMINION PRESS
> Ottawa, Ontario Canada
>
> FROM: Lawrence Benson
> Hong Kong
>
> Re: Renco query. Unable to identify as company name in Hong Kong. Two Rencos in Hong Kong phone book. Both U.K. businessmen and brothers. Both principals in travel agency with U.K. headquarters. No connection with Canada. Checked out name with H.K. Businessmen's Association. Nothing listed.

As last resort ran the name through the H.K. office of Industry, Trade and Commerce. Renco International listed as investment consultants. No list of company officers obtainable with exception of president Wong Nei Chong, Manager of Foreign Exchange Department, Kowloon International Bank, H.K. Branch. Attempted to contact him at his home and office but he is on vacation and not expected to return for another three weeks. As far as I could find out he's in the U.S. Bank would not discuss Wong or Renco except to confirm that it is an account in good standing. Was able to confirm that Renco was incorporated in Panama two and a half years ago. Do you wish further investigation?

Ingram whistled. "It could be something."

"Don't let your imagination run wild. It could be nothing more than an umbrella operation for washing Red Chinese money. They are a dime-a-dozen in Hong Kong."

"If that's what it is why would it have an Anglo name and a Chinese president and be incorporated in Panama? And why incorporated just around the time the payments for the reactors would be made?"

"The precise questions I'd like answered. How good are your RCMP contacts?"

"Better than average."

"Could you get Renco run through Interpol without someone asking too many questions?"

"It's worth a try. Interpol could probably get a full report from Panama in a matter of hours."

"The one thing I want to know is, who are the directors and why was the company incorporated in Panama if it's doing business in Hong Kong? Also see if you can tie Renco in with Canada. If it has any dealings with a Canadian firm or individual it could prove interesting. What were you doing on the Hill?"

"Trying to track Cairns down."

"Any luck?"

"I finally got the bastard to come to the phone. He's in Belleville drumming up votes. He sure didn't want to talk to me. I had to put the heat on his executive assistant. Does Garfield Logan ever protect his boss."

"What did he say about McBride?"

"It's what he didn't say. At first he denied all knowledge of McBride having his private number but when I kept hammering him on it he suddenly remembered that McBride had asked for an exclusive interview. He said he told him to call for an appointment and use his private number."

"Why wouldn't he tell McBride to go through his press secretary?"

"I asked him that and he said that because he trusted McBride he did it that way."

"Do you believe him?"

"About as much as I believe you when you say I'm getting a raise."

Both men laughed.

"Follow it up," ordered Warner. "Let's make Cairns squirm. He won't know how we got the lead and what we're going to do with it. Let the bastard sweat. Does he expect to hear from you again?"

"He'll be back in his office at nine on Thursday. He's expecting me at nine thirty."

"Good, damn good," said Warner with relish.

30

Adam Sutton felt like he was back in school as he silently sat in front of Dr. Louis Panzica's desk and awaited his approval or rejection of the story he had written on nuclear technology. The warming glow of the mid-morning sun that flooded the office did little to alleviate his apprehension as Panzica silently read with little or no change of expression. As the minutes dragged on Sutton began to realize with a heightened awareness how much depended upon Panzica's approval. Approval would enhance his standing with Ambassador Wu and Lao Chengtu. Rejection could seriously damage his financial future. While he felt secure in what he had written he was insecure about being placed in the position of having an acknowledged opponent adjudicate something that under normal journalistic standards he had no right to pass judgment upon. Pre-clearance of a story by anyone other than an editor was totally unacceptable to a professional journalist.

Panzica flipped back a few pages, ran his finger down the page and mumbled under his breath. Quickly turning to the page he was reading, he lapsed into further infuriating silence as he continued to read. Finally he placed the pages on his desk and looked at Sutton. Removing his glasses, he said in measured tones, "You surprise me, Mr. Sutton."

"I had no intention of surprising you, Doctor."

"It's a compliment or aren't you accustomed to being complimented on your work?"

"I've had one or two in my day."

"Has Rogers seen this?"

"Yes. He read it over."

"I thought I recognized his nitpicking. Did it bother you?" Sutton shook his head. "I won't compound the problem. With the exception of a slight suggestion on page four, which covers A.P.C.'s philosophy on the controls of the Bonnaventure, I can't quarrel with what you have written. In fact it is very good. It's the best I've seen by a non-informed outsider. Again, my compliments."

Sutton allowed his body to relax. "Thank you."

"You are very thorough and surprisingly accurate. You accept the fact that I'm not in total agreement with such articles being written for foreign consumption, especially within Communist countries. But, if they are to be written I prefer them to be of your standards."

"Then it's cleared for publication?"

"If Rogers has passed on it so will I. We have a running joke with Rogers and his red felt pen. No one within A.P.C. has ever submitted a report, paper or memo to him that hasn't come back without something being altered. Believe it or not we have a pool going to see if anybody can get something passed by him

183

without it being marked up. Each time something is submitted we throw a quarter into the pot. It hasn't been claimed yet."

"If I'd known that I'd have tried to get in on it," replied Sutton.

"You certainly came close," said Panzica as he fanned the sheets and handed them back.

Sutton picked up his attaché case and snapped the locks. "Thank you, Doctor. I appreciate your co-operation."

"Are you in a hurry, Mr. Sutton?"

"Not especially."

"I'd like to ask you a very personal question."

"Certainly."

"How would you feel if your story was the means of furthering the Communist program of world domination?"

Sutton placed the attaché case on the floor beside his chair and locked eyes with Panzica. "I'm afraid I don't quite follow you."

"Let's not play games. I believe you do. Professionalism notwithstanding you are being used by a system that is dedicated to the overthrow of our way of life and you damn well know it."

"Look, Doctor, I damn well don't know anything of the kind. I am being paid to do a job and I'm doing it to the best of my ability. Just because you don't agree with the philosophy of my employer is no reason to be insulting." Sutton picked up his case and stood up.

"Sit down, Mr. Sutton. Aren't you curious to know why I'd make such a pejorative statement?" Sutton sat down. He was intrigued. "Thank you," said Panzica. "You could have told me to go to hell and walked out."

"The thought had crossed my mind."

"You interest me, Mr. Sutton."

"I return the sentiment."

"I think it might help if I explain something to you. Come here." Panzica walked to the wall and looked at a picture that was at eye level. "I want to show you something." Sutton walked slowly toward the picture. "See that gawky child in the second row?" said Panzica as he tapped the glass. "That's me. I was ten and a half. It was just before the war." Sutton looked closely at the picture. Four rows of neatly dressed and well scrubbed children stood in front of an old building. Standing to the left

184

with his hands folded in front was a benign looking priest in cassock and birett.

"That priest was Father Guiseppe De Gasperi. He was the principal and the most Godly man I have ever met. Are you Catholic?"

"I'm afraid I'm not much of anything. I was brought up Baptist but once I became old enough to think for myself I left. I couldn't stomach their brand of religion. Why do you ask?"

"If you were Catholic you'd appreciate what a saint was. If God ever made one it was Father De Gasperi. I never knew him to raise his voice in anger. It's hard to believe that a merciful God would allow a life like his to be taken and taken so violently. He would have gone far in the church. Who knows, he might have made it to Cardinal. He had all the attributes."

"Why are you telling me all this?"

"It's quite a story. You're a man of stories. I read yours now do me the courtesy of listening to mine."

"I'm listening."

"Before I begin I want to make one thing clear. I am not apologizing for what I said. I still feel you are being used and I'd like to think that you are too smart to be made a fool of unless you are a fellow traveller."

"Now wait just a goddamn minute."

"Hear me out, then I'll let you have your say. That picture was taken in my home town of Riesi in the south of Sicily. I want you to look at Father De Gasperi and never forget his face."

"Why should I?"

"Because he was murdered by the Italian Communists."

"A lot of people were murdered by the Communists."

"Not many of them were like Father De Gasperi. He committed the unpardonable sin. He opposed them and all they stood for. The people of my village loved that man. When he told them that Communism was evil and Godless they turned their backs on anybody who tried to subvert or indoctrinate them. He was the most powerful man in the community. I said a few minutes ago that I couldn't ever remember Father De Gasperi raising his voice in anger. That's not quite true. He never raised it with us children, even when disciplining, but he thundered at Communism. Do you remember your war history?"

"Slightly."

"During Mussolini's dictatorship the Communists laid low. But once it was obvious that Fascism and El Duce were through and the Allies had won the war they began to make their move to consolidate power out of chaos. They had long memories and a longer list. Father De Gasperi was near the top because of his pre-war opposition. At first they were friendly and suggested that times were changing and it would be wise if he retired from making political statements and concentrated on his school and students. Naturally he refused. The friendly suggestions soon became physical threats backed up with broken windows, fires and finally the bombing of a shed at the rear of the school. Instead of frightening Father De Gasperi it made him fighting mad. I know the Italian soldier hasn't a good image as a fighter but an Italian priest, especially if he is Sicilian, is another matter. Father De Gasperi felt that his flock was being attacked and he was their anointed champion and defender. At the time I don't think he realized it would be a fight to the death, his death. Even if he had, I honestly believe he would have changed nothing."

Sutton lit a cigarette. He was pleased that he had controlled himself and had not stomped out of Panzica's office.

"I remember the night. It was two days before my youngest brother was born. Five members of the local Communist cell broke into Father De Gasperi's flat. They gave him an ultimatum. Either he give them his sacred word as a priest that he would cease speaking out against them or they would have no alternative but to take strong action to silence him. He adamantly refused and called upon them to renounce their Godless ways and return to the Church. They told Father that they were under orders and proceeded to drag him into a car and drove about 40 kilometers to an abandoned farm. They tied him up and left him in the barn for three hours to think over their final offer which was to leave Sicily immediately and never return.

"He asked for his rosary to be placed in his tied hands. They wouldn't even give him that. When they returned he was in prayer and refused to either look at them or answer them. The leader took out his revolver and ordered one of his men to pull up Father De Gasperi's cassock. He blew off his right kneecap. Father didn't cry out or beg for mercy. The second kneecap was blown off. He never murmured. His bravery and silence sent the leader into an insane rage. He grabbed Father De Gasperi's right hand and placed it on a chopping block that was used for cutting off the heads of chickens and hacked it off above the wrist. Still Father didn't cry out. Instead he said a prayer for his tormentors. Realizing that his life's blood was ebbing from his mutilated body, he looked the leader in the eye and placed his left hand on the block and began to slowly recite a Hail Mary as the axe came crashing down.

"They found his body the next day. Father De Gasperi," tears welled up in Panzica's eyes, "died praying for his murderers. Do you understand now why I hate Communists with such a passion. I don't care if they are Italian, Russian or Chinese. If they are Communists they represent a vicious, Godless regime totally dedicated to world domination at any cost. It goes against everything I believe and stand for to be party to anything that will help them reach that goal."

"You have made significant contributions to the Bonnaventure reactors and they are going on-stream in China. Doesn't that bother you?"

"Of course it bothers me. It bothers me greatly but I am a scientist. If our government wants to play fast and loose with a nation that would devour us that's their problem. I have no control over where they sell their goddamn reactors."

"That's a convenient rationalization."

"Possibly, but remember one thing. When we began designing the Bonnaventure it was for Canada. The fact that it became the best in the world and in demand from other nations is not my responbility."

"That's a credit to you and your colleagues."

"Of course it is but it doesn't ease the pain. I almost quit when I heard that they had sold them to China."

"Why didn't you?"

"Because I have something to contribute and it would be foolhardy to cut off my nose to spite my face."

"Don't you think it's possible that there are nuclear scientists in China who feel exactly the same way you do as far as peace is concerned?"

"You don't honestly believe that do you?"

187

"Did they find the murderers?" asked Sutton in an effort to change the subject.

"Yes. About three years after the war. One of the men had an attack of conscience and confessed to a priest who turned him in."

"I thought anything told a priest was privileged?"

"Normally that's true, but the priest did what he felt he had to do to see justice done."

"What happened to them?"

"The one who confessed received life imprisonment, the other four were hanged. I would have gladly sprung the trap." Panzica's face was a mask of hate. Sutton lapsed into brooding silence. He was not only beginning to understand Panzica he was beginning to like him. "Well, Mr. Sutton," said Panzica. "I do not seek you approval but I do ask for your understanding."

The McCadden Poll could not have been released at a worse moment for James Cairns. The day before he was scheduled to address the Western Wheat Federation in Winnipeg every major newspaper in Canada gave front page prominence to the results.

The Winnipeg *Guardian*, the most influential Conservative newspaper in the west, did the most damage with its lead story and headline. "MORE DISAPPROVE OF JIM THAN CHRIS." The Cairns organization was seething.

The results were damaging at a time when it was hoped that the campaign was beginning to build to a crescendo which would peak on the eve of the election. Eight percentage points separated the two men. The only encouraging aspect for Cairns was in the regional results. His approval quotient exceeded Jennings' in the west but it was not sufficient to offset his dismal performance in Ontario, Quebec and the Maritimes.

Senator Humphrey Ross bit so hard on the stub of his unlit cigar that he was forced to remove it and, following a deep throated hack, he spat pieces of tobacco into his handkerchief. Ignoring the gross breach of good manners, he rammed the cigar back into his mouth and glowered at James Cairns who was sitting in front of his hotel room window in the Downtown Winnipeg Holiday Inn.

"Well!" thundered Ross as he began pacing back and forth.

"Well what, Humphrey?" replied Cairns as he laid the torn out front page of the *Guardian* on the end table beside his chair.

"You tell me. This is the worst goddamn campaign I've ever been in. We've been eating dust since the very first moment. It's about time we showed Jennings and his boys our ass for a change. How do we do it?"

"Ignore it," suggested Garfield Logan who was sitting on the end of the bed.

Ross glared at Cairns' executive assistant. "Ignore it! Are you that simple minded that you think Jennings and Harrison will let us ignore such devastating figures? Because if you are, nephew, I hereby suggest to our leader that he replace you without further delay."

Logan flushed. "It's worked before. If you ignore something distasteful it lessens the importance."

"Is that a fact," replied Ross with obvious disdain. "Is that a goddamn fact."

Logan was not about to be demeaned in such a cavalier manner by anyone, including his uncle. "All right," he said in a firm voice, "if you don't agree with ignoring the bloody poll what do you suggest?"

Ross was taken back by Logan's outspokenness. He was unaccustomed to being challenged especially by a member of his family. He rather enjoyed the experience. In typical rejoinder he answered the question with a question. "I'm not running for office. What do you suggest?"

Logan sucked wind through his clenched teeth. "A diversion. Just get media attention away from the poll."

Ross smiled. He recognized the ploy immediately. It had worked for him many times before he was appointed to the Senate in reward for services rendered. It had also backfired on occasion. "There is only one thing that will move the poll off the front pages and that is the Bonnaventure Reactors."

"Forget it!" snapped Cairns. "I am in no position to speak to the question."

"When will you be in a position?" asked Ross as he flopped on the bed beside Logan.

"Maybe never. I have come up against a blank wall."

Ross glared at Cairns. "What in hell do you mean a blank wall?"

"Exactly what I say. I have everything I can get on the subject. There is no more and what I have is not enough to speak out on."

"This is incredible," stormed Ross as he walked back and forth. "You mean you have nothing more than the little you told me the last time we met at my place?"

"That's about it."

"Did you ever have anything?"

"Senator," said Cairns choosing his words carefully. "If you are implying that I made it all up you'd better be prepared to back up such a statement."

"I don't have to back up anything. You do!" Ross jabbed his index finger at Cairns.

"If I thought I had enough I'd go to the press with it tonight. You know that!"

Ross sat down with a labored sigh. "O.K., Jim. We're not going to solve this predicament by breaking ranks. We have to stand together if we're to beat it. Let me rephrase my question. I thought you gave me a firm understanding that you were on the verge of having irrefutable proof which would support your allegations?"

"Allegations is not the fitting word, Senator."

"What would you prefer?" asked Ross sullenly.

"Charges, hard charges."

"My profound apologies."

"Look, Senator, as you said, we won't get anywhere if we fight one another. I honestly thought I had Jennings by the balls. With any luck I'd have got him and he wouldn't have had to call an election; we could have brought him down. Goddamn! I was so close." Cairns pounded a closed fist into his hand.

"Isn't there any way?"

"If it's any comfort, we're not the only ones interested in the Bonnaventures."

Ross looked up at Cairns in total surprise. "Who?"

"I can't say at this point. It's privileged."

"Shit! You have more privileged information now than when you were Prime Minister."

"If I could tell you, I would. Please accept that."

"Does he know?" Ross jerked his head in Logan's direction.

"No! I don't know and when I should know Jim will tell me," Logan interjected before Cairns could reply. Cairns was grateful for the support. He hadn't expected it.

Ross realized that if he destroyed Logan's creditability, he would sever his connection to Cairns. He had no intention of living to regret a hasty word. For the moment he needed Logan. In a gesture of reconciliation he affectionately patted his nephew's leg. "Of course, my boy. My profound apologies. I am sure that when the time comes we'll both be told. I had no right to ask or imply." Logan flinched at his uncle's touch. Ross stood up and flexed his shoulders slightly. It was an unconscious reaction. He made it every time he stood up in the Senate to give a speech. "Let me put all my cards on the table. The poll just about seals this party's fate. Unless it can be reversed we might as well mail Jennings the election and save everybody a lot of work and grief."

"I'm not going to mail that bastard anything. I'm surprised at your defeatest attitude, Humphrey."

"Jim, I'm only being realistic. You're trailing badly and the party's trailing even worse. We'll be lucky if some of the less experienced candidates don't throw in the sponge and say to hell with it. I was on the phone for an hour and a half with some of the provincial party leaders and the mood is one of resignation and defeat. It's about time you faced up to it."

"Granted it is a hard pill to swallow but we're a long way from being defeated."

"No, Jim," said Ross shaking his head. "Time's running out. The only thing that will save the day is a gesture, a magnificent gesture, which will shoot you back into the spotlight and keep you there until election day. If that happens we might be able to either win or come so close we can make a deal with one of the splinter parties and form a coalition government. At least it would keep Jennings out of Sussex Drive and put you back in."

"I'm fresh out of gestures."

"Now who's being defeatest? Keep in mind that you won't have another day to fight if you lose. That will be it. You'll be through."

"You mean you'll see that I'm through. Isn't that right, Senator?"

"I wouldn't put it quite so bluntly," said Ross as he inspected his fingernails for dirt that wasn't there. "You've been around long enough to know that if we go down to defeat someone will mount a call for a leadership review as soon as possible."

"Would that someone be you, Senator?"

"I wouldn't enjoy it, but if I thought it had to be done for the good of the party I'd have no choice. I did it once before."

"I am aware of what you did."

"You were a backbencher then and if memory serves me right you supported me."

"That's correct, but circumstances were different. John Collins was well into his seventies and no one could look to the future with a leader who would be in his eighties when the next election came around. I'm not into my sixties."

"Jim," said Ross in a patronizing tone. "Face facts. You may have problems holding onto your own seat."

"My seat's safe."

"No seat is safe in this or any other election. We all talk about safe seats but we're just sucking wind." Cairns began cracking his knuckles. "For Christ's sake leave your knuckles alone. My first wife used to crack hers just before she started to give me hell about something. It nearly drove me crazy."

Cairns turned and stared out the window at the endless lines of traffic snaking their way through the downtown Winnipeg streets. The silence in the room was oppressive. Ross and Logan stared down at the floor. Each man was waiting for someone to break the silence. Cairns turned slowly. "Well, we agree upon one thing. I need a strong speech and good press tonight."

"That goes without saying," said Ross. "Did they write you a good one?"

"It's my best speech of the campaign. I'll have those wheat producers on their feet. How much time do you think I have?"

"For what?" asked Ross.

"To come up with what you term the magnificent gesture."

"I suppose if you want to be technical, the day before the election. But the sooner the better. The way Jennings is rolling he'll be next to impossible to stop within a week to ten days. What have you got in mind?"

192

"I wasn't kidding when I said there are others who are looking into and asking questions about the China sales. It's a long shot, a damn long shot."

Ross stood up. "I won't ask you who or what. If it's got the slightest chance of working I'd recommend that you give it a try. We have nothing to lose. I'll back you."

"Gar!" commanded Cairns. "Get on to Air Canada and CP Air and book a seat on the first available flight from Ottawa to Winnipeg. Pull strings if you have to. Make it a return ticket and leave the return open. Book the ticket in your name and use my Master Charge number. I'll pay for it personally."

"I could put it through campaign expenses."

"No, I'll pay for this one. Let me know the details as soon as possible, then I'll make a phone call. If we're lucky we could have a meeting as soon as I'm finished tonight. Don't plan for anything after my speech. You could be in for a long night."

Logan was on his feet and scribbling in his note pad. "Anything else?"

"How long do you need to set up a snap press conference?"

"About two hours, especially if I can say it's more than election hot air and you're going to drop a bomb."

"If I get what I want they'll hear the explosion all the way from St. John's to Victoria."

"What about radio and TV? Will you give interviews?"

"Yes, within reason."

"Do you want them screened?"

"No. I'll handle any questions."

"I'll get working on the ticket right away. I should be back to you within the half hour."

"It's got to be tonight. I've made up my mind. I want this over and done with by the time we leave Winnipeg tomorrow. Don't take no for an answer. I don't care if they have to bump somebody. If they do, make sure it's a Cabinet Minister."

The three men laughed. It broke the tension that had been building between them.

"Don't worry. I'll get a seat on the first possible flight out. Just to be on the safe side I'll double book. Will you be giving out any hard copy at the press conference?"

"No. I'll make a statement then answer questions."

"Do you want me to moderate it?"

"Yes. Somebody has to keep those vultures in line."

"Any objections if I have a supply of tonight's speech available? We might as well milk it for all it's worth. It's a dandy."

Ross enjoyed what he was seeing. The renewed enthusiasm was what was needed to get the campaign rolling into high gear. The calculated goading of Cairns, while distasteful, reaped the desired results. The situation was getting desperate and if the Liberals were going to catch the front-runners they had to be led by Cairns at his positive best. Galvanizing Cairns into dramatic action was the goal of the moment and it appeared that it had been reached.

"Well," said Ross. "I shall take my leave. Good luck tonight. I shall be third row center and the unofficial leader of your cheering section. I'd be grateful if I could be present at the press conference."

"Of course, Senator, and thank you."

"The day is not lost."

"One thing, Humphrey."

"Yes."

"You will keep this conversation privileged. I'll speak to you prior to the press conference."

"Surprise me instead. And above all, surprise Jennings."

31

It had taken Inspector Aubrey Pickard twenty-two years to rise through the ranks of the RCMP. During that period his dedication to the force grew in concert with his reputation as a stickler for rules and regulations. More than one errant constable vowed to never again offer excuses when in the wrong. It was preferable to bear the brunt of Pickard's monumental wrath which rose and fell like a tidal wave than to endure at rigid attention the convoluted lecture on his philosophy that the strength of the force was in its rules and regulations and the weakness in those who broke them.

Pickard looked up from his desk at the sound of a knock on his office door. "Come," he said in an affirmative voice.

Staff Sargent Eric Briddle entered and stood at attention. "You wanted to see me, Inspector?"

"Sit down, Briddle," said Pickard as he opened a file and removed a sheet of computer printout. "You made an inquiry through Interpol on a Panamanian company named Renco. Is that correct?"

"Yes."

"I have Interpol's reply but I fail to see any file number indicating that the inquiry was concerning an active case. Could you explain?"

Briddle coughed slightly. "It was an independent inquiry, sir. There is no file on Renco."

"Did you clear the inquiry with your Inspector?"

"No, sir."

"May I ask why not?"

"Inspector Kerr was on a week's leave."

"Who was in charge during his absence?"

"Inspector Vary."

"Did you ask him?"

"No, sir."

"Briddle," said Pickard as he leaned back in his chair. "Rules are made to be kept not broken. This appears to be a flagrant disregard of rules. Do you have an explanation?"

"Kevin Ingram of Dominion Press called me and asked if I could have Renco checked out through Interpol. He said he was working on a story and would appreciate my co-operation."

"Did he say why he was making the request?"

"No. All he said was that he would appreciate it if I could help him. Since he has always been positive about the force in anything he has written I felt it would be good public relations to do him this favor."

Pickard slowly read Interpol's reply then looked up at Briddle.

"Renco is a very interesting company. Ingram didn't say why he wanted to know its history?"

"No, sir."

"I wonder what story he's working on?"

"I have no idea. Do you want me to find out?"

"It would be interesting."

"Do I have permission to inform him of Interpol's reply?"

"Why not? No sense in wasting good time and effort." Pickard handed the printout across the desk.

"Don't you want this for your report?"

"I have the original."

Briddle regretted asking the question. Of course Pickard would have a copy for his report which undoubtedly would end up in his file to support the reprimand.

"Is that all, sir?"

"For now, Briddle. Please keep me informed once you have spoken to Ingram."

Briddle stood up. "Of course, sir."

As he reached the door Pickard looked up and removed his reading glasses. "Briddle."

"Yes, sir."

"I won't be making my report until I hear what Ingram has to say. Your apparent disregard for rules and regulations might turn out to have positive ramifications. We'll reserve judgement, shall we?"

"Thank you, sir," replied Briddle with great relief. "I'll call Ingram immediately."

"Do that," responded Pickard as he replaced his glasses.

32

Eight minutes before James Cairns completed what the press was to term his finest speech of the campaign to the Canadian Wheat Producers Association in Winnipeg's Fort Gary Hotel, Christopher Jennings was receiving a standing ovation from the Alberta Oil Producers Association in Calgary's Four Seasons Hotel.

The enthusiasm of his audience was as marked as the differences in political attitudes of the wheat farmer and the oil producer. In Manitoba and Saskatchewan he was never allowed to go on the attack and was constantly placed in the position of defending his government's wheat policy. In Alberta there was very little if any opposition to his energy policy which, in effect, gave Alberta sovereignty over its natural resources and guaranteed the oil producer just slightly under world prices for its oil.

The presence of Diane and the girls had little or no effect upon the tone of the Manitoba or Saskatchewan meetings. The farmers blamed Jennings for their plight and no woman or children would deter them from making their feelings known to the man they held personally responsible.

It had been a trying ten days for the campaign team and tempers were running short. It was no less trying for Diane and Harrison, who maintained a reserved politeness whenever they were together which was only when absolutely necessary and never alone.

Even though Harrison had attempted to convince him that he and Diane were through, Jennings was not certain if their indifference was nothing more than a well planned and well executed act or an honest reflection of their relationship. Had he given it careful thought, based upon their friendship of earlier years, he would have recognized the pattern. Harrison was not a man to keep fanning the fires of a dying or dead love. Past history gave ample testimony to his ingenuity at being able to divorce himself from all encumberances yet somehow maintain a tenuous thread in case the individual might become useful in the future. Harrison often joked that there was not a woman who shared his bed who would not be pleased to hear from him again. He had no reason to believe that Diane might be the exception.

The fact that Diane was something more than a brief one-night stand or weekend to Las Vegas affair did not affect Harrison's decision to terminate the relationship. He regretted letting it get out of hand and he regretted allowing himself to become so involved with someone as closely identified with his career. The old cliché that dictates 'if you screw the help, you end up screwing the company' flashed through his mind with increasing regularity.

The very nature of their relationship dictated the ground rules under which Jennings could operate. When and if the breakup of their marriage came about, it would have to be done in such a manner that he, as Prime Minister, would remain totally innocent and the wounded party.

To Diane's credit she played the public role of loving wife and mother with great panache. More than one photograph of her adoring smile as she watched her husband campaign became the art for a number of the personality stories on the Prime Minister and his family.

Jennings wasted little speech time in attacking Cairns' energy program. His oratorical prowess kept the attentive audience keyed up from the first sentence. "You know this party's views on energy and you know exactly where Alberta stands with Ottawa. If you want to change that working relationship you'll have your opportunity to do so but I think not. Alberta wants to be master of its own house and it is the intention of my government to let it be precisely that within the confines of Confederation." Jennings stood back from the lectern to thunderous applause. Time after time he was interrupted by shouts of encouragement and standing ovations as he fed his Albertan listeners precisely what they came to hear.

"I believe that I have clearly laid out what I and my party's views are on energy and where Alberta fits into the grand plan. Now I'd like to bring you into my confidence on the question of the firm stand I intend to take on future nuclear sales.

"If you listen to Liberals they would like the government to lower safety standards and non-proliferation controls that my government imposed upon overseas buyers of our Bonnaventure nuclear reactors in order to increase sales. This I say will not be done. Canada is in the business of selling to foreign buyers but only with conscience. We will not be a party to contributing to world instability for a few dollars.

"We will, my friends," continued Jennings, "always be conscious of our responsibilities not only to Canada but the global community. If this means that we lose some orders for our Bonnaventures so be it. At least Canadians will be able to sleep at night. Give that message to Mr. Cairns and those in his party who feel that conscience can be bought. Nobody has offered Canada enough for its nuclear conscience, and nobody ever will as long as I am Prime Minister."

"What about China?" called out a voice from the rear of the room.

Jennings flipped over the remaining pages of his speech and reached into his inside coat pocket and took out an envelope. Knowing that all eyes were on him he made the most of the moment by slowly extracting the contents of the envelope and smoothing out the creases.

"It's no secret I demanded that Mr. Cairns come forward with proof at the very earliest moment. He owed it to the House and Canada to stand up and speak to the question, but he did not. Why? I think I can tell you why. He has nothing to back up his charges. He is not man enough to say 'I'm sorry, I was wrong, please accept my apology.' If he had done that I would not be talking to you like this tonight.

"I did not let the matter rest. If there was misconduct I wanted to know. I ordered a full investigation by the RCMP into the sale of the Bonnaventures to The People's Republic of China. I was so determined that any investigation be totally objective that I personally called in Commissioner Chambers and instructed him to oversee the investigation with no strings attached. Commissioner Chambers was given carte blanche to audit what he wanted audited, speak to whomever he felt he should speak to, and bring in his findings. I have those findings in my hand." Jennings waved the sheets of paper.

It was an electrifying moment. Diane was sitting beside him

at the head table and Cole Harrison was standing behind the press table to the right of Jennings. Diane glanced at Harrison. He did not change expression. Jennings had taken him completely by surprise.

"Normally such an investigation would be conducted by the Solicitor General, but I felt that if it was to be unhampered it had to be conducted by someone with no vested interest. Since the Solicitor General is a member of my government I decided upon Commissioner Chambers. He's a man for whom I have the highest regard. I won't read the entire report. It will be made public in due time. However, the closing paragraph tells it all:

Finally, sir, it gives me great pleasure to submit this report to you as requested. The investigation as conducted by a team of my most experienced men from the commercial crime division, headed by Superintendent Roy Yardley, was thorough and complete. It is their consensus that there were no irregularities connected with the sale or payment of the Bonnaventure Nuclear Reactors to the People's Republic of China. All monies have been received from Peking and they balance to the cent. It is my opinion that in this instance both the spirit of the contracts and the letter of the law have been adhered to without deviation.

"Based upon what I have here I think it only fair to all Canadians, regardless of whether they are Progressive Conservative supporters or not, to ask Mr. Cairns to either make a public apology or withdraw from the election. A man so irresponsible in such a matter is questionable as leader."

Jennings sat down. Diane reached for his hand and gently squeezed it. The squeeze was returned. It was the first physical contact between them since the night she professed her love for Harrison.

Jim Cairns was in a relaxed mood as he stretched out on the oversized chesterfield in the sitting room of his Winnipeg hotel suite. Five minutes into his speech he knew it would be the best one of the campaign. The standing ovation confirmed it. Slowly, he sipped his drink. He was grateful for the few private moments before wrestling with the problem of the press conference which he now felt duty bound to hold.

Garfield Logan had hurriedly told him as he left the platform that Air Canada Flight 181 had arrived on time from Ottawa and that his guest was in his room, two floors below his suite, awaiting instructions. Cairns instructed Logan to send him up, alone, half an hour after he got back to the hotel. Cairns was startled by a sharp knock on the door. Looking at his watch, he stood up and drained the remaining contents of his glass. It was 12:34 a.m.

He opened the door, extended his hand and smiled broadly. "Thank you for coming on such short notice, Mr. Ingram. I trust you had a pleasant flight."

"It's not very often that I get to fly first class. I must say Air Canada certainly turns on the service. It's been quite a day."

"Would you care for a drink?"

"I assume it will be a late night or early morning."

"Quite possibly."

"A rum and coke will be fine."

Cairns began mixing the drinks from a well stocked bar on a credenza at the side of the room. "Have you any idea why I arranged for you to come here on such short notice?"

"I have a few, but I'd rather you tell me."

Cairns sat down and faced Ingram. It was an uneasy moment. To begin on the wrong note could not only seriously affect the meeting but his future. "You requested a meeting with me and indicated that you wanted to discuss Tom McBride. Is that correct?"

Ingram nodded.

"Before I tell you what is on my mind I'd be grateful if you'd enlighten me about your involvement with Mr. McBride."

"The late Mr. McBride," said Ingram.

"Of course. I was shocked to hear of his untimely death. What was the cause?"

"Officially, it was put down as a massive stroke but the police are looking into it."

"Why?"

"Foul play is suspected. The pathologist found a toxic substance in his body that cannot be identified. It is possible it contributed to his collapse and eventual death."

"Will an inquest be held?"

"If there is sufficient question the coroner will order one.

201

The decision won't be made until the pathology reports are in."

"He was a fine journalist."

"One of the best," responded Ingram.

"What led you to me?"

"His contact book. He had your name, address and private telephone number and it was flagged with an asterisk. I was curious why he would isolate your name in such a manner. It had to be for a reason."

"How did you come by his contact book?"

"For the moment let's just say it fell into my lap."

Both men were jousting and waiting for an opening. Neither was about to give one unless he could score a point.

"I see nothing curious in the fact that a well respected journalist would have my number. I dare say that you have some surprising numbers in your contact book."

"Quite possibly, but we are not talking about my contact book, we're talking about McBride's. In any case the very fact that you brought me to Winnipeg reinforces my curiosity. Excellent as the flight was and the drink is, what's this all about?"

Cairns placed his drink on the coffee table separating their chairs. "The hour is late so let's place our cards on the table. Tom McBride supplied me with some very startling information. He was in the process of collecting evidence to support what he told me prior to his untimely demise. I need that information and I need it immediately."

"The Bonnaventure sales to China," said Ingram in a firm voice.

"Precisely. The Bonnaventures. It's no secret that unless I can clear up the controversy in a satisfactory manner I and my party could be in serious trouble. I haven't seen a transcript of what Mr. Jennings had to say tonight in Calgary but from what I've been told he lashed out at my credibility and came up with a little RCMP surprise. I do not intend to sit back and have him assassinate my character any longer. What I said to Winston Morrant on television was said in all honesty. I have no idea of where your political loyalties lie, Mr. Ingram, but I assure you I am no fool and do not run off at the mouth."

"What did McBride tell you and why did he single you out?"

Cairns was expecting the question but dreading it at the same time. To open up to Ingram, who owed him nothing, would be a calculated risk. There would be no way that he could stop Ingram from using anything he could tell him. He decided to appeal to his spirit of fair play.

"Before I answer, could I request one thing?"

"What?"

"Could this conversation be totally off the record?"

"That depends. I have always worked on the premise that nothing is off the record. If an individual wants to tell me something then I should be free to use it as I see fit. I'm sure you understand that I had to inform my editor of this trip. He's expecting a story upon my return to Ottawa. If what you are going to tell me forms the basis of a story I can give you no assurance that I won't use it. However, if what you tell me can be classified as deep background for a future story it does not necessarily have to be used. I can go no further."

Cairns began cracking his knuckles. The popping sound echoed in the stillness of the room. "You are placing me in a very difficult position, Mr. Ingram."

"I'm sorry, but you seem to want ground rules established before we continue."

"But it would appear that all the advantages are on your side of the table."

Ingram shrugged. He was about to pull back and suggest a compromise but before he could reply Cairns resumed speaking.

"All right. You leave me no choice. If you won't give me your personal guarantee could I ask for a time consideration in what you may or may not publish."

"Providing I get whatever you have as an exclusive."

"Agreed, you've got an exclusive. Tom McBride came to me with an astounding story a few weeks prior to his termination as press correspondent for the Chinese embassy." Cairns stopped abruptly as Ingram opened up a notebook and began writing. "I'd prefer if you didn't take notes at this time, Mr. Ingram."

"It would be much easier if I did. I never like relying on memory alone. But if you're uneasy I give you my assurance that if I decide to not use anything I shall tear out the pages and leave them with you."

"Very well, I accept your guarantee," said Cairns reluctantly.

"McBride told me that he had been given an assignment to puff, as you journalists call it, the use of the Bonnaventures in China. Evidently Peking wants to assure the world and Canada that they are being used for peaceful research and not involved with the military in any manner. While researching the story he found that this was not the case, and he also came to the conclusion that something questionable was going on involving the financial aspects of the sale."

"Such as?"

"That was as far as he would go at our initial meeting. I told him to get back to me if he had anything concrete as there was nothing I could do with pure speculation."

"Did he give you any indication on what he based his suspicions?"

"Not initially but he did a week and a half later."

"What was it?"

"He said that there was collusion between people in high places in Peking and Ottawa and he could prove it. He was quite definite."

Ingram whistled. "Did he name names?"

"No. He said he'd not name names at that time but would at a later date when he had hard evidence to support his suspicions."

"What did he want you to do?"

"The one thing he couldn't do – stand up in the House and demand that a Royal Commission be formed to look into the matter. In other words, blow it wide open."

"Did he mention anyone in government or the civil service?"

"I told you he didn't mention names but it would have to be person or persons in either, perhaps both. It would take more than one person to organize whatever has been done."

"Did you hear from Tom again?"

"Yes, he called me after his arrest on the drunk and disorderly charge. He said that once he got the matter settled he was taking off and would get back to me. He never called again."

"Did he indicate that he thought he was in any kind of personal danger?"

"Not really. As I recall he was pretty hyper when he called and I assumed that he'd been drinking. But he didn't indicate that anybody was after him, if that's what you mean."

"Did you try to get to him?"

"Yes, but he'd dropped out of sight and I had no luck."

"I'm curious. Why did you speak out on the Morrant show?"

"For a very good reason. I thought it would bring McBride out of hiding, if that's what he was doing. I wanted him to get back to me."

"It was just a calculated ploy?"

"Of course it was. I never do things on the spur of the moment without first thinking them out."

"You fooled a lot of people. That was quite a can of worms you opened up."

"Now I want to close the can, hopefully with Jennings in it. I'm going to nail him to the goddamn wall."

"That's politics for you," said Ingram with a chuckle. "I can't blame you for trying. What do you want from me?"

"I need what you have. You're obviously the only one McBride would trust. I'll be frank with you, Mr. Ingram, I need it badly and I need it now. I am scheduled to appear at a press conference and when I do I will have to say something about the Bonnaventure sales that will get me off the hook. It's that simple."

"When's the press conference?"

Cairns looked at his watch. It was 1:38 a.m. "In about nine and a half hours. Will you help me?"

"Why should I?"

"Because you are a Canadian and because Canada appears to have been ripped off."

Ingram smiled. "Politics has nothing to do with it. Your motives are purely altruistic."

Cairns could feel his anger rising. "Look, Mr. Ingram, I'm not asking for your approval. I'm asking for your help in exposing a situation that affects every law abiding Canadian. It would appear that a serious crime has been perpetrated. If men in places of trust are involved they should be exposed and made to pay."

"The fact that those men might be Progressive Conservatives doesn't lessen your zeal, does it?"

"I'm a politician and an honest one, whether you agree with me or not. I'd do the same thing if my party or government was involved. You can accept that or not, but it's the truth."

205

Ingram looked intently into Cairns' face. "I believe you. I don't agree with your politics, but I believe you."

"Thank you for that much," replied Cairns with biting sarcasm. "Now that we understand one another and now that I have been totally candid with you can I expect the same in return?"

Ingram closed his notebook and returned it to his jacket pocket. "Very well. What do you want to know?"

"Why are you so interested in Tom McBride?"

"Very simple. He called me and asked me to see him."

"When?"

"Right after your appearance on the Morrant show."

"You've talked to McBride?" asked Cairns with surprise.

"No. I never spoke to him after he called and arranged the meeting."

"You've lost me. You say you never spoke to him after the initial call. Why not?"

Ingram related the events that surrounded his finding McBride at the cottage and up to his death in the Ottawa Civic Hospital. Cairns listened without interrupting. "Why didn't he call me?"

"I have no idea, but I can speculate. Tom knew I'd written the China story and had a good understanding of the subject. As you say, he trusted me. I would assume that he was working on the story up to the time you blew it on television. If I'd been him I'd have everything ready to file the moment you stood up in the House. He was out of a job and this would make him a good buck, to say nothing of offers of more work."

"I still can't understand why he didn't call me."

"Again, I can only speculate, but if I had been Tom I wouldn't trust you. I'm sure that he felt he'd been betrayed. The story was blown and half the journalists in the country, including me, would be working on it. He'd lost the advantage."

"I only did what I thought was right."

"We know that, but Tom didn't. He never trusted politicians and always said that he wouldn't believe one if he swore on a stack of Bibles ten feet high. You're a politician. Need I say more?"

"O.K., you've made your point but it doesn't do me much good. I can't hold a press conference on what I have so far. I'd be laughed out of the room."

Ingram unconsciously patted his breast pocket. "Does Renco mean anything to you?"

"Renco? No, should it?"

"Perhaps. It's a financial investment firm registered in Panama. Evidently it is connected with the Bonnaventures in some manner. Did Renco ever come up in the House or committee?"

Cairns shook his head slowly. "Renco," he repeated. "To the best of my knowledge, no. Where did you hear of it?" Ingram told Cairns about McBride's last attempt to communicate before he died. "Why would a Panamanian firm be involved with a Canadian government transaction?"

"That's what I'm asking." Ingram reached into his inside pocket and pulled out the Interpol reply. "I had a friend of mine in the RCMP run it through Interpol. The reply is very interesting." Cairns leaned forward as Ingram spread the paper on the coffee table and read with interest. "It could be a dummy firm. Do you recognize any of the principals? Two are obviously Chinese, one a woman with an Anglo-Saxon name, and the other sounds Italian."

"They mean nothing to me. You can't go by names, especially in countries like Panama. They could be phony to protect the real people. It's an interesting corporate mix. But why," said Cairns tapping the paper with his finger, "would they use two Chinese names if they were phony? It doesn't make sense. Why not make them all John Does or John Smiths if all they wanted to do was hide the identity?"

"There must be a tie-in, otherwise why would Tom use his last breath to get the name to me?"

"Shit," muttered Cairns, "we must find the tie-in before the press conference."

"You can't go with this much. Suppose Tom meant something else and there was no connection?"

"I know, but it's tempting. What do you plan to do with this?"

"My editor is having it traced back through Hong Kong. The company is operating there . . ."

Cairns stood up quickly. "Why didn't you say so? That's it! Renco is a front for something connected with Peking. I'll bet my life on it. We have to find out what it is. How soon will you know anything?"

"I have no idea. I might mention that we are trying to

establish who the two non-Chinese principals are and see if they have any Canadian connections."

"Perhaps I can help speed up the investigation. I'll call Jerome Demeraise, my former Solicitor General. He could get things moving immediately with his connections. Will you back me?"

"Depends upon how far and how much."

"I want to mention Renco at the press conference. I give you my personal guarantee that I will not reveal my source. I intend to make a statement to the effect that now I can speak to the question because additional information has come to me."

33

Beads of sweat trickled down the nape of Lao Chengtu's neck and disappeared into the collar of his shirt, which was fast becoming soggy and stained. For the past ten minutes he had been on the phone laboriously instructing First Secretary Yuan Tzu on what to say should the press contact him personally for a statement on the Bonnaventure sales. He was now holding a dead receiver while Tzu had his call transferred to Ambassador Wu Tai Shan's private office. The air conditioning in Lao's apartment was turned up high. He found the atmosphere sweltering and oppressive.

Spread across his cluttered desk were numerous newspaper clippings. Each one featured either Christopher Jennings' Calgary speech or James Cairns' Winnipeg press conference. The bold headlines were pointed and at times caustic.

"Comrade," said Wu in his low, well modulated voice.

"Excellency," replied Lao.

"I am most distressed by what is happening in the Canadian press. What is your evaluation?"

"I am in the process of analysing the articles and editorials. I will have a summation on your desk in the morning."

"I asked what is your evaluation?" repeated Wu in a firm tone.

"I too am distressed, Excellency. I had hoped the Bonnaventure matter had been put to rest and would not be raised in the election. I do not know what prompted the outburst by Cairns or Jennings. It would appear that it was done for self-serving purposes rather than to embarrass our nation or Canada."

"How can you be sure?"

"I can't, Excellency, but until I have made my evaluation, this is my initial reaction. Both men are in deep political waters, their campaigns are not going well. They are getting desperate."

"Whom do you see as being in the forefront?"

At the moment, Jennings, without question. Unless Cairns can make a major impact on the voter Jennings will continue to be Prime Minister."

"I would like to think so. You should know that Peking has placed its fourth order for a Bonnaventure reactor. The official announcement is scheduled to be made jointly by Peking and Ottawa four days before the election. Mr. Jennings suggested the timing and Peking agreed. It will be a tremendous plus for his election. It's no secret that Canada's domestic nuclear industry can use what North Americans call a shot in the arm." Wu chuckled at what he considered a clever turn of phrase.

"You are quite right, Excellency. Since nothing has been firmed up with Bulgaria, the sale should result in additional votes for the Conservatives. Have the terms been worked out?"

"The new Bonnaventure will be a more sophisticated version of the three we have. The hardware and software will be significantly upgraded. Naturally the sale price will reflect the upgrading and inflation. Mr. Sutton's excellent story could not have come at a better time. It was well received. In light of the positive reaction it is distressing to see Mr. Cairns muddy the waters at such a sensitive time."

"Will you be making the announcement of the sale or will it come directly from Peking?"

"I shall be making it."

"I will have a draft press release plus background material for the press prepared for your approval immediately. With your permission I shall ask Mr. Sutton to work on the wording. His input could be beneficial."

"Please do. Of course it will be necessary for Peking to give final approval of anything we release but I see no problem. I have to advise Peking as to my evaluation of what is happening. How do you see it? Shall I suggest a formal statement denying all knowledge of what either man is talking about or do we just ignore it and let them battle among themselves?"

"To even allude to the problem is tantamount to admitting there could be validity in what Mr. Cairns is saying. It is my strong recommendation that the matter continue to be nothing more than an internal squabble and be totally ignored by us. In that way we are not drawn into the debate. I have suggested to Comrade Tzu that in the event he is contacted for a statement he says nothing more than it is the policy of The People's Republic of China to refrain from commenting on domestic issues. If he is pressed, he can mention the fact that according to Mr. Jennings the RCMP has investigated the matter thoroughly and found that both Peking and Ottawa have adhered to the letter and spirit of the agreements. I feel that nothing more need be or should be said on the matter."

"I concur with your counsel. So be it."

Lao stroked one side of his head with his free hand. "Thank you, Excellency."

"One thing more, Comrade. I am still awaiting your report on the progress you have made in retrieving the missing documents. What is the status?"

"I am preparing a detailed report of what I have done in order to reach that goal, Excellency," lied Lao who had not begun his report because he had nothing of a positive nature to say.

"Summarize please."

"My friend at the Ottawa Civic Hospital was most co-operative and was able to carefully go through Mr. McBride's personal effects. She found nothing remotely connected with the documents. Frankly, I did not expect that she would. It is highly unlikely that a man of McBride's experience would carry around something which would lead anybody to the documents."

"They are someplace and it is your responsibility to find them."

"Accepted, Excellency, but have you considered that it is just possible the documents might have, in effect, died with Mr. McBride?"

"Explain," demanded Wu.

"Assuming that he did not have time to have them translated he would have no way of knowing their real importance. That's a question only Mr. McBride could answer. Again assuming that he did have them translated and did realize their importance he would most certainly deposit them in a safe place until he could make use of them."

"In what manner do you think he would make use of them if he realized their value?"

"By selling them back to us or the highest bidder. It is no secret that Mr. McBride was in dire financial straits. It would be my thinking that we'd be the first ones contacted with an offer to buy them back with no questions asked. I submit that he died before he had the opportunity to make any contacts."

"Interesting hypothesis, but it doesn't change the situation. Those documents have to be found and if you can't do the job I shall ask security to take over. your failure will certainly have to be included in my report on the matter. Peking will not look favorably on what they will consider to be gross laxness on your behalf."

"I shall not fail, Excellency," said Lao weakly.

"I trust that you won't, Comrade, for your sake. I shall withhold my report to Peking for the time being in order to give you ample time to successfully conclude your assignment."

Lao was fully aware that Wu was being self-serving in delaying a formal report to Peking. He was protecting himself. To report the documents stolen would necessitate a full disclosure that they were in his office file cabinet rather than the embassy safe. This would be interpreted as a direct breach of security. Peking would certainly view such laxness by an Ambassador in a negative light. A reprimand would be the very least he could expect; the worst would be a recall with no further foreign postings.

"I shall keep you informed, Excellency."

"Goodnight, Comrade," said Wu.

The click in Lao's ear indicated the termination of a most unpleasant conversation. As Lao replaced the receiver his eye fell on a clipping from the Saskatoon *Register* next to his open suitcase. It was the lead story on the front page. He winced as he read the four column bold face headline.

ELECTION TO BE WON OR LOST
OVER BONNAVENTURE SCANDAL

34

Cole Harrison entered the Duke of Kent Room on the lower level of Victoria's Empress Hotel. His eyes were red-rimmed and he needed a shave. He gave all the appearance of a man who had not been to bed the night before. Sticking out of his pocket was an Air Canada timetable, dog-eared and obviously well used.

Harrison had been on the phone constantly from six in the morning trying to reach Diane Jennings. It was the first time since Diane had told Jennings that she was leaving him for Harrison that he had called 24 Sussex Drive. Placing a handkerchief over the mouthpiece in an effort to disguise his voice, he spoke to a sleepy and disgruntled Copeland who advised him that Mrs. Jennings was not in residence and, no, he did not know when she would be back or where she had gone. Since she had left the campaign after the swing through Alberta, her movements had been kept secret.

The more he pressed for information the more obstinate Copeland became, to the point of rudeness. Marcie Peckman was slightly more pleasant but of no help either. She suggested that he ask Jennings, if he was that determined to reach her. In desperation he placed a person-to-person call to her at Dr. Desmond McConnell's residence in Renfrew. Mrs. McConnell answered but refused to call Diane to the phone saying that she was under doctor's care and could not be disturbed. Harrison left a message for her to return the call. He gave the name Coleman Williams and arranged with the hotel operator to be paged under that name the moment the call came in.

Some heads turned as Harrison was seen and identified. The undercurrent of conversation died down as he moved quickly towards the front of the room where a small table with a green cloth was set up. A large full-color picture of Queen Elizabeth, resplendent in royal robes, hung on the wall. It was framed by a British Columbia provincial flag on the right and a Maple Leaf flag on the left.

Hurriedly, those standing around drained their coffee cups and stuffed the remnants of Danish pastry into their mouths before they took their seats. The room was set up theatre style and capable of accommodating nearly 100 people. It was just over half filled.

Harrison sat down, adjusted the table microphone and waited patiently. Once satisfied that he had the attention of those assembled he said, "Thank you, ladies and gentlemen, for coming at what must be an ungodly hour for some of you. We regret the early call for this press conference but the Prime Minister is scheduled to speak at a luncheon meeting in Fort Nelson and must get away by ten to catch his plane. He will make a statement and then be pleased to answer as many questions as time permits. If you'd like to position your micro-phones on the table and get your cameras ready I'll bring the Prime Minister in in a few moments."

Harrison left the room as reporters and cameramen quickly positioned their equipment. The door to the room opened and Christopher Jennings entered, followed by Harrison. With a broad smile and nods to those he recognized he walked with firm steps to the front of the room and sat down behind the table. The television lights were turned on and illuminated the front half of the room.

Jennings opened a file and looked around the room before

speaking. He was pleased to see such a good representation from the media.

"Thank you for taking the time to be here this morning," began Jennings. "I have a brief statement to make. As you are well aware, Mr. Cairns some time ago publicly charged that there were serious illegalities connected with Canada's sale of Bonnaventure nuclear reactors to The People's Republic of China. He never substantiated those allegations and I feel that I can do nothing less than answer them and disperse this cloud that is hanging over so many honest, hard working elected members as well as those in the Civil Service who have had their reputations blackened by innuendo.

"I, as Prime Minister, took great pride in the fact a Canadian reactor was chosen by China. To be singled out in such a highly competitive field is recognition of being the best in the world. I would like to announce now that China and Canada have agreed to the purchase of another reactor.

"Mr. Cairns alluded to some sort of payoff connected with the previous sale. I don't have to tell you that we do not have to pay out taxpayers' dollars to sell our products. I accept the fact that it was done in the past but it has not been done during my time as Prime Minister. I issued a directive to this effect shortly after taking office. As for an under-the-table deal, call it what you will, I can also say that this did not happen."

Jennings held up Commissioner Chambers' report. "What I have here is the detailed report on the sale of the Bonnaventures by Commissioner Chambers. There will be copies for you as you leave. This report is detailed and exhaustive. To repeat, every aspect of the financial transactions was audited and Commissioner Chambers summed up his findings by saying, 'It is my opinion that in this instance both the spirit of the contracts and the letter of the law have been adhered to without deviation.'" With a theatrical motion Jennings returned the report to the file and closed it. "There is nothing more to say on the subject. The file is closed and in closing it I challenge Mr. Cairns to do the honorable thing by coming forward and publicly apologizing and saying he was in error. That, ladies and gentlemen, is my final word on the matter."

Hands went up all over the room. Jennings nodded in the

direction of a man sitting in the middle of the second row.

"Phillips, *Southam News*. Mr. Jennings, I covered the Cairns' press conference in Winnipeg. During his statement he mentioned a company called," Phillips glanced down at his notes, "Renco. He said it is a Panamanian company. Are you aware of a company called Renco, and if so what is its connection to the Bonnaventure sales?"

"The name Renco means absolutely nothing to me and I have no idea as to why Mr. Cairns raised it. Perhaps he would be in a better position to answer your question."

"I asked him precisely the same question, sir, and was given a noncommittal answer. He said that Renco's activities were being looked into and as soon as he had something definite to announce he would make a statement."

"Until proven otherwise, I shall also put Renco into the collection of his flights into fancy." Jennings was pleased that the questioners were bringing Cairns into the picture. As long as he could throw the spotlight on Cairns' credibility he had achieved his goal.

Jennings smiled in the direction of a tall immaculately dressed man in the second row who held his hand high. Dwight Gibbon was immediately recognizable. His stature as Canada's foremost columnist was celebrated. His columns appeared daily in over forty major Canadian newspapers and he was the author of six definitive books on politics and economics. He had a reputation for jugular questions and all eyes were on him as he stood up.

"According to the latest McCadden poll it would appear that you have a sizeable lead on Mr. Cairns. As I recall, you were quoted as saying during the last election, when you were trailing by a sizeable percentage, that you placed little or no importance upon public opinion polls. Do you still hold that view?"

"To some extent I do but I feel that this one is a true reflection of Canadian thinking. I have tried to give Canada firm leadership and for the most part take great pride in the accomplishments of my government. It has been a productive parliament. While we still have far to go we are all well underway and should the Canadian voter place its faith in the Progressive Conservative party for another term we shall achieve many of the goals we set out in our long-range plans."

Gibbon was just warming up and those in the room, including Jennings, waited for him to strike. "You have publicly challenged Mr. Cairns to either retract and apologize or resign. Are you still prepared to stand by what you said?"

"Absolutely."

"In the event that Mr. Cairns can support his allegations, as he claims he will do, would you be prepared to resign?"

An ominous silence fell over the room. Everyone moved forward in their seats. Jennings licked his lips. It was the first indication that he had ever given in public to being nervous. "That is a hypothetical question, Mr. Gibbon. Based upon the RCMP report I do not feel that such a question deserves an answer."

"Anything is possible, Mr. Prime Minister," replied Gibbon emphatically. "Should Mr. Cairns be proven to be correct in his allegations would you resign?"

Harrison moved toward the platform but a quick glance from Jennings made him stop. This was not the moment to remind Gibbon that he only had two questions. "The question of resignation would be one my party would have to answer. I have the full support of my caucus and party executive."

"You did not offer that option to Mr. Cairns. You simply said that if he could not substantiate his charges then the only honorable thing to do would be resign."

"Mr. Gibbon. The question at hand is not whether I should resign or not but whether Mr. Cairns is telling the truth or just creating mischief. Based upon what we have seen and heard to date I would say the latter is probably closer to being the case."

"Are you concerned about the possibility of him being right and that persons or persons unknown have been involved in some kind of conspiracy?"

Jennings stiffened. His face flushed. "I do not know why you are still pressing on this issue. I have Commissioner Chambers' word that nothing questionable is connected with the financial dealings between Canada and China. What more do you want?"

Gibbon relaxed slightly and dropped his hands. "Very well, sir. Accepting what you have just said as a statement of total confidence in the report, I ask you again for an answer to my question. In the eventuality of Mr. Cairns being proven right would you resign on a matter of principle?"

Jennings looked at Harrison. His face was ashen. He scanned the faces of those staring at him and in a firm voice said, "Yes!"

35

The gruelling pace of the 60-day campaign took its toll on both candidates and workers who found their nerves to be at the breaking point. One point upon which the three leaders agreed was for an immediate reduction of the election span to 40 days or less, thus saving the public and politicians alike from another repeat of an archaic election campaign.

Jennings was concerned that because of the inordinate demands upon his time for the national campaign he had neglected his home riding of Bonnachere/Renfrew. He was not worried about being re-elected as he considered his seat safe, but the Liberal candidate was running a strong campaign and zeroing in on the absentee representation the riding was receiving. Some voters were being swayed.

To re-establish a high profile he ordered Harrison to locate his campaign headquarters in the Armory at the Renfrew Fair Grounds and arrange for a victory celebration on election night. There would be refreshments and music supplied by a local country and western band. It would help to counter what his opponent was terming his 'callous indifference to those who put him in office'.

Harrison vigorously fought the suggestion, but was over-ruled. He would have preferred to have election headquarters in the Chateau Laurier which had more prestige, better facilities and was traditional. Jennings was adamant and refused all discussion. He also directed Harrison to stay in Ottawa on election day and co-ordinate the media coverage from the national headquarters of the party. This would be a total departure from the norm as campaign managers generally hovered close to the candidate on election night and ran media interference.

Harrison guessed that there was more than political motivation prompting Jennings' unorthodox decision. To separate him from Diane and himself on a day of victory which he helped orchestrate would be a final indignity in the terminal days of their relationship.

Harrison also reacted heatedly to the suggestion that instead of staying in the Hotel Renfrew the entire Jennings family would take up residence in the same modest frame house they occupied during the time they lived in Renfrew. He cited many considerations and problems from security to communications but Jennings' mind was made up and he issued orders accordingly. It was an easy request to fulfill. The owners were flattered and agreed to temporarily turning their home over to the Prime Minister and his family.

All the details were finalized before he told Diane what he had in mind. He asked her to come but gave her the option of refusing. She was delighted, especially when he told her that outside of the mandatory RCMP security there would be no staff coming from Ottawa. She would have to cook the meals and look after the children. Not only did she accept the invitation, she offered to do anything he asked of her if it would help his re-election.

Following her acceptance, Jennings was on the verge of asking point blank what her plans were following the election but he held back. He sensed a dramatic change in attitude. He also sensed a growing ambivalence towards Harrison. He first became conscious of it just before she and the girls boarded the Armed Forces jet in Edmonton for the flight to Ottawa. When it came time to say goodbye she kissed him warmly on the cheek but virtually ignored Harrison. At the time he thought the coolness between them could be nothing more than role playing for his benefit but now he wasn't certain.

As the election drew nearer a dramatic change came over

Harrison. The ebulliency that had marked his personality over the years gave way to preoccupation and moroseness. While his efficiency level didn't drop, he avoided many friends and acquaintances. He had a perpetually worried expression on his face and Jennings often wondered if he had more on his mind than just his relationship with Diane.

The 156-kilometer drive from Ottawa to Renfrew was scheduled for late evening. Jennings wanted to arrive with as little attention and commotion as possible. He needed time with his family to settle in, relax and get a good night's sleep before a final whirlwind pre-election day tour of his riding. With Diane at his side, along with the children, he would show a high profile and counter the impression that he was taking his re-election and riding for granted.

Harrison, in his meticulous manner, timed his itinerary to the minute. Following a leisurely 43-minute mid-morning stroll down Raglan Street to shake hands, talk to people and wave at passing cars he would drive 11 miles to Olmstead Lake for a box lunch picnic with an invited group of local farmers. Precisely at 1:50 he would begin touring the riding, returning home for dinner at 5:45. He looked forward to the day with relish. It would bring back waves of nostalgia for times when all was well with his marriage and the world was his to conquer. He was especially looking forward to revisiting the many picturesque hamlets and villages such as Haley's Station, Cobden, Douglas and White Lake. When he and Diane first discovered them they had the luxury of anonymity. They could move about at will without the encumbrance of the ever-hovering security who watched their every move and the moves of those close to them.

Diane was like a new bride as she entered her former home and inspected each room. Many of the furnishings were still in place and she excitedly pointed them out to the girls or Jennings. She was walking back in time and was the happiest she had been in months.

Following goodnights to the two security officers who would remain on duty until relieved in the morning, Jennings and Diane took their daughters upstairs and put them to bed in the front room. The hour was late and the girls fell asleep almost the moment their heads hit the large feather pillows. After securely tucking in the eiderdown comforter, they turned off the light and quietly closed the door.

"Well now," said Jennings softly as they walked down the hall, "shall we flip a coin?"

"For what?" asked Diane.

"To see who gets the back room with the double bed and who gets the middle room with the single bed."

"Do we have to?"

"I suppose not. Ladies first. You choose. Either one is fine with me. The way I feel I could sleep standing up in the corner."

"That's not what I had in mind, Chris. Remember the last night we spent in this house?"

Jennings nodded. He remembered it vividly. It was filled with warmth, tenderness and lovemaking. It was almost spiritual and became a joint imprimatur on their marriage and future together.

"It's been a long time," observed Diane.

"A lot has happened since then," replied Jennings. He immediately regretted making the statement. From the abrupt change of expression on Diane's face he knew he had fractured the moment. "I was not referring to the past; I was referring to us generally," he countered.

"I know. It's all right. I understand."

The low wattage bulb in the small hanging tiffany light accentuated Diane's still beautiful face and near perfect complexion. As Jennings looked deep into her eyes he could feel a stirring within his body. He desperately wanted to take her in his arms, feel her body close to his and tell her that he still loved her no matter what had happened between them. He also wanted to tell her that he was twice the man Harrison was, in or out of bed.

"Thanks for coming and bringing the girls. I was hoping you'd come. The election looks good. Unless everyone is off in their predictions we'll win it by a country mile. Even some Liberals are saying I could go back in with a bigger majority than either Diefenbaker or Trudeau ever had."

"I'm pleased for you, Chris. I really am." Diane gently touched his arm. "You've earned it. You've worked hard. What about now?"

Jennings could feel himself once more being backed into a corner. The last time it was Dwight Gibbon and the stakes were high. Now it was Diane and the stakes were even higher. All Gibbon could have done, had he been successful, was take the election away from him. That danger had apparently passed. This time his personal future could balance on how he handled the situation.

His first inclination was to take Diane by the hand and lead her to the large double bed in the back room for a repetition of their last night in the house. It would wipe out all the bitterness and hurt of the past months, but nothing would be changed in the morning. Diane had said nothing to indicate that in two days she would not be stamping 'finished' on their marriage and embarking upon a new life with Harrison. To weaken for the sake of momentary self-gratification went against his fibre. He had been profoundly hurt. He was a proud man and a very stubborn one.

The thought flashed through his mind that in her own curious way she was just being kind. She was a compassionate woman and it would be totally in character for her to make their few remaining private hours memorable, pleasant and fulfilling. Should this be the case he did not know if he was emotionally equipped to accept such a gratuitous act of kindness.

The other and most distasteful consideration was whether or not she wanted one final intimate relationship as a signature to their marriage. It would not be unlike setting up a bridegroom with a prostitute on the eve of his wedding for a final fling at bachelorhood or to establish a benchmark on which to measure his new bride.

Jennings moved sideways and looked into the darkened middle room. Running his hand down the side of the wall, he found the switch and flicked on the light. The room was pleasantly furnished. A single brass bed with a brightly colored bedspread in a quilted sunburst design looked inviting. A refurbished wash stand with china basin and pitcher was beside the bed and a three-drawer oak dresser completed the furnishing.

"This will be fine," he said. "You take the double bed. The way you roll around you can use the extra room." Jennings leaned toward Diane and gently kissed her on the cheek. It felt warm and inviting. "Thanks," he said quietly.

Diane's eyes glistened. Reaching out, she took both of his arms above the elbows and pulled herself close. Tenderly she kissed him on the lips. It was a lingering kiss, not passionate but meaningful. Without saying anything she turned, walked into the back bedroom and slowly closed the door.

The ringing of the doorbell and the sound of muffled voices wakened Jennings from out of a deep and refreshing sleep. He rubbed his eyes and looked at his watch. It was 6:47 a.m.

Muffled footsteps and the creaking of the stairs were followed by a quiet voice calling, "Mr. Prime Minister. Are you awake, sir?"

Jennings reached for his robe and shoved his feet into a pair of slippers. "Yes," he replied as he struggled into his robe and opened the door.

Sergeant Dan Shortt, the senior security officer, was standing at the top of the stairs.

"What is it?" asked Jennings. He could hear Diane moving about in the back bedroom.

"Commissioner Chambers is in the livingroom. He would like a word with you, sir."

"At this hour?" replied Jennings as he followed Shortt down the stairs. His added weight made the stairs creak like an old ship.

Chambers stood up as Jennings entered the room. "My apologies for the hour, Prime Minister."

"It's quite all right, Commissioner."

Chambers looked at Shortt. "Leave us alone and see we are not disturbed, by anybody" he ordered.

"Sit down, Commissioner," said Jennings as he made himself comfortable in the large easy chair that matched a well used chesterfield. Chambers sat on the edge of the chesterfield and placed an attaché case beside him.

"It is a matter of grave urgency and I wanted to brief you personally."

Diane called from the top of the stairs. "What's the matter, Chris?"

Jennings walked to the bottom of the stairs and looked up. Diane looked beautiful in a flowing white peignoir that covered a low-cut revealing night gown. The hall light behind her silhouetted her slim torso and legs. The tousled hair added a sensual touch to her appearance. "Stay with the girls and don't let them disturb me. I'll be up shortly," replied Jennings in a soft voice.

Returning to the livingroom, he sat down and looked at Chambers' worried face. "What's the problem, Commissioner?"

Chambers snapped the locks on the attaché case and removed a large file marked 'Confidential'. "I regret to have to inform you that Cole Harrison and Dr. Louis Panzica of Atomic Power were arrested late last evening. A warrant is out for Lao Chengtu of the Chinese Embassy but it appears he has fled the country. We have alerted Interpol and the F.B.I. to be on the lookout for him. Even if we get him he'll probably plead diplomatic immunity."

All the color drained from Jennings' face. He stared at Chambers. "Harrison! Are you absolutely certain?"

"There's no mistake. We have a full confession. Dr. Panzica has been most co-operative and he's implicated Lao and Harrison. They were all in it together."

"What's the charge?"

"Murder, for openers."

Jennings shook his head in total disbelief. "Murder? Who?"

"A reporter named Tom McBride. According to Panzica, he deliberately put some obscure, tasteless drug into his food and drink. It took a while but it eventually killed him. Dr. Chester Wainwright of the Ottawa Civic will substantiate the fact."

"I heard he had died ... I knew him ... Look." Jennings moved to the edge of the chair. "Harrison has done some questionable things in his career, nothing illegal mind you, but questionable. Murder's something else, even for him."

"It is a classic situation. According to what Panzica told us, McBride was a threat to their operation. Since he was a threat it was decided to put him out of commission for a short time while one more payoff could be engineered. Instead of temporarily incapacitating him, they killed him."

"What made them suspect McBride?"

"Just a lucky chance, apparently. He contacted Panzica and told him that he was working on a freelance article and wanted an interview. It was right after he was either fired or quit the Chinese Embassy and he needed the money. During the interview he asked some pointed questions that in Panzica's mind he had no business asking unless he suspected something. Panzica panicked and told the others. They began imagining the worst and that's when they decided to take action. They couldn't run the risk that McBride was on to them or so close that he might stumble on to what they were doing by accident. From what we know so far, I really feel sorry for Panzica. Of the four he was the only one in the scheme who did not personally benefit."

"You're losing me, Commissioner," said Jennings with a tone of irritation. "What exactly is it that you think they have done?"

Chambers removed a handkerchief from his trouser pocket and blew his nose three times. There was nothing to blow. It was a device he used when in need of a few moments to collect his thoughts and choose his words carefully. He was curious about Jennings' reaction. He had fully expected him to explode in shock, outrage or total disbelief. Since his close personal relationship with Harrison was celebrated he was fully prepared to have him jump to his friend's defense. This did not happen and he was puzzled.

Slowly refolding the handkerchief, he replaced it in his pocket. "We don't think Prime Minister; we know. The scheme is the slickest I've come across in many years. The Canadian government has been defrauded of hundred of thousands of dollars and a man is dead because of it. Just how much money is involved I can't say until we have conducted a full investigation and have heard from Interpol who are making inquiries in Hong Kong and Panama."

Jennings shifted uncomfortably in his chair. Chambers had not come to the point. He wished that he would stop rambling. Noting Jennings' agitation Chambers said, "If you will bear with me, sir, I shall start at the beginning. The picture isn't totally clear yet but based upon our own investigation, what we have so far from Interpol and Panzica's confession, it all began about three years ago. Lao approached Harrison and sold him on an idea which could make all of them independently wealthy with little or no risk. He told Harrison that he had no intention of returning to China when his posting in Canada was over and wanted to build for a comfortable future in the West. He used the same line with Panzica. He was aware that Harrison was in deep financial trouble. Evidently his debts were monumental and he was being pressured by creditors. Apparently he got in over his head in some wheat futures deal that didn't pay off. He had used inside information on pending sales and Lao knew it through his contacts. In effect, Harrison was blackmailed into accepting the deal, though he may have become involved anyway. It was an imaginative scheme," continued Chambers. "With the recognition of China by Canada both countries entered into huge trade programs and the money began flowing from Peking to Ottawa in the millions. All Lao had to do was set up a tight network whereby the payments from Peking to Ottawa were short-circuited for a few days to be used by him.

"Once the funds were received in the Hong Kong branch of the Kowloon International Bank they were placed in a blind account for a few days and put out into the short term money market to earn interest. As near as we can tell, the longest they were used was seven days but that has to be confirmed. Just to give you an idea of what's involved, one million dollars loaned for seven days at 15 per cent, which is a conservative figure, would result in a profit of $410.00 per day or a tidy $2,870.00 for a full week. And there were hundreds of millions involved here.

"God only knows how much this quartet managed to skim off over the years. They also had the option of holding the funds until the exchange rate appreciated in their favor to cream off two or three per cent more, but I'm inclined to believe they went the short-term money market route for the most part."

"You told me that Canada received full payment from Peking."

"To the penny. There's no question about it."

"Then it's not technically theft?"

"Technically no, but morally yes."

"What will the charge be?"

"We're looking into that now. We have them on murder which is more than sufficient to hold them. I feel confident that we can also get them on conspiracy to commit fraud, breach of trust in Harrison's case, and possibly theft. Even if they beat the murder charge they will certainly be convicted on conspiracy and because of the careful planning and protracted length of time involved they could get up to twenty years."

"If they are guilty I hope they get what's coming to them, but something bothers me."

"What's that, sir?"

"It's common practice for business to use the short-term money market. It's done all the time. Since every cent of the principal was forwarded to Canada, was a crime committed?"

"That will be up to the courts to decide. As far as I am concerned they defrauded Canada of interest that Canada could have realized."

Jennings nodded his head. "I agree with you, Commissioner. I only put the question to you as I'm sure that point will be argued in court. They must have had a tight operation."

"Very tight. Lao planned it with the precision of a military operation. He left nothing to chance. By only allowing three others into the scheme he maintained a total control and lessened the possibility of a weak link. First he needed someone in Hong Kong who had access to the Peking account and could set up a blind account without drawing attention and questions. Wong Nei Chong is the Foreign Exchange Manager in the Hong Kong branch of the Kowloon International Bank. Kowloon International is the official bank for Peking's business with the non-Communist countries, so he was an ideal choice. He also happens to be Lao's second cousin.

"Next he needed someone close to government in Ottawa who could keep an eye on what was happening in order to give advance warning should the balloon burst. Who better than Harrison? No one is closer to the Prime Minister's office and no one has better access to what's happening inside government than he."

Jennings winced. "That's the understatement of the year." Lowering his voice he mumbled, "First Diane, now Canada."

Chambers strained to hear what he had said. "Beg pardon, sir."

"Nothing. I was just thinking out loud. Where does Panzica come in?"

"Lao couldn't work in a vacuum once it was decided to concentrate on the Bonnaventure sales and use the money they generated. He had to know what the scheduling was so that he could alert Wong to be ready for the movement of monies. Panzica covered that end."

"What was his motivation?"

"It was not self-serving. He never saw a dime of the money personally. He has a passionate hatred for Communism and used their money to finance the building of a new school in his home town in Sicily in memorial to a priest who was murdered by the Italian Communists shortly after the war."

"Neat, very neat," observed Jennings.

"The final link was Peking and Lao covered that. From his vantage point within the Chinese Embassy he was able to monitor what Peking was doing as far as the Bonnaventures were concerned. Once he had the mechanics set, the four formed a company in Panama." Chambers ran a finger down a page in the file. "It's called Renco."

"Then he was right, the bastard was right!" said Jennings. The lines in his face deepened.

"It was just by accident that we learned of Renco. Kevin Ingram, a reporter for Dominion Press, asked one of my officers to have Interpol check out Renco. Such unofficial requests are frowned upon but in this instance it paid off. One thing led to another in our investigation and we were able to tie everything together very neatly. It wasn't easy, it took a lot of hard work by Interpol before it was confirmed that all four are corporate officers of Renco." Chambers leafed through the file. "The President is Lao Tai-fu of Taiwan. He is Lao's uncle. The Vice-President is Wong Nei Chong of Hong Kong. He's Lao's second cousin. The Secretary is Mrs. Mary Scribner of Chatham, Ontario and the Treasurer is Piero Oriciani of Palermo, Sicily."

"Hold it," interjected Jennings. "Mary Scribner. Harrison's mother remarried and her new name was Scribner."

"The very same."

"She's been dead for seven or eight years. I attended her funeral."

"Her name was used as a blind to protect Harrison. Countries such as Panama do not check too carefully. As long as the taxes are paid and money comes into the country they don't

227

bother anyone. They had no reason to check out the name because Renco operated totally within Panamanian law."

"You said that there were only four in the scheme. Who is this Oric . . ."

"Oriciani. He's a lawyer in Palermo who set up the company. He was given a title without voting rights to protect Panzica. He is also a school chum of Panzica and the chairman of the new school that is being built."

"Did he know where the money was coming from?"

"I've no idea. Interpol is checking him out. It's my guess that he is innocent and only interested in Panzica's philanthropic venture. Panzica absolved him of all complicity in his confession."

"No wonder Harrison pushed me to approve the sale of the Bonnaventures to China. It was one of the most difficult decisions I have ever had to make."

"You mean you didn't support the sales?" asked Chambers in surprise.

"Not at the beginning. I had grave reservations about selling 70-megawatt research reactors plus weapons grade uranium. I held out for supplying them with a different design of fuel which is called 'carmel'. It's only enriched 10 per cent instead of the weapon's grade of 92 per cent, but I backed down."

"Because of Harrison?"

"Partly. He insisted that if I held out for the carmel fuel the sale would be cancelled and they'd get it somewhere else. At the time his argument made sense. I still have problems with China. While they are becoming more open they are still opposed to our system. I privately question their motivation."

"Why did you give in?"

"Because it would be good for the Canadian nuclear community and would generate more sales. Thousands of Canadian jobs rely upon the successful marketing of the Bonnaventures. I don't have to tell you that we are not setting the world on fire with our reactors. If the industry goes down the drain we'll lose many of our finest scientists. They'll go to the States for work. Remember what happened to the aerospace industry when Diefenbaker cancelled the Avro Arrow. Outside of DeHavilland and a few small manufacturers, Canada has no aircraft industry. I didn't want a repeat of that disaster."

Chambers took out a blank piece of paper and began writing. "You say that Harrison pushed for the sales?"

"Yes. He made a strong argument that if Canada didn't sell them to China they'd get them from some other Western nation such as Great Britain, France or the States, and why should we lose out on a principle that was obsolete in the light of a changing world. At the time it made sense. Now I can see why he was so insistent. The bastard."

"Did anybody else pressure you?"

"Some in caucus supported the sales but that was to be expected. All they're interested in is keeping their constituents happy and making brownie points that will pay off on election day."

"Did Harrison push for other sales?"

"Wheat, but that wasn't contrary to what I was pushing for. My government was in serious trouble over the sale of surplus wheat. If you don't believe me just ask any Saskatchewan wheat farmer. Why are you asking?"

"I think we are only seeing the tip of the iceberg, Prime Minister. We'll want to find out if they had similar arrangements in other countries."

"I thought you said they were only interested in the Bonnaventures."

"That's what Panzica said but I'm not so sure. They made it work on one and what's to say they wouldn't have expanded. Greed does funny things to people. They are never satisfied."

"Where's Harrison and Panzica?"

"In custody. They'll be officially charged this morning."

"Will they get bail?"

"I doubt it. Since Lao has skipped, the Crown will fight bail. If they get bail the figure will be so high they'll have trouble raising it."

"Any idea where Lao is?"

"We've traced him to south Texas. He left Ottawa for Toronto via Air Canada." Chambers consulted his notes. "From Toronto he flew to Chicago via American Airlines. From Chicago to Houston via Braniff and from Houston to Brownsville via Texas International. He worked through contacts in Toronto's Chinatown, but oddly used his own name. He's the only one who doesn't have to worry, at least not worry about us. He's protected by diplomatic immunity. Anyway, it looks like he'll get his."

"What do you mean?"

"I talked to Ambassador Wu and they want to get their hands on the Honorable Mr. Lao. Seems there are some missing documents that they now believe he has in his possession and they want them back. They've asked us to advise them where he is if we find him and they'll take it from there. From what the Ambassador said it would appear that he was working both sides of the street."

"I don't follow."

"It looks like he was in the employ of Taiwan."

"A mole?"

"Exactly. I wouldn't want to be in his shoes when they catch up to him."

"If you know his route, don't they?"

"I doubt it. They can't trace him the way we can."

"Going to tell them?"

"Not until we get to him first, if we can. I've sent a couple of men to Texas to see if they can catch up with him but the chances are slim. It's my guess he's crossed the border at Matamoros and is in Mexico. He'll head for Panama, get his money and disappear. At least that's what I'd do."

"What a hell of a mess. Are you sure about Lao being a double agent?"

"Reasonably so. Panzica told us that he and Lao purposely fed Peking false or misleading information about the Bonnaventures in order to make things more difficult for them to get them on-line."

"Now the pieces begin to fit. As you know, my trip to China was postponed. I didn't want to go just before I began fighting the election and Peking didn't seem the least bit upset by the delay. They said it would give more time to get the reactors working properly. I didn't think too much about it but evidently they are having their problems."

"Thanks to Lao and Panzica."

"It would seem so. Based upon what you say Panzica said in his confession, you have him cold on passing classified information to a foreign power."

"Possibly, but if the defense attorney can prove that the information was inaccurate by design it could be a difficult conviction."

"Was Ambassador Wu privy to what Lao and Panzica were up to?"

"He'd certainly know that Lao was obtaining assumed classified information from Panzica."

"External Affairs should be so informed. There are grounds for a strong protest to Peking," said Jennings. "I'll certainly support such a note. It's my guess that External Affairs will recommend a status of *persona non grata* for the Ambassador. It will mean his recall."

"So it should."

"Too bad it couldn't have waited another two days until the election is over. The timimg couldn't have been worse."

"I'm sorry, Prime Minister, but we had to move. If we'd delayed we'd have lost them all."

"I'm not blaming you, Commissioner. You did your duty. One last question. I've got to know. Are you absolutely certain that Harrison didn't kill McBride?"

"Harrison didn't do it but he is an accessory to it and so is Lao. At the moment, I'm convinced it was an accident. No one intended to murder McBride. Lao traced McBride to the cottage and Panzica shadowed him for quite a while. He's quite a fisherman and McBride never realized that he was being watched by a man in a boat. It didn't take Panzica long to plot a pattern. McBride was a creature of habit and every morning and afternoon he would take a walk then return to sit on the dock and drink. Panzica just waited his chance and while he was out slipped into the cottage and doctored his food and drink."

"What was it?"

"Some obscure Chinese drug that Lao gave him. Evidently it can simulate a stroke. The effects are only supposed to be temporary and gradually wear off. All they needed was time to complete the final transaction. Unfortunately they didn't consider McBride's condition. Through heavy drinking and poor eating habits he was in a weakened condition and couldn't fight off the drug. He died. There's always a chance that he died of natural causes, but until proven otherwise we are laying a charge of murder. If the drug Panzica administered caused his death

231

they'll go down on second degree murder."

"Is that all, Commissioner?"

"For the time being. I'll keep you informed. I wanted to be the one to tell you before the press came beating down your door. At least you'll be able to answer their questions knowing the full story."

Jennings stood up. "I'm grateful to you, Commissioner. Pass my compliments along to your staff. I'd better get moving. I have an election to fight."

"I wish you well, sir," said Chambers as he rose and walked to the front door.

Jennings shook his hand and watched as Chambers walked down the front walk and stopped to talk to one of his men who was standing by his car. Turning, he tugged at the sash of his robe and called out, "Diane, would you please come down. I have something to tell you."

36

By 8:30 on election night the mood of the packed Renfrew Armory was somber and subdued. Shocked faces stared at television sets that were scattered around the floor. Tears streamed down the faces of many exhausted workers and supporters.

With the polls closing one hour earlier in the Maritimes than in Ontario and Quebec, the networks were racing one another to be first in predicting the election outcome Unless Quebec, Ontario and the west reversed the trend it appeared that a Liberal sweep was assured. The Conservatives were wiped out in Prince Edward Island. The Liberals took three seats, the

NDP one. In Newfoundland only two Conservatives were elected out of a total of seven. Nova Scotia elected three out of eleven and New Brunswick, one out of a possible ten. It was a disaster.

Accepting the fact that traditional Tory strength lay in Ontario, and especially the west, the figures were adjusted to reflect that strength. The early predictions gave the Liberals 152 seats, the Conservatives 98 and the NDP 32. The more optimistic Tories tried to raise flagging spirits but it was a hopeless venture. With each updating it was apparent that the day had been lost.

Christopher Jennings and Diane, along with a few senior party members, were in the Commanding Officer's quarters and watched the television set in stunned silence. No one spoke above a whisper and no one spoke to Jennings, who was sitting on a chesterfield with Diane, unless spoken to directly. Jennings held a remote tuner in his hand and switched back and forth between networks. The projections were practically identical and both were predicting a Liberal victory.

Diane walked over to the far end of the room to where her daughters were sitting at a small table playing with their dolls. She cautioned them to play quietly.

Jennings was more interested in the riding up-dates than most but when anchorman Winston Morrant's face filled the screen all whispered conversation ceased and full attention was given.

"We're back", said Morrant. "We don't generally begin analyzing returns so early on election night but because of the dramatic turn of events we have asked Liberal Senator Humphrey Ross and Mr. Brian Beacom, Chairman of the Conservative Strategy Committee, to give us their impressions of the Maritime voting trend." Morrant turned in his chair toward Ross. "You first, Senator."

Ross entwined the fingers of both hands and placed them firmly on the desk. With a broad smile he looked straight into the camera and said, "Thank you for inviting me, Winston. This is indeed a very exciting night for us. It would appear that we are well on the way to a resounding victory. I think it is safe for me to predict that we will form the next government with a comfortable majority." Ross had great difficulty controlling his delight.

Morrant swung toward Beacom. "Not such a great night for Conservatives, Mr. Beacom. Beacom cleared his throat but said nothing. "Why, gentlemen? Was it just the Bonnaventure scandal or something more?"

"I feel the reason we did so poorly in the Maritimes is a direct result of the Bonnaventure scandal," Beacom said. "Had it not broken the day before the election I dare say Senator Ross would be wearing a much more subdued smile than he is tonight."

"No question about it," said Ross. "While most politicians will take a win any way they can get it this one is not quite so sweet. It is more like winning by default and I am sure Brian will agree that if the shoe was on the other foot he'd feel the same way."

"Want to try me?" asked Beacom with a half smile.

"Do you think the voter is punishing Mr. Jennings for the sins of Cole Harrison or because he so steadfastly denied any impropriety and has been proved wrong?"

"Could I speak to the question first, Winston?" asked Beacom. "I believe it is more the latter than the former. Anyone who knows Christopher Jennings knows that he is a man of honor. To imply that he is being punished for the sins of a man close to him is ludicrous. To imply that he is being punished for sticking by what he thought to be the truth only to be proved wrong is open to debate. There is no question the voter, especially the uncommitted voter, has swung away from our party. I can't deny it. But, no Prime Minister or leader should be held responsible for the actions of those around them if they are not privy to those actions and would not approve if they knew of them."

"Tell that to Richard Nixon," interjected Ross.

Beacom leaned forward so he could look around Morrant and fixed Ross with a blistering stare. "That's a specious statement, Senator, which I would have thought was beneath you. Nixon broke the law! He was up to his ears in Watergate. Christopher Jennings is totally innocent of any complicity. He knew nothing whatsoever about what Cole Harrison was doing.

234

Had he, he would have been the first to see that justice was done. To even imply that he . . ."

Ross held up both hands. "I'm not implying anything, Brian. All I'm saying is that in the public's mind the leader must be held accountable for what those under him do. You must agree that Mr. Cairns sounded a word of warning right on Winston's weekly show."

Morrant nodded in agreement. He was enjoying the moment. It was good programming.

"Of course I accept that," responded Beacom. "However, tonight would have been much different had Mr. Cairns been able to back up what he said with hard facts instead of just painting with a wide brush."

Ross shrugged his shoulders. "I still remember what Harry Truman said about the buck stopping somewhere."

"What about the west, Senator? The Liberals have not done particularly well west of the Lakehead."

"You're right about our western strength but, if the Maritimes is any indication there could be a reversal of our fortunes."

"Do you agree, Mr. Beacom?"

Beacom scowled. "I think George Eliot said it better in *Janet's Repentance*. 'Any coward can fight a battle when he's sure of winning; but give me the man who has pluck to fight when he's sure of losing. That's my way, sir; and there are many victories worse than a defeat.'"

Morrant leaned back in his chair and laughed heartily. Ross pushed out his lower lip and looked over his glasses.

"On that note gentlemen we'll pause for station identification and return to election center in just a moment."

Jennings exhaled a lungful of air slowly as the station credits came on the screen. Placing his head on the back of the chesterfield, he closed his eyes. He was bone tired. The events of the day, beginning with his call to Marcie Peckman minutes after he had left Diane in a flood of tears, flashed through his mind.

With magnificent presence, Marcie immediately took charge of the press room and brought order to chaos. All requests for interviews were channelled through her and refused outright or stalled. She also wrote a formal statement for Jennings to release to the press. He approved it without change.

Mrs. Jennings and I were shocked and distressed upon hearing of the arrest of Mr. Cole Harrison and Dr. Louis Panzica. It is premature for a statement to be made on the charges at this time. However, I have instructed the Minister of Justice to look into the matter personally. He will be working closely with the RCMP and the Ottawa Police. Should the law have been broken those responsible will have to face the full penalty, without exception. Mr. Harrison submitted his resignation as Executive Assistant to the Prime Minister at one this afternoon. It was accepted with profound regret.

By 11:20, Renfrew time, the early results were beginning to come in from British Columbia. The trend which had been set in the Maritimes held across the nation. Christopher Jennings and his Progressive Conservatives had lost the election and would return to Parliament as the official opposition with somewhere between 97 and 99 seats. James Cairns would head a Liberal government with a better than 25 seat majority over the combined totals of the Conservatives and NDP.

Jennings finally made his appearance on the Tory blue bedecked platform. The applause was thunderous and he was greeted with shouts of encouragement. Diane was at his side holding the hands of her two sleepy daughters who blinked in the glare of the television cameras. Marcie Peckman stood off to the side with a drawn face.

Jennings waited patiently for the ovation to die down and finally, holding up both hands for quiet, said, "Friends and fellow Progressive Conservatives, I want to say something to those who are here in the Renfrew Armory first before I speak to the rest of Canada.

"I thank the untiring workers and supporters of Bonnachere/Renfrew for making it possible for me to return to the House of Commons as your Member. The events of the last twenty-four hours certainly did not give my personal campaign any encouragement. However, we won and for that I'm grateful. Thank you."

His statement was greeted by applause and the release of balloons which floated to the roof of the armory.

"What can I say to the rest of my fellow Conservatives across Canada? We lost. While we lost badly in many areas we are still

Her Majesty's Loyal Opposition and we will fight the new government tooth and nail for what we feel is right. To those who lost their seats I extend my profound regrets and sympathy. We shall miss you in caucus and in the House. To those who won, enjoy the next few days because we are all going to have to work twice as hard. The new government will never be able to take us for granted. If I were them I'd be watching over my shoulder all the time. Being second isn't as good as being first but I'll tell you something. We've nowhere to go but up. I give you . . . I give you," repeated Jennings over the applause, "my solemn promise. We shall repeat tonight in about four years, but there will be a difference. The band will not be allowed to play 'Help Me Make It Through The Night'. We'll send the music over to the Liberals because they'll need it."

Jennings stepped back with a wide smile. He had seemingly turned despair into hope. Stepping forward to the microphone again, he signalled for quiet.

"I just called Mr. Cairns in Ottawa and congratulated him on his victory. I know he is waiting to make his formal statement to the nation so I'll be brief. These have been trying days, especially the last two, but I tell you what I told Mr. Cairns. He was right about the Bonnaventure affair and I was wrong. I was wrong, but I was wrong in good faith. I apologize to Mr. Cairns and his colleagues and assure them of my full co-operation in seeing that justice is done."

Holding up his hands again, he continued. "I was fully intending to announce my resignation as the leader of the Progressive Conservative Party tonight." His next words were drowned out by calls of No! No! No! Jennings reached out for Diane's hand and squeezed it. "Thank you for that vote of confidence. I was hoping you would give me such a message."

The applause exploded and Jennings raised his arms in a victory salute.

It was a quarter to two before Jennings and Diane finally tucked their daughters into bed. It was a repeat of the previous night as they stood in the hallway and looked at each other.

"Well," said Diane as tears welled up in her eyes. "Do you still want me as your wife?"

Jennings looked deep into Diane's eyes. Without saying a word he took her by the hand and led her to the back bedroom and closed the door.

Their lovemaking was gentle. There was no passion. That would come later, much later.